THE VINYL ENIGMA

By Robert Love

The Vinyl Enigma
by Robert Love

Published by eBookIt.com

ISBN-13: 978-1-4566-2149-0

CONTENTS

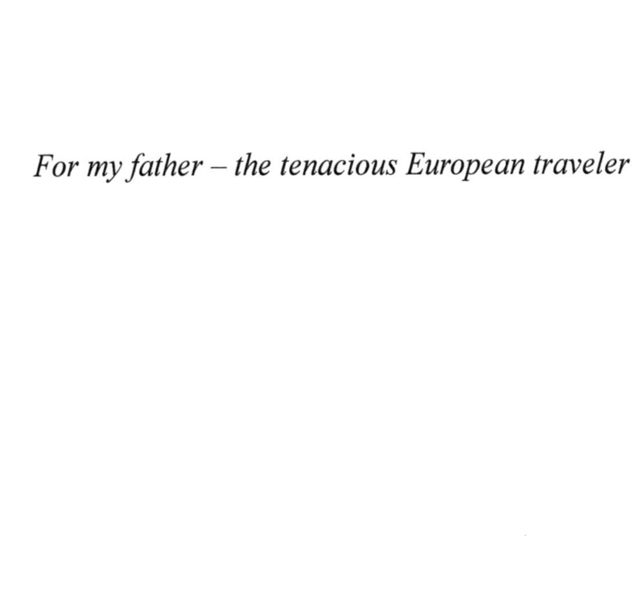

For my father – the tenacious European traveler

PART I

THE DISCOVERY

Chapter One

Have I really chosen this strange journey for nearly a decade, or has it been forced upon me by powers I cannot imagine? I am compelled now to pen a brief account, regardless of how others may judge my sanity.

I live alone in London's Chelsea district, occupying a moderate-sized apartment with a partial view of the Thames River (partial enough to bring about a much higher rent). I work part-time in a music-publishing firm, which provides basic sustenance. Prior to this, I studied music at Juilliard (focusing on cello, and later composition), and once held a position in the London Symphony Orchestra as first cellist.

In May of 1989, I traveled to Leningrad with the LSO as part of a rare tour of Eastern Europe and the Soviet Union. It was a time of remarkable thaw, politically and weather-wise, and I often had the liberty of roaming the streets without escort. I even heard rumors of the city being renamed to its original Saint Petersburg. One chilly evening, I left Shostakovich Hall and strolled past Arts Square with its statue of Pushkin, eventually reaching an old, narrow street with a small record/book store tucked under the first level of a crumbling apartment building. After I'd entered and browsed through stacks of Soviet-era recordings, the owner appeared – a small, thin fellow with scrambled gray hair and long, slender fingers, which suggested the hands of a musician.

To my surprise, he began a conversation in English. "I saw you play last night, and enjoyed your interpretation of the controversial Shostakovich Fourth Symphony. It was presented as nicely as our own orchestras did in the sixties."

"Well, thank you very much," I said, humbly impressed with his historical perspective. "I'm fond of twentieth century Russian composers, and I'd like to purchase this collection of Prokofiev piano sonatas."

The owner nodded, but then seemed distracted by a flash of intense thought. He tugged slightly on my sleeve and motioned toward a back exit. I followed him along a dimly lit, tunnel-like hallway, which looked disproportionally long for the building. His words echoed off the hard, plaster walls as we walked. "I have a very special item that may interest you." Soon we entered a storage room cluttered with a variety of dusty containers and books. I wondered if I was the first foreigner to stand there.

With trembling hands (from age or anxiety?), the old man handed over a thin cardboard box labeled in Russian: Classical Music. I carefully pulled out the standard-sized LP phonograph record and scrutinized it for obvious defects, as I always did before purchasing. It appeared perfectly round, yet the disc's thickness was difficult to assess by touch, which I blamed on the stiffness in my hands after the cold walk outside. The black surface had a strange, featureless character, but I dismissed the perception as a consequence of poor lighting in the room. At least the album had no obvious scratches, nicks, or breaks. Out of sheer curiosity, and because of the low price he was offering (perhaps too enthusiastically), I included this item with the sonatas and paid the owner.

As I exited into the crisp night air, he stood in the doorway and shouted one last comment. "Would you believe that I played violin with the Moscow Philharmonic in 1961 at the Fourth Symphony's world premiere under Kondrashin? Perhaps one day you will hear that performance." I made a mental note to check on any documentation of the event.

I didn't examine these purchases again until I returned to my flat in London the following week. As I mounted the generic record on my turntable for the first time, I noticed an absence of two things: a sheen normally arising from multiple grooves, and rings indicating separation between tracks. Therefore, I placed the tonearm down somewhere near the middle. The total silence that followed was surprising, given the unlikelihood of randomly finding a break between movements. Also odd was the lack of background noise typical of vinyl records.

Suddenly a confusing mixture of sounds greeted me; not quite music, but more like rapids in a large river. This transformed quickly into a series of identifiable, though extremely short, pieces of music in many styles. Occasionally I could pick out bits of classical music. Then, silence again.

I was beginning to view the disc as a practical joke when orchestral music emerged. It was a symphony, starting from the beginning, which I recognized as a work by Haydn. The performance and recording quality were so impressive that I sat transfixed in my chair, listening to the entire piece. The lack of any text accompanying the LP made it impossible to identify the orchestra, location, or conductor with any certainty.

Immediately afterward, I tried to reseat the needle in the same position, but a different selection emerged – a Mozart violin concerto from the same time period; again starting from the beginning. Driven by sudden exhilaration, I moved the needle close to the record's end (near the center), and heard contemporary performances by composers like Steve Reich and John Adams. Moving the needle to the start (outer edge) gave early Renaissance music, not all of which I could identify, but which had apparently been performed in large cathedrals with distinctive reverberation.

After many weeks of trials, it was clear that the record contained an unknowably large number of performances of "Western" classical music, in roughly chronological order. The selection to arise was unpredictable, except for approximately the time period in which it was written, and ranged from solo instruments and quartets to concertos and operas. To the best of my memory, I never heard the same performance twice, no matter how accurately I tried to return the tonearm to its original position. Thus, each listening event became a unique moment in time, not to be interrupted unless its permanent "loss" was acceptable.

An equally disturbing observation was that the tonearm, once in play, never advanced noticeably in a radial direction across the record, even with very long pieces such as an opera. Nor could I see the small needle itself riding on the disc; instead it seemed to become enveloped in the ill-defined black surface, as if dipping into a pool of smooth, black tar.

Occasionally, I had an acquaintance drop by for dinner, and played some "background music" from the record, to exclude the possibility of auditory hallucinations. On these visits, I didn't reveal the disc's extraordinary nature. With audiophile friends, who might intuitively recognize and question the continuous playback of a long piece from the single side of an album, I allowed only short works to reach completion.

In the beginning, I naturally assumed I was hearing performances from the previous fifty years or so, during which time reasonable quality recording equipment was available. After several months I was less sure, and began to ponder the unthinkable; that with this record I might (eventually) hear all performances ever given of any composition, including events that were centuries old.

Each day brought new questions. Would this album include even rehearsals, or performances at small venues in someone's home (e.g., Chopin playing in the salons of Paris)? After several years of intense scrutiny, such diversity seemed unlikely, since I always detected some audience noise, and the acoustic character (ambience, echoes) always suggested a sizeable room. I concluded I was consistently hearing live, formal performances in large halls with significant attendance (even during solo instrument recitals).

Nevertheless, the number of events available for playback seemed exceedingly large. I was comforted only by the logic that the total number of performances must be finite. I often found myself asking: Is the disc an advanced storage device, or some kind of time portal linked to specific musical events? Why (thus far) does it offer only performances involving larger venues with audiences? Is this related to some necessary critical mass of listeners forming a "collective consciousness," if such a thing exists?

In any case, the seeming impossibility of a vinyl record encoding so much information was soon forgotten as the wonderful presentations filled my modest living room. I eventually adjusted my daily schedule to revolve around playback, and didn't initiate any session without adequate preparation for listening to its entirety. All my attempts to document playback using magnetic tape mysteriously failed. Each event was like viewing a magnificent sunset – never to be repeated. In short, I became obsessed with the disc.

The uniqueness of each experience led to a number of frustrating moments; for example, during an electrical storm when power was interrupted and the stereo system shut down during an exciting version of Beethoven's Ninth Symphony. I also vividly recall one instance during the second year, when an enchanting rendition of Mahler's Das Lied von der Erde was underway. It featured a soprano's voice more beautiful than any I had heard before, yet I chose to walk away and sleep, since I was tired and had concerns over business matters. Of course, I was never able to locate this piece again, and deeply regretted the decision for months, as if I had passed up a perfect opportunity to make love with someone I desired greatly and who was in my presence for only one night.

Several incidents besides the Record (as I have come to call it) have influenced my routine over the last decade, yet these have always seemed trivial compared with the disc's impact. Not long after my return from Russia, I broke off an engagement with a woman (a fellow musician) whom I had known for several years. A car accident in 1993 ended my professional career with the orchestra because of nerve damage to my left arm, although the limb remained functional for everyday activities. An unforeseen family inheritance in the mid-nineties permitted me to end full-time work at my firm and devote more attention to the Record, and thus better chronicle each listening session. All of this only fueled my growing isolation. Eventually, I yearned for a sign that my "duty" (if that is the appropriate word) toward study of the Record had expired.

One intriguing prospect emerged this week. I heard a performance of Shostakovich's Fourth Symphony, almost certainly under Kondrashin and perhaps the 1961 live world premiere, but not the first taped recording from 1962 (the album of which I own). If correct, then I have witnessed what the Leningrad shop owner referred to long ago. Unfortunately, no further information from that source is now possible. In 1997, I traveled back to St. Petersburg and conducted a futile search for the store. Not surprisingly, the entire block had been converted into modern housing units, and the shop was gone. The old man's whereabouts were unknown to local residents.

At this point, it seems inappropriate, perhaps even perilous, to hand over the disc for objective scrutiny such as scientific analysis at a university or museum. I fear I have become a confidential guardian of something sacred, like a successor in a long chain of ancient priests assigned to oversee and pass along a holy relic. Perhaps I was indeed "chosen" by the Leningrad musician, who may have been the previous "keeper" (and may have studied the disc for a longer period than myself). Should I now seek the most promising apprentice for scholarship?

In the last couple of years, my thoughts have evolved toward an even higher level of speculation: Could the Record's music be a manifestation of some profound message? Thoreau wrote, "Music is the sound of universal laws promulgated." Perhaps the selections available are a code, waiting to be deciphered for the delivery of some incredible revelation to humankind (or at least to musicians!). This hypothesis leads to even greater anxiety regarding the disc's fate. I may have a unique opportunity in the history of civilization to unlock a momentous secret, if only I have the patience to continue listening. But for how long? And for what, exactly?

The uniqueness of each event on the Record, the regret of lost listening opportunities, and the sacrifices required to listen patiently, all mirror aspects of everyday life, yet they lack one simple and critical component: sharing the experience with others. There is a loneliness I have ignored almost completely over the past decade. This is the revelation for me – the need for human interaction. I must now part with the disc and return to the world I knew before, even at the risk of abandoning some insight hidden within.

Therefore, I have packaged the Record with great care. My plan has been made and I have contacted the appropriate people to help accomplish the final steps. Soon I'll be free of this miracle and curse, and shall begin the slow, painful, but necessary process of putting my life back together.

Nigel Thompson
London, 1998

Addendum: It is now the summer of 2000, and the "London Eye" has become a fixture on the horizon. To me, this magnificent Ferris wheel, with its endless, circular route, symbolizes the Record and its boundless potential. Yet I believe the Record embodies something far beyond our ability to comprehend at this time. Furthermore, the task of finding the proper heir has been daunting, and the responsibility on my part overwhelming, given the burden that ownership would place on a friend or colleague.

It was thus my decision last year to bury the Record beneath this glorious symbol, until at a later point in history it can be uncovered and relished as an archeological treasure. I recruited a friend who was an engineer on the Eye project, and who had access to the large pit dug for the foundation. I obtained a strong steel box to enclose and protect the Record. On the night before the first of many layers of concrete was poured, I instructed my friend to place the container at the bottom of the pit. I am confident that some future technology will allow detection of an odd metal object embedded deep beneath the Eye, just as the pyramids of Egypt are scanned today for inner chambers.

Meanwhile, I return to my intended role in the present – namely, efforts at musical composition. As Mahler stated, "To write a symphony is to construct a world." Through my scores, I hope to create emotional worlds for all, and if I am fortunate, a few performances of my work will be immortalized on the Record, for the ears of a distant generation.

Chapter Two

Three bloody degrees of tilt. The words smoldered inside the British engineer as he stared up at the giant Ferris wheel, towering 440 feet above him. His field technicians had just reported the deviation from perpendicular, using laser-based survey equipment. As an accumulation over fifteen years since the attraction had opened, the measurement fell within the normal range of settling for such a large structure. However, the object in question was the famed London Eye; Europe's tallest observation wheel, perched on the Thames across from Westminster, with 1800 tons of steel designed to hold 800 passengers. Any abnormality had to be documented and reported to various city organizations.

The engineer shook his head in disbelief and stepped aside to remove his helmet under the warm sun, revealing gray hair matted against a balding scalp. The Eye had been closed all morning for inspection, despite the obvious conflict with the tourist season and a steady stream of 20,000 riders per day. There was urgency to complete the work, since an angry mob of international visitors had formed at a roped barrier along the street. Many were yelling about tickets purchased for a morning ride.

This wheel should not have been built on a riverbank, he grumbled to himself as he walked alongside the Thames, gravel crunching beneath his work boots. But another thought was even more troubling. He had been here when a large pit existed and the earth was impaled with sixty-foot pilings, before 3000 tons of concrete were poured to form the wheel's massive foundation. He knew what lay at the bottom of the pit, alongside ancient Roman ruins. It was something that should never have been left down there.

For the moment, however, he found no need to correlate this memory with the superstructure's readjustment. Eventually, and only if absolutely necessary, he could guide investigative teams to a specific section under the foundation. He logged his final report on the firm's website, along with his conclusion. Date: 16th June, 2015; all measurements within normal tolerance; no further action required; signed, David Rollins, Chief Engineer.

The group of managing companies did not agree. Within a week, an oversight committee was demanding that Rollins hire an independent contractor to re-examine the Eye's parameters and verify his report. Fortunately, the choice of a consultant was his, and he did not hesitate to select a name. He was going to do everything in his power to resolve this situation quietly.

The nightclub was dark except for several spotlights trained on a small stage where a jazz quartet had been performing for an hour. While not professional artists, the musicians were quite talented, and clearly at ease playing together. Featured instruments were electric guitar, piano, drums, and acoustic bass, while songs included classic melodies like *Take Five*, *Stormy Monday*, *Honeysuckle Rose*, *Straighten Up and Fly Right*, and *Lullaby of Birdland*, along with a few jazz fusion inventions. The mixture of music, background chatter, clinking glasses, and outbursts of laughter lacked only one thing – a thick haze of smoke. With that, the place could have been any famous jazz establishment from a bygone era. However, this was Boston in the year 2015, and the sign outside read 'About Midnight,' an allusion to the song *Round Midnight* by Thelonius Monk. The audience consisted of college students, local residents, and a few refugees from outlying suburbs who had ventured downtown on a warm July evening.

On piano was Evan Blake, professor of engineering at MIT. His light brown complexion was framed with short, dark, wavy hair and a close-cropped beard revealing specks of gray. Thin, wire-rimmed glasses were almost invisible except when capturing and reflecting the spotlights. Though of medium height and build, he seemed dwarfed beside the baby grand piano occupying almost half the stage. At the moment, he was lost in improvisation. His left hand hammered out complex chord progressions while the right sketched an intricate melody line; all with the same ease he had shown earlier on guitar. The band had a routine of switching guitar and piano players midway through the set, and Evan alone was equally skilled at both instruments.

The show concluded with Evan delivering the minimalist solo piano tune, *Peace Piece*, written by Bill Evans. The coincidence of personal names only added to the intrigue. His audience was hypnotized, and applauded enthusiastically at the end. Several students occupied a spot near the stage, and Evan was impressed with their attentiveness toward songs written many decades before they were born.

The musicians retired to a table and ordered a round of beers, after which one student approached Evan. "Excuse me, Dr. Blake? I'm Allen, a student at MIT. I really enjoyed hearing you play tonight." He cast nervous glances at the other performers. "Actually, the whole band was great!" They all smiled and raised their drinks in appreciation.

"Thanks, Allen," said Evan. "We don't get out here very often, so this was as much a practice session as anything."

"I'm looking forward to your course on Materials Science next fall."

Evan winced slightly, uncomfortable with mixing talk of work and play, but managed to keep a relaxed expression. "Well, I hate to tell you this, but I'll be gone on sabbatical this fall, at Imperial College in London." He turned to address his fellow musicians. "Also, I'm flying over there this weekend for a quick contract job, so I won't be able to rehearse until next month."

Evan faced Allen again. "Professor Atkins will be taking over the class, and he's an expert in the field, so you're in good hands. You'll be a senior?"

"Yes. By the way, I was wondering how you got into music, and jazz in particular."

"I heard it often growing up in London. My dad had a huge record collection, with all sorts of American jazz and blues. He's African-Jamaican, so I was also exposed to ska, a Jamaican fusion sound. In Europe there's always been an interest in jazz, even very old and fringe material – sometimes long before it was appreciated in America. I learned to play piano and guitar with encouragement from my mother, who's a musician from Scotland."

Evan finished his drink and set the glass down soundly. "Well, I wish you luck in the fall. Cheers!" He walked behind the stage, where the musicians were packing up their instruments. Evan cased his tan, 1970 Fender Jazzmaster guitar, which he had found languishing in a South London pawnshop in the late nineties. It had a unique, mellow tone, perfectly suited for informal venues like tonight. The club owner strolled over and thanked the group for making his weekly 'amateur night' another big success.

After driving to his townhouse in Cambridge, Evan entered a cluttered study and collapsed into the comfortable armchair at his desk. He gazed at two framed photographs of Rosina. One showed their early days together in London, as she pursued advanced classes at the Royal Conservatory of Music and he studied at Imperial College. The other was taken as she sang at a 2008 music festival in Bologna, Italy, close to her hometown of Milan. Audiences and critics had ranked her among the best sopranos of her generation. Two years later, while they were both in their mid-thirties and married only five years, she was diagnosed with ovarian cancer. Although several new regimens of treatment had offered hope, she was gone within a year.

He reviewed documents related to his upcoming contract – an unusual assessment of the London Eye. David Rollins had sent emails urging him to text as soon as he arrived in London. Evan recalled his days as a new graduate student at Imperial, working under David on Eye-related projects for course credits. The rationale for Evan's selection now as a consultant remained unclear, since civil engineering was not his specialty. In any case, David had been a supportive mentor and friend, the two having remained in touch over the years, so Evan was happy to return the favor.

The next two days raced by as he readied himself for the trip. He had arranged a residence exchange with a London professor who would be working at Harvard during the fall semester. Luckily, that professor had already vacated his London flat for a summer vacation, providing an opportunity for Evan to view the overseas accommodations early. Traveling was straightforward for him these days – no spouse, no children, not even pets. *Keep life simple,* he reflected.

After only a few hours of sleep on his final night at home, Evan looked forward to a long nap in the first-class airline seat offered by the contracting firm. As he stepped outside and climbed into a taxi bound for the airport, he heard someone playing blues on a harmonica far down the street. He felt an unusual reluctance to leave, but dismissed it as fatigue.

Evan's experience at Heathrow on Saturday afternoon was uneventful; he was still a British citizen. While passing through customs, he received the usual double glances, which always reminded him of his parents' fortitude. Without apology they had entered an interracial marriage considered taboo in many cultures. The glances directed at them had often been tinged with hostility rather than curiosity. They now enjoyed a peaceful retirement in South London.

A taxi took Evan to the furnished but unoccupied apartment on a quiet lane in West Kensington. He obtained the key from a neighbor, and then climbed the steps to the first floor, which in London meant one level up from the street. David had offered a ride to dinner, so Evan freshened up and ventured outside to wait. After living for a decade in America, he had to think twice about which side of the street the car would approach. David pulled up to a screeching halt in a Volvo station wagon, and soon they were speeding off to an Indian restaurant not far from the home of Evan's parents.

They entered the noisy, humid establishment and staked out a relatively private table near the back. The air was thick with the sweet and pungent aromas of masala dishes and baked breads. After small talk of weather and English politics over a round of Indian lager, their food arrived, and David transitioned to more formal topics. "It's really nice to have you here for this job."

"You do know that I'm into advanced applications now, like nanotechnology," Evan stated, as diplomatically as possible.

David replied quietly, avoiding eye contact, "Oh yes, I remember, but my main reason for picking you was that I needed a confidant."

Evan studied his friend's face, which suddenly seemed much older than his fifty-five years. Additionally, his voice conveyed a degree of stress far beyond anything Evan could recall.

David continued in a more positive tone. "I don't really keep up on all the new stuff, you know. I've stayed at the larger end of the spectrum; I worked on several 2012 Olympic designs."

"Well, nanotechnology is not really so new," Evan said. "It's become a buzzword for almost any research on a scale up to a hundred nanometers – the size of many viruses, or a thousand times thinner than a human hair, as they like to say. And it's been around for several years now. A lot of commercial products already have nanoscale additives: cosmetics, sunscreens, house cleaning products, batteries, surface treatments for fabrics and glass, and so on."

They paused while a strong coffee was served. David stared suspiciously at the powdered creamer, in light of their previous discussion. He ordered milk instead.

Evan resumed. "Around the time we were raising the London Eye, the Americans were setting up a National Nanotechnology Initiative to coordinate funding – some of my money comes from that. Several whole journals are devoted to the topic now, and last year when I attended a Materials Science meeting, half the presentations were nanotechnology related."

"But your department is called Nanoengineering?"

"Right. Designing functional devices on a nanoscale. You already know how computer chips and data storage are shrinking, but there's much more going on. Take solar energy, for example. Instead of thick panels, we can now print out flexible rolls made of nanostructured solar cells. Pretty soon, solar converters will be paintable. I've also seen nanofilms and nanotubes, just one atom thick, serving as electronic components and sensors."

David adjusted several rolled documents lying next to his chair, and then looked back at Evan. "Didn't you also mention you're moving into biology now?"

"Bioengineering – building electronic devices out of organic materials instead of silicon. Smartphone displays and televisions have already used organic, light-emitting diodes for years. But the newest organic transistors can mimic features of the nervous system itself, like the connections between neurons known as synapses. We're designing 'neuro-inspired' computers that can adapt to their surroundings."

"All very interesting stuff, Evan, but if you don't mind, I'd like to show you these schematics now."

They cleared off the table and David spread out several large sheets, reminding Evan of a scene from an old war movie where the enthusiastic British general proudly presents his latest battle plans. "We've dug a shaft parallel to the foundation's outer wall, here at this corner, where I believe there's a disturbance, based on radar tomography. I'd like you to take a look; I'll need you as a witness on the official report."

"Are you expecting to find a den of moles?" Evan quipped, "I hear they outnumber humans in the UK now." David did not smile, or even look up, so Evan adopted a serious demeanor. "Okay, when do you want to do this?"

"How about tomorrow night?"

"Actually, I was hoping to catch a live show in Soho."

"The entire site will be closing early to the public, so it's an ideal time to deal with any . . . special circumstances."

Evan sighed. "All right, then, let's give it a go."

"Brilliant!" David said with relief.

Once they left the restaurant, Evan requested a ride to his parents' home in the neighboring borough of Lewisham; he would take the tube back to his flat later. Foremost on his mind was hearing a good jazz performance during this short visit.

Chapter Three

The men approached the base of an eerily vacant London Eye at ten o'clock, looking like two ants compelled to inspect a recently parked bicycle. Few clouds obscured the sky, still glowing dark blue after a late sunset, and providing an opulent background for the enormous ring of lights that defined the ride's circumference. Even for a Boston resident, it seemed like an impossibly long day. David began chatting like a tour guide, gesturing here and there while emphasizing key facts, despite Evan's previous experience with the site. The only other sounds were the pleasant gurgling of the nearby Thames, and the ever-present hum of traffic across the river in Westminster.

Although larger observation wheels had been constructed since the Eye, this creation was special. While indeed resembling a giant bicycle wheel, with a central hub and spindle connected to the outer rim by fine cable spokes, it was two hundred times larger than the average racing bike wheel. The design employed a unique suspension principle, with the wheel's weight supported solely by an A-frame on one side; the frame in turn was stabilized through cables planted firmly in the ground. Numerous engineers and factories had cooperated on the construction. All the main components were built offsite in different countries and then transported in pieces up the Thames on enormous barges. The Eye was assembled horizontally on temporary support platforms built in the river.

Raising it to an upright state was accomplished in several stages over a week. Although Evan had played only minor roles in the entire process, he felt pride and awe every time he stood beneath the gravity-defying structure.

The newly prepared vertical shaft was three feet in diameter and equipped with a sturdy metal ladder attached to one side. David descended first, gesturing for Evan to follow just before disappearing into the abyss. After several minutes of cautious climbing, they reached a small room featuring an unbroken, vertical expanse of concrete, where a section of the foundation's outer surface had been exposed. A single incandescent bulb burned in a dangling work lamp, so David pulled out several flashlights from a nearby locker. Evan remained puzzled; what exactly were they trying to assess? Surrounded by damp earth in this claustrophobic space, he felt like one of those moles he had mentioned earlier.

David's eyes darted around, surveying the scene. He finally pointed to a small area of the wall. "The concrete here is weak. There may be some kind of defect behind the surface. I made some measurements last month, but delayed digging until you could arrive."

"Last month! Well, I'm here now, so what's the next step?"

David used a small pick ax to attack a spot where any rational observer would expect to find only solid concrete. It conjured the image of a madman attempting an impossible escape from a basement prison cell. Yet the tool broke through, a hole appeared, and it became clear that only a thin shell had separated them from some kind of cavity. After expanding the hole by several inches, he redirected his flashlight, peered inside, and then spun around. "Incredible! The original seismic study showed a uniform density distribution, but it looks like this space didn't fill up when the cement was poured."

"Or maybe those older methods couldn't detect a small bubble," Evan replied.

They broke away more of the thin wall to get a better view. The chamber was spherical in shape, several feet in diameter, and featured a smooth inner surface. Prominently occupying the center of its volume was a black metal box, seemingly suspended in space, but actually supported by dark, crisscrossing, steel rods – the original rebar matrix used to reinforce the concrete. The box itself was a little over one foot square and about six inches high.

Evan stared in disbelief. "What the hell? This box must've been here when the foundation was poured. But how did a round cavity form? The liquid concrete should've encased the box completely." Evan's first impressions were disturbing. It looked like the concrete had been pushed away from the center under tremendous heat and pressure, in a perfectly symmetrical pattern, leaving the box clean and lacking any crusty residue.

Before Evan could pursue his train of thought, David began whispering, even though no one could possibly overhear them. "Evan, there's something I need to tell you. *I* put the box here, during the construction phase. I was hoping that this location, inside the rebar, would prevent its immediate crushing."

Evan was nearly speechless, and suddenly concerned for his friend's sanity. "Dave, why—"

"I did all this for a friend who wanted to bury something. Something that nearly destroyed his life – those were his words. He said it should be hidden from humanity for a long time." David looked back into the chamber, unblinking. "I never dreamed I'd see this again in my lifetime. I hope you'll help me."

They chipped away more of the concrete until they could reach their arms inside. Despite an awkward angle of approach, Evan was able to negotiate the box toward the opening and both men grabbed hold. It was a heavily constructed steel container weighing about twenty pounds and having two small latches with keyed holes. After they sat the box down at their feet, David staggered back and wiped his forehead with his sleeve. He was sweating profusely, more from anxiety than exertion. "I can arrange for the cavity to be filled with a liquid polymer that hardens, to stabilize this part of the foundation."

"What's in this box?" Evan asked, despite his reluctance to hear an answer. He reached over and tried opening the latches, but they were locked. He also noticed that the top of the box was bent inward slightly, as if it had undergone deformation under extreme pressure.

"I honestly don't know. I asked that question myself many times, but my friend refused to explain. He just said it was some kind of relic or artifact he brought back from Russia. He obsessed over it for years, and then finally decided to get rid of it."

Evan peered into the cavity once more, scanning the perimeter with a flashlight. To his disappointment, he saw no skeletons, treasure chests, or anything of an exotic nature.

David regained his breath and tugged on Evan's sleeve. "Let's take it up now."

"Wait. Something strange happened here, but the metal rods, even the metal box, haven't been affected. It doesn't make any sense."

"Evan, I really need to get all this behind me, as soon as possible. Just leave the rest to me."

They slowly climbed up to the surface, with David holding the box tightly. As they emerged from the shaft, Evan first, they were startled to find a nighttime security guard waiting for them. His expression changed when David came into the light. "Mr. Rollins! Didn't expect to see you out here so late, sir."

"Oh, hello. Uh, a worker left some expensive equipment down there, so I had to retrieve it before I left tonight. This is my colleague Dr. Blake. Well, thanks for your prompt attention, and have a good night!"

"Good night to you too, sir," the guard mumbled, hesitating slightly before wandering off into the shadows.

At the car, David placed the box into his trunk while checking all around, as if expecting a SWAT team to spring from nearby bushes. They drove back to Evan's flat in silence, with David wringing his hands on the steering wheel. It was now past midnight, yet Evan was fully alert, being on East Coast time. It did not help matters that the sky had become black only an hour before.

"Come inside and let's talk about this," said Evan. "I'll fix some tea."

Opening the trunk lid, David motioned toward the box, inviting Evan to be the carrier. With the metal container tucked under his arm, Evan approached his door while looking around self-consciously, feeling like a terrorist smuggling a handgun case onto an airplane. After setting the contraband down with a loud thud on a coffee table in the living room, he stumbled into the kitchen to prepare refreshments. David hovered around the small dining table, stealing glances at the mystery in the next room.

Evan brought out two servings of tea and grimaced as he sat down, his muscles aching from the night's unexpected manual labor. The two men studied their cups for several minutes without speaking. The citrus-tinged scent of Earl Grey permeated the space between them. A clock ticked somewhere down the hallway, then chimed softly.

David finally looked up. "Evan, please take the box and do whatever you want with it. I know it's asking a lot, but I can't take responsibility for it anymore. It was stressful enough just hiding the damn thing in the first place. I don't want to know what's in it."

"Why didn't your friend destroy it?"

"Who knows? Maybe he was afraid to try, or saw it as too important to trash."

Evan was wary, but his curiosity had been sparked. "Okay, I'll take it, but I may just throw it in the river." Yet he knew these words were only meant to console David. Evan's imagination was already on an exhilarating roller coaster ride. This finding might offer a one-time opportunity to experience something extraordinary; perhaps a mystery he could solve himself. An artifact from Russia, David had said – maybe a fabulous archeological discovery?

Evan walked back into the kitchen and stood at the sink, gazing through the window. He spoke without turning around, thinking out loud. "What would be the best way to make a huge impact on the world; something that would last for thousands of years? Something beneficial, of course."

"Well, aren't you trying to do that now, with your career? I mean, you're in a position most people would envy."

"Contributions from scientific research are so incremental, and the hottest topics are very competitive. Few people have the skill or luck to pull off monumental advances."

"I'm not sure what you're getting at," David said.

Evan was reluctant to elaborate. He wondered what type of immortality ordinary people could achieve. Then he thought of Rosina's voice – recorded for all time.

"I think we're getting too tired for philosophy, my friend," said David while yawning. He stood up and walked slowly to the door. Just before exiting, he turned toward Evan. "If you decide to share your discovery with the world, please don't include my name, or where you found it. However, I do ask that you sign off as my witness today," he added with a grin.

"Whatever you say, chief," Evan replied, using his old nickname for David while patting him on the back.

Evan closed the door softly, wondering if he would ever see his friend again. Returning to the living room, he sank down into the couch and stared across at the metal box, debating his next move. His reaction was now mixed. It was interesting, yes, but it encompassed another person's world of problems, while his own was complicated enough. The container was a symbol of every doubt and uncertainty at this point in his life.

This is ridiculous, he decided. *What could possibly be so dangerous?* It was probably just a harmless souvenir buried as a practical joke. He searched several drawers for tools, and found a chisel suitable for prying open the two latches. Presumably the original owner would not be poised outside, waiting to press charges of vandalism. However, a few cautionary images flashed through Evan's mind; he had seen enough movies in which boxes were booby-trapped. After breaking the two latches easily, he opened the lid just far enough to confirm the absence of wires that might indicate an explosive device.

Upon raising the lid fully, he found a wide, flat, cardboard container, along with a sealed letter envelope. Inside the container, a paper sleeve held what appeared to be a single vinyl record, though the black disc felt much thicker than the usual LP. *That's it? Surely something's missing*, he reasoned. Perhaps back at the car, when David put the metal box in his trunk, he'd unlocked it and removed a priceless object using a secret key. *Crazy thought.* Evan quickly dismissed the suspicion. Opening the envelope, he found a handwritten manuscript, which began, '*Have I really chosen this strange journey . . .*'

Before reading any further, his eyes jumped to the last page. It was signed 'Nigel Thompson' – a fairly common name in the UK, but where specifically had he heard this? After a moment, it dawned on him. It was the name of an English composer who had achieved worldwide fame over the last dozen years. Evan returned to the beginning, and read one of the most remarkable tales he could remember. *Surely just speculative fiction, or the diary of a lunatic*, he concluded. Disgusted with the whole affair, he resigned himself to sleep, and lay on the bed, pondering his upcoming sabbatical. Besides scientific research, there would be renewal of old relationships, and the accompanying awkwardness of bringing everyone up to date on his personal life.

After a few hours of half-sleep, Evan awoke before dawn to the sensation of faint music, yet after walking to the window, he found no source; the streets were still dark and empty. He glanced back at the opened box. As an audiophile who had seen his share of rare, old records, he was curious about the disc, and so without further deliberation he carried it over to a turntable in the flat's modest stereo system. He placed the record on the platter, set the needle down near its beginning, and returned to the couch.

After a few moments of silence, he was startled by a dense cacophony of tones, resembling white noise. Several seconds later, the assault slowed to a rapid sampling of multiple types of music, as one might hear while spinning an analog radio dial rapidly through dozens of channels. He felt dizzy, yet as a musician was determined to listen. The stream of music slowed further until finally some sound bites lasted long enough to register a pleasurable sensation. Then, as suddenly as it had begun, the presentation ceased. He sat frozen, like someone anticipating the blast of sound from a symphony as the conductor's baton plunges downward. How much time passed, he could not have said, but eventually he heard something astonishing, yet completely natural. Early American jazz was coming from the speakers.

Evan sat back and listened, and he continued listening throughout the next day, not venturing outside. After a week had passed, he issued requests for some of his belongings to be shipped over to

London immediately, explaining that he wanted to start his sabbatical early. During the subsequent fall months, he devoted long hours to working in the labs at Imperial, interacting with only a few, carefully chosen scientists. In mid-December, he sent a letter to MIT requesting a leave of absence for the spring semester, citing health issues for himself and his parents, though none in fact existed.

Early the next year, Evan ceased communication with everyone he had known before, and left London without revealing his destination. His only regret, hovering in the air like the final note of an enchanting musical performance, was the memory of a woman he had befriended in Boston. But the relationship would have to wait; a monumental advance was calling.

Chapter Four

Jeanette Menard knew that early April in Boston meant erratic weather, so she was not surprised to see a frosty morning transform into a relatively warm day, with temperatures climbing into the sixties. She glanced out of a large window while making a final tour of her laboratory, checking on the activities of staff and students. Jeanette was a newer faculty member in Boston University's Bioengineering Department, having joined in 2011 at age thirty-two. After only five years, she had built up a sizeable, high profile research group, exploring new methods of therapeutic drug formulation.

Today she was eager to leave work early and address a few personal matters, including an odd request to meet with the head of MIT's Nanotechnology Department. While she often visited faculty at nearby institutions for academic collaborations, she suspected that the director's invitation had something to do with Evan Blake. Evan's recent disappearance was a hot topic among gossip circles in the engineering world. Some also knew that Jeanette and Evan had dated on several occasions.

First, however, she had to deliver an hour-long lecture starting at eleven. As she left her research lab to walk across campus toward another building, one of her graduate students chased after her with a question about an ongoing experiment. In his excitement at describing a new result, he broke into

Mandarin Chinese. Jeanette interrupted to point out that she was actually of mixed Vietnamese and French descent, and even so, had received only limited exposure to her mother's Asian language while growing up in Montreal. He vented a nervous laugh and finished his inquiry – in English.

Arriving at the lecture hall several minutes late, she faced the small and familiar group of advanced undergraduates who attended her weekly class on medical technology. A quick connection of her laptop computer to the projector revealed a PowerPoint slide entitled 'Nanomedicine: Applications of nanotechnology for novel drug delivery.' Still out of breath from the walk over, she pulled back and tied her long, brown hair, then beamed at the class. "Today I get to talk about my own area of research." Presenting this topic was easy for her, and she rarely glanced up at the slides for cues.

"Imagine a Trojan horse the size of a virus particle, which has been constructed from materials of our own choice. Buried within its core is a chemical compound toxic to cells. The surface is coated with soap-like molecules – lipids and related biopolymers, which increase solubility, prevent degradation, and block attack by the immune system. This object can also have antibodies attached, which guide it to a specific target such as the surface of a cancer cell. We call this a nanocarrier, or nanoparticle, if its final size is around 100 nanometers or less. Once at the target site, the nanocarrier can release its payload, or better yet, get pulled inside the cell. The cancer cell is then destroyed without damaging the surrounding tissue, helping to reduce side effects."

She displayed a list of nanoparticle-based therapeutics already approved for use, as well as several in progress. "Here are a dozen drug-loaded nanocarriers on the market now, mainly for cancer therapy, along with several dozen more in clinical trials for cancer as well as diabetes, infectious diseases, and even neurological ailments.

"Now, other things can be packaged into a nanocarrier besides a cytotoxic agent. There's a nanoparticle formulation of insulin for absorption in the mouth, which releases the protein into the bloodstream within minutes. Nanoparticles loaded with 'short interfering RNA' can enter cells and shut down the synthesis of a particular protein; for example, an enzyme promoting high cholesterol levels. We can also package genes themselves – segments of DNA – into nanoparticles, for delivery into the cell's nucleus, to start production of proteins that are lacking due to some disease."

The next figure was a schematic of colorful spheres covered with wiggly lines representing the biopolymer coat. "We can take all this a step further, and design even more exotic devices, with even more sophisticated weaponry. Gold nanoshells can absorb light or radio waves of a certain frequency, and then generate intense heat, killing tumor cells without disturbing healthy cells nearby. Nanotubes made from a single, thin wall of interconnected carbon atoms are being used as drug carriers and thermal agents. Nanodiamond particles can enclose drugs, insulin, and even DNA."

She paused and walked around in front of the desk, addressing her audience in a more casual manner. "In summary, things are pretty exciting in nanomedicine right now. Are there any questions?"

"What's the availability of grant money in this field?" asked one senior, clearly thinking ahead a few years.

"Typically, you have to do some hunting, but several sources do exist. I receive funding from the National Cancer Institute through their Alliance for Nanotechnology in Cancer."

Then, there was a question Jeanette always welcomed, and one she heard often. "How did you end up working in this field?"

"I was motivated by several family experiences, starting with my parents. Both went to medical school, and my father is a practicing physician in Montreal. When I was in college, my mother was diagnosed with a rare bone cancer. She fought the disease for several years, but after trying all sorts of treatments, she finally lost the battle.

"Another person who influenced me was my aunt – my father's sister, who lived in Montreal. She helped raise me while my parents worked, and was especially supportive while my mother was sick. About a dozen years ago, she began showing signs of Parkinson's disease. It advanced rapidly, and she now lives at a special care facility in France.

"Seeing a number of traditional therapies fail over the years made me realize how desperately we need truly novel approaches. I switched from a music program at McGill to biology at the University of Toronto, followed by biochemistry in graduate school at the same place. After that, I worked a couple of years in a large pharmaceutical company, but found the corporate environment too distracting – even counterproductive, in terms of innovation. So I returned to academia, which brings me to the present."

Stopping to study her audience, she noticed everyone's eyes riveted upon her, with a couple of students beginning to tear up. She had ventured further than usual into a personal realm, forgetting the potential impact of her story on younger listeners. She tried to wrap up. "Well, feel free to stop by my lab any time, if you want to see what we do. That's all for today."

At ten minutes past noon, Jeanette left the classroom and headed directly for her car, avoiding a return to the lab where some issue would undoubtedly delay her departure. Her first stop was MIT, just across the Charles River, and she felt a tinge of guilt for not walking over the short distance on such a nice day. Parking was not a problem with her adjunct faculty sticker, and she began a short hike to the newest building on campus, dedicated to nanotechnology. She paused briefly at the entrance, feeling lightheaded, and wishing she had grabbed a snack before facing the unknown. Fighting the urge to turn around, she mentally prepared herself to steer the meeting toward a rapid conclusion.

Richard Atkins had risen to the head of his department with ease. Besides forging advances in solar energy conversion and computer design, he was noted for his skill at obtaining research funds through contracts with corporate and industrial sources, a growing opportunity for many universities. Jeanette knocked softly on his open office door, and he rose to greet her warmly. She was invited to sit at a round conference table in the corner of his large office overlooking the river.

After small talk regarding their respective institutions, his tone changed and he spoke with a hint of melancholy. "Jeanette, I'm sure you've heard the news about Evan. He's been one of our most valued faculty members for a decade, and his research was at the cutting edge of our group. But more than that, I'd grown quite fond of Evan; he and Rosina were close friends of my wife as well. When Rosina died, I knew Evan would need time to adjust, but he never regained the same level of enthusiasm, even after five years. Also, he let many of his friendships and scientific collaborations slip away."

As if only now aware of his guest's identity, Richard hastily added, "Evan mentioned your name several times over the last year, and in those moments I saw his face light up."

Unsure how to respond, Jeanette remained silent and stared at the table's centerpiece – a chintzy, glass solar panel donated by a commercial vendor.

There was something about Richard's delivery that seemed more perfunctory than she had expected from one of Evan's friends.

He pulled out a brochure listing scientific conferences in Europe during 2016. "I see you're speaking at the Nanobiotech meeting in London next month. I'd like to ask a favor. I'm sure you've got a lot going on here, but would you mind staying over there a couple more days to do some detective work? I believe you're connected with people at universities around London. Of course, I'd offer to pay for the extended visit."

"I was planning to stay in Europe after the meeting anyway, to see some relatives in France. So yes, I could ask around about Evan while I'm in London."

"Wonderful." He walked over to the window, and then continued after a brief sigh. "I've already gathered some information, but it's scattered and doesn't make much sense. Evan did in fact pursue research at Imperial during his sabbatical, but it didn't include anything from his original proposal. Instead, he was involved in some bizarre Materials Science project, which he didn't publish or even present in a seminar. You could inquire at Imperial, but there's another lead I've learned about."

Richard whirled around, his eyes wider now. "Evan was seen in the company of Nigel Thompson – the London composer, of all people. I realize Evan is very much into music, but I always thought his preference was jazz. In any case, it's possible that Nigel will have some clues as to Evan's whereabouts."

Jeanette was astonished; this was a name she knew well. Critics had hailed Nigel as the new Shostakovich, for having created a rich and diverse body of neoclassical work over the last fifteen years. Twice, she had seen him conduct his own symphonies in Toronto, and had developed quite a crush on the statuesque icon, even though he was twenty years her senior. Momentarily thrilled at the prospect of meeting Nigel, she nearly forgot about Evan. She refocused. "Yes, Nigel sounds like a good person to contact. I'll let you know my progress."

"Thank you so much, Jeanette." He walked her down the main hallway, and then disappeared into a lecture hall where a seminar was underway. Still dizzy from skipping lunch, Jeanette walked to an outdoor food court, where she planned to meet her friend Susan Henderson, a member of Harvard's Anthropology department. Susan, in her fifties, was a force of nature in the group. For decades, she had led numerous expeditions documenting the world's remaining indigenous peoples, at locations ranging from Asia to South America. She was also an amateur violinist, and their mutual love of classical music had drawn them together as they sought venues for practice, such as impromptu quartets formed in the Boston area.

"Jeanette, over here!" Susan yelled from a small table, sipping a drink with one hand while the other anchored papers in the blustery wind. Jeanette bought a sandwich from a vendor and made her way through a large crowd of students, many in shorts and T-shirts on what was clearly perceived as a balmy day.

"They're predicting nice weather for the Marathon next week," Susan said. "I hear you're not running this time, after doing it several years in a row, right?"

"I just couldn't work in enough training this year to qualify. My stamina has really taken a hit," Jeanette said between bites of food.

"So how did your mysterious meeting go?"

"Even weirder than I expected. Atkins asked me to check on Evan Blake while I'm in London next month."

"Really? Now *that* sounds interesting," said Susan in a teasing voice. "You've mentioned his name enough recently."

"I have? Well, yes, I did find, I mean . . . I *do* find him attractive. But I was reluctant to barge into his life. Anyway, I've been so busy over the last few months with new projects. I haven't had much time for dating."

"It's been, what, four years since your divorce?" Susan asked. "Still no regrets?"

"Absolutely not. I heard that my ex is trying to start a biotech firm in Toronto. Maybe he'll find someone up there willing to put her career on hold for him, since that wasn't me."

The women ordered espresso drinks from a nearby kiosk and continued their chat. Clouds were beginning to paint themselves onto an otherwise perfectly blue sky, making it feel cooler, so they moved to another table better sheltered from the wind.

"Say, how Asian do I really look?" Jeanette asked, thinking back to the encounter with her student in the parking lot.

Susan studied Jeanette's face in mock scrutiny. "It depends on the day, even the time of day, and also who you're with. Seriously though, you should just enjoy looking so exotic. Now, fill me in on Evan, since you're on a crusade to find him," she said with a grin.

"We first met back in 2012, but a lot was happening in our lives at that time. His wife had recently died, and I was in the middle of a divorce, not to mention starting up my lab at BU. We started going out occasionally for lunch only last summer, before he left on sabbatical. I felt comfortable around him. There's a lot we share, besides an interest in science. For example, each of us had parents with different ethnic backgrounds, so we can relate to growing up in-between two cultures. We both love music, of course, and both play piano. In fact, each of us considered music as a career, but instead it became just a hobby; we always regretted that decision a little."

"Well, it certainly sounds like Evan is on some kind of adventure. What do you think happened to him? Entered a monastery? It must be something incredible for him to give up everything."

"It's not clear he's given up. But I can't imagine what's going on. I don't even know if he'll respond to my efforts to reach out."

After lunch, the women strolled down a quiet, tree-lined sidewalk on campus. "Oh, I forgot to mention," Jeanette said with excitement. "I'm supposed to contact Nigel Thompson in London for possible leads! Do you know how many people try to grab him for interviews without success? I might as well call the royal family and invite them out for tea."

A link between Nigel and Evan was certainly the strangest notion Jeanette had heard in years. The thought of her life becoming entangled with both men at once was even stranger. She brushed off the idea as nonsense, and began a discussion of music that she and Susan would play together over the weekend.

Chapter Five

It was day five of the week-long bioengineering conference, and Jeanette longed to begin the next segment of her journey. Her presentation had gone well, generating interest among scientists with whom she could strike up future collaborations. The meeting was held at King's College, on Guy's Campus just south of the Thames. Numerous attractions were available in the area, including the Tate Modern Museum and Shakespeare's Globe theater. She walked whenever possible, enjoying the multitude of flowers blooming in the unusually warm May climate. She also rode on the London Eye one sunny afternoon, taking in the spectacular views.

Throughout the week, it did not escape her attention that she was near the suburb where Evan had grown up, and even closer to the flat in Kensington where he had stayed the previous year. Venturing over to Imperial College after the conference, she questioned a number of faculty members, ranging from old acquaintances to persons recommended by Atkins. Most were polite yet aloof, perhaps suspecting that she was a private investigator posing as a scientist. In any case, a palpable concern over Evan's disappearance could be felt on campus.

Her emails to Nigel Thompson's agent went unanswered until she mentioned being Evan's friend. Near the end of her stay, she received a message from Nigel himself, proposing lunch on the following day at a café near Lincoln's Inn Fields. It seemed too good to be true.

Ignoring the light rain and cooler weather that had arrived overnight, Jeanette left her hotel by taxi on Saturday morning for the café. She arrived early in order to first visit Sir John Soane's Museum, an eclectic assortment of art, sculpture, and artifacts packed into a multi-story house on a quiet street bordering the park. The claustrophobic labyrinth of small galleys and narrow passageways, teeming with works from multiple cultures and periods, only magnified the surreal nature of her mission that day.

With some relief she stepped out of the museum and into the lushness of the park, which evoked memories of her first encounter with Evan. It was during a 2012 conference in San Francisco. The irony of the two meeting there, when each worked in the same city so far away, had been an effective icebreaker. One free afternoon they chose to explore Golden Gate Park in his rental car. Their destination was merely the Japanese Tea Garden, yet the drive seemed like the crossing of some vast frontier, given the low visibility from fog, a winding, tree-lined road, and a dash of anxiety from mutual attraction. At the pagoda-crowned main gate, they hesitated, and then plunged through into another world, greeted by scenes straight from an ukiyo-e woodblock print. Mossy lawns bordered by tightly sculpted hedges. Dwarf trees shaded by larger Japanese maple and cherry. Mirror-like ponds dotted with miniature islands supporting stone lanterns. Peaceful waterfalls and elegant bridges, especially the unique drum bridge that formed, along with its reflection in the water, a perfect circle.

A loud car horn blared directly in front of her, snapping her back to London. She had almost stepped out into a busy street against the red light. Her mind nevertheless fought to complete the memory. The two had sipped tea in the ornate Tea House, agreeing to meet again soon. But career building took its toll, and their lunch dates had begun only much later.

After reaching the designated bistro and waiting in a long line, she ordered soup, hoping to warm up from the damp walk. Carrying her bowl into the dining area, with its long wooden tables and benches, felt like entering an old English boarding school. She immediately recognized Nigel, sitting alone at the end of one table, apparently unnoticed by the dozens of patrons. He wore a simple, collarless black shirt and light rain jacket. His medium-length dark hair was swept back across his ears and highlighted by gray streaks. The aura of his presence matched her expectations for a worldly artist.

She sat directly across from him, yet he continued looking down at his meal. Feeling a bit star-struck, she recalled her mother describing a chance encounter with opera singer Maria Callas in Paris in the mid-seventies.

"Hello Mr. Thompson. I'm Jeanette Menard."

His eyes lifted slowly, and he stretched a hand over to shake hers. He spoke in a deep, soothing voice. "Please, call me Nigel. Do go ahead and start your soup; it's their specialty."

"Thanks for meeting me. For a while I thought you'd be impossible to find, but here you are, quite public!" she said, feeling clumsy with her opening line.

"True, inaccessibility is not a good thing. But sadly, I have many distractions these days. I can't accommodate everyone who wants to talk."

Between sips of vegetable soup, Jeanette described her activities in London, as well as her musical background. But when she introduced the topic of Evan, Nigel seemed reluctant to continue.

"Many people in Boston have missed Evan," said Jeanette, wondering whether her tone revealed herself as one.

"Of course. The question is – what do they really want from him?"

The response stumped her, but she pressed on. "Can you tell me where he is?"

"During the first few months of this year he went to America to make some inquiries. I believe he's back in Europe now, but I don't have any further details."

"America!"

Nigel was watching her closely, and she sensed he was the type who could read others quite well. He smiled slightly. "Do I detect a personal motivation behind your quest?"

"Yes. I guess it's obvious," she said with a sigh.

"Let me assure you, Evan's all right, but he's decided to pursue something that goes far beyond his other responsibilities."

"What do you mean? And why have you two been collaborating?" she asked, her voice growing louder.

Nigel glanced around, checking for eavesdroppers. He then lowered his voice, apparently hoping she would follow suit. "Jeanette, there's no 'collaboration.' Each of us had a similar, and very unusual, experience. We simply chose to communicate about it."

"Could you describe the experience?"

"It's a long story, and one I can't discuss now."

"Why did you agree to meet me, if you won't share any details?"

"I wanted to learn whether you harbored some hidden agenda. I'm guessing the answer is no. Yet people in Boston are asking you to search for Evan, correct?"

She decided not to mention Atkins; that would only fuel his suspicions. "It's nothing more than what I said. I just want to know why he took off, and when he's coming back. He's a friend who I care about."

"He'll return when he finishes his current project."

"At least give me a hint of what's going on, so I can estimate a timeline."

"Look, Jeanette," he said in a near whisper, "I can't disclose what Evan has discovered. That must be his decision."

Jeanette stared down at a half-empty bowl. Her emotions were jumping between anger and anguish, and her patience had become a tightly wound spring. She felt her face flushing, yet no longer cared what anyone thought. Finally something snapped.

"Fine. Thank you for your time," she said, grabbing her things and standing abruptly. The bench scraped loudly against the floor. She walked briskly out through a side door and into a long alleyway designed for pedestrian traffic. Halfway down the deserted alley, she stopped, and then leaned against a wet brick wall, the umbrella dropping to her side. She found herself crying quietly for a few seconds, the tears camouflaged among small raindrops on her face. Apparently Evan had affected her more than she realized. Yet it was not like her to become emotional in this way. *Must be jet lag*, she concluded.

After shifting her thoughts to other plans of the day, she was startled to see Nigel standing a few feet away, watching silently. He approached cautiously, but with a compassionate smile. "Jeanette, I think I've misjudged you. Obviously, I couldn't know your true motivation when you contacted me. You see – Evan believes that people with ill intent are searching for him because of what he's found. However, I'm willing to trust my intuition and tell you more. Come, let's get out of the rain."

Nigel led her a few blocks to the Ship Tavern Pub, which at that moment was nearly empty. He ordered two pints of ale while she settled into a table at the rear. After returning with their drinks, he sat patiently while she composed herself and took a few sips. Both were more relaxed now.

“Did you know this pub is over five hundred years old?” Nigel said, glancing around. “My father and grandfather frequented the place.” On the menu’s back cover, Jeanette read of outlawed priests conducting Mass from behind the bar during the reign of Henry VIII. A few priests, caught hiding in a cellar tunnel, were executed on the spot. She mused over the image of Evan lurking in the cellar, waiting to be seized, though with less dire consequences.

Once again, Nigel’s voice was incredibly soothing, almost maddeningly so. “Let me ask you something. What if you had a chance to reveal something extraordinary to the world, with profound implications? Isn’t that the ultimate goal of a scientist?”

She nodded, toying with her napkin.

“You would want to be sure, though – to gather solid evidence.”

She responded with another nod.

“Well, Evan is on such a path right now,” he said.

“That’s still pretty cryptic,” she replied.

“You’re a musician, so let me summarize it this way.” Nigel paused, searching for words. He then leaned over and spoke almost theatrically. “Music is the means through which Evan will share the most incredible discovery in human history.” He paused again before adding, with apparent sincerity, "I hope you'll be part of it."

At this point, Jeanette had given up any hope of a clear statement from Nigel, but at least she felt better about their meeting. Half an hour later, they emerged from the tavern and faced one another. Suddenly his voice sounded more down to earth. "I'll find some way to reach Evan, and give him your contact information. And I'll emphasize your desire to see him. He might respond, but I can't guarantee it."

Nigel took a step forward and gave her a hug; it was warm and comforting. She could feel her schoolgirl crush transforming into a mature friendship, and she was grateful for his genuine concern. They exchanged goodbyes, not knowing if they would ever meet again. Walking away without looking back, she braced her umbrella against a strengthening wind.

At the hotel, Jeanette began thinking about her trip to France, where she would visit relatives in Paris, and then travel to Lyon to see her aunt. She had decided to abandon further inquiries about Evan when, the following morning, she received an email from someone claiming to be him. The sender was asking her to go to a specific Paris bookstore at six that evening. She decided it was a low risk proposal, given the public location, and scheduled it into her overall agenda.

Chapter Six

On Sunday, a Eurostar train roared through the Channel Tunnel to drop Jeanette at Gare du Nord in Paris within three hours. A few metro stops later, she arrived at a small hotel owned by her cousins and situated just east of Luxembourg Gardens. She had visited Paris many times, and was elated to dive back into the warm waters of a familiar culture and language. After strolling through the gardens for an hour, she sat in a chair near the large toy boat pond and consumed the obligatory scoop of ice cream.

Mindful of her rendezvous with Evan, she started out from the hotel early and made her way through the Latin Quarter toward Shakespeare and Company bookstore, located across the Seine from Notre Dame Cathedral. As she passed alongside twelfth-century Saint-Séverin church, the stone gargoyles lining the roof seemed to leer down at her as never before.

Stopping briefly at 22 Rue Saint-Séverin, she peered up at the city's narrowest house; a tall sliver of plaster, only two windows in width, seemingly compressed between adjacent apartment buildings. It was once home to eighteenth-century author Antoine François Prévost, whose novel, *Manon Lescaut,* described the ill-fated romance of a Parisian couple. The book was controversial in 1731 but later inspired several operas and ballets. Jeanette remembered reading it, and pondered the outcome of her own forthcoming tryst.

Reaching the bookstore early, she negotiated a narrow, wooden stairway up to the second floor, and then occupied a cloth armchair located below the front window. A randomly chosen book of French literature provided solace.

An hour passed, and Evan had neither appeared nor called. *Don't I ever learn?* She marched outdoors and onto the sidewalk. A poster at the neighboring Saint-Julien-le-Pauvre church advertised a Chopin piano recital starting at eight, and she was sold. There was just enough time to grab a sandwich and eat in a small park outside the church, while keeping an eye on the bookstore – just in case. Clouds were moving in, and rain seemed likely.

Paying a modest entry fee, she entered one of the city's oldest churches, predating even Notre Dame. She loved the intimacy and charm of these small, medieval sanctuaries, especially ones hosting secular solo or chamber music performances, though large churches like Notre Dame and Saint-Sulpice remained ideal for organ concerts and choral works. Taking a seat near the rear to better appreciate the acoustic ambience, she was enthralled as the recital got underway. A local pianist interpreted some of her favorite ballads, scherzos, and preludes.

At intermission she wandered up to the front row of higher priced seats, looked around several times, and then sat down nonchalantly; it seemed permissible given the low attendance. As she studied her brochure, waiting for the recital to resume, she felt a hand come to rest on her shoulder from behind, and assumed someone wanted her to move. Instead, it was Evan. He had surmised her interest in the recital.

"My apologies," he said in a hushed voice, "the metro lines were running late, and my bloody cell phone refuses to hold a charge."

"That's okay. I got to hear something nice, and it starts again soon."

"I'd like to invite you to an even *more* interesting musical event. But we need to leave right away."

"Well, I am enjoying this a lot."

"Please, it starts soon. You won't be disappointed. It's unlike anything you've ever heard."

"All right. That's a pretty convincing sales pitch."

As they emerged from the church into dusk, light sprinkles were beginning to fall. He gave her a quick welcome hug. "Oh, by the way, hello!"

"Hi, Evan," she said with slightly less enthusiasm. After long days of investigation, this was a somewhat anticlimactic encounter. She was almost too exhausted to ask questions.

"Wow, check out the view," he said, which relieved her of trying.

The lights of Notre Dame reflected off the Seine, as well as his glasses. After a few moments of silence, he turned and led her down a side street, where the towering walls of connected buildings engulfed them like a narrow canyon from the

American southwest. They huddled together under Evan's umbrella while avoiding puddles of water. Foot traffic had thinned, the cool rain discouraging all but the hardiest pedestrians.

Soon they entered old neighborhoods surrounding Sorbonne University. Evan stopped in front of a building less obvious than most, slightly recessed and in shadows, with steps leading down to a lower level apartment. He did not seem surprised to find seven individuals gathered at his door, patiently awaiting his arrival. The small group was politely ushered inside, where they removed damp coats as he prepared hot coffee and tea.

Evan whispered to Jeanette how humbled he felt among this distinctive crowd, composed of older jazz and blues musicians of world-class reputation. Most were French but two were American. Selection and screening had been a long and careful process, and all were sworn to secrecy about this location and the purpose of their visit. None had brought instruments; they were here solely to listen and give their opinion.

The group assembled in his large living room, which was unusually spacious for the apartment's overall size. Evan had set up padded folding chairs on one side, while the other featured two mid-sized, stand-mounted loudspeakers. The speakers were powered with audio equipment located in a smaller adjacent room, hidden from view by means of a black curtain stretched across the top of a doorframe. The audience sat in hushed anticipation as Evan stepped behind the curtain and started the music. Jeanette remained on her feet and leaned against the back wall, remembering magic shows she had seen as a girl. She almost expected Evan to reappear wearing tails and a top hat.

Their ears were soon greeted with a selection of highly improvised jazz piano. Based on the musician's style, several participants recognized this as a solo performance by Thelonius Monk. Background chatter in French was evident on the soundtrack. Following a lively discussion, the group turned toward Evan and offered opinions. Jeanette stepped forward to translate as necessary. This was Monk playing at the 1954 Paris Jazz Festival – the first time he had visited Europe. Two of Evan's guests had actually attended; one was an Amcrican, who noted that no recording of this performance had ever been formally released.

Evan furiously scribbled down all their comments. It was critical to document what this group was saying; namely, that to the best of their knowledge, they were hearing actual historical events and not contemporary recreations. No one questioned the source of Evan's music. Early on he had stated that the technical details would not be revealed, and they were happy with the compromise.

When Evan started the next selection, the response was immediate and widespread. Most recognized the venue as the first European jazz festival, held in Paris in May 1949. The set featured Miles Davis and several other Americans playing at the *Salle Pleyel*. Some of these concerts had been broadcast and released later, others had not. The consensus in the room was that this piece fell into the latter category.

Next up was an ensemble of acoustic guitars, violin, and bass, playing in a distinctive bouncy style. One audience member jumped to his feet and said "*Quintette du Hot Club de France! C'est fantastique*!" Jeanette stepped in again, telling Evan what he already guessed. Since the 1920s, jazz had been a significant part of cultural life in Europe, and with the *Quintette's* creation in 1934 by guitarist Django Reinhardt, France became one of its leading supporters. Since the players introduced themselves specifically as *Django et le Quintette du Hot Club de France*, this was likely a gig during World War Two. Yet formal recordings were not practical at that time due to widespread shortages. The man now standing owned all known albums of the *Quintette*, yet had never heard this particular performance.

One final selection caused jaws to drop in astonishment. Jeanette could hear the guests quietly debating how any recording of this event could possibly exist in such pristine condition. It sounded like a performance by clarinet/saxophone legend Sidney Bechet and his band as they played at the opening night of *La Revue Nègre* in Paris in 1925, where exotic dancer Josephine Baker had danced wearing nothing but a feather skirt. While none of Evan's guests had been present, there were many clues to confirm the venue.

After about an hour, Evan's guests began to exit, each deeply moved and thankful for the opportunity to hear the genius of past masters at work. One musician named Jean-Paul recommended a new member for their little club; namely his nephew, who supposedly possessed a large and rare record collection. Evan promised to initiate the necessary 'background checks.'

As they filed out, the two Americans addressed Evan affectionately as 'kid,' since he had recently turned forty. Evan was proud to share a tiny piece of the miracle that had entered his world quite accidentally. Small teams like this one tonight were part of a large-scale validation he was building, prior to the great announcement. But there would be no rush toward full disclosure. Nor would he allow himself to become socially isolated in his special knowledge, as had befallen the previous owner.

Evan and Jeanette were alone now, and she surveyed his face closely for the first time that day. He certainly looked different; not in an entirely negative way, but as one appears after aging several years, or experiencing a stressful incident. However, his voice was calmer than she could remember.

"I'm glad you came," he said. "Sorry for all the mystery."

"Evan, I'd like to know what's going on; why you disappeared; what you've found."

"It's a long story. How about some coffee while we talk?"

"Maybe later. Can't you just start somewhere?"

He paused for several seconds, looking away. "It was all so unexpected. I don't know where to begin. Wait, let me show you something." He led her into the adjacent room, filled with stacks of audio equipment, optical disks, vinyl records, laptop computers, and a high-end turntable. "Tonight you heard digital recordings I made using a *single* record as the source." He pointed to a black, unlabeled disc sitting idly on the turntable.

Her eyes continued to dart around, expecting some extraordinary sight, but she found none. "I'm confused. What's so unusual about that?"

"It's probably best to just spit it out. This record," he said boldly, as if introducing a person, "contains jazz music. But much more than any LP would normally hold. Some performances are very old, even before recording equipment was available, yet the quality exceeds modern-day standards."

Jeanette was now even more baffled. But her greatest concern was that Evan might be suffering from some delusion of grandeur, manipulating the group of visiting musicians for some bizarre reason. She decided to remain a passive spectator for now, and not challenge his claims.

"Where did you find it?"

"In London. Afterwards, I used my sabbatical at Imperial to study it. I'll tell you about those results later. I felt I needed to verify as many of the performances as possible, so I flew over to the States earlier this year. I returned to Europe just this month to wrap things up. Jazz has always been popular here, and older fans can help me to confirm what's on the disc, as you saw tonight."

"Evan, what's the significance of jazz being on this record?" she asked cautiously, avoiding confrontation.

"It plays jazz now because I'm the current owner."

"I don't understand."

"Jeanette, let me show you a letter written by the previous owner, Nigel Thompson." She was amazed, yet somehow not really surprised. Evan grinned while viewing her reaction. "Nigel called me after meeting you in London the other day. That's how I knew you were in Europe and coming to Paris. I don't really follow conference proceedings anymore to see who's speaking, you know. But I'm curious why you decided to contact Nigel."

"Richard Atkins."

"Ah, of course," he said, nodding his head at the inevitable. He handed her a yellowed manuscript several pages long, which she carried over to a comfortable sofa in the living room. Evan watched her through side-glances while preparing refreshments.

As she read, Jeanette sensed a metamorphosis. She was no longer simply Jeanette in Paris; she had become Alice in Wonderland.

Chapter Seven

Handing back the pages penned by Nigel, Jeanette's face begged for elaboration.

"I found the Record during an inspection of the London Eye last summer," said Evan, "obviously many generations earlier than Nigel had planned."

He sat beside her and continued. "I contacted Nigel and told him I'd found the disc, but was hearing jazz instead of classical music. That renewed his interest. He was willing to hear about my research, but refused to see the Record again, or even visit me. He said it was a closed chapter in his life. However, he admitted that those years of listening inspired him to compose, and gave him fresh ideas."

"It *would* be amazing to hear Mozart conduct his own works in Vienna," she said. Evan looked surprised by her endorsement, which she quickly amended. "If it's all true, of course."

"Now, just as Nigel wrote, I hear live performances rather than studio recordings, which would be redundant anyway. And I never experienced the same performance twice, maybe just because there are so many selections available. Some of the material on the Record was never captured using any conventional method. Nigel had few opportunities to verify the performances *he* was hearing. But I was able to do more research, since so much of jazz comes from the twentieth century. Also, for some reason, Nigel wasn't able to transfer anything to tape. But I've made high resolution digital recordings during playback, using my analog-to-digital convertor."

Evan stood up and walked around while he spoke. "Of course, it can't be a vinyl record as we normally think of it. But I don't think it's a 'time portal,' as Nigel speculated. It must be some kind of media player, like an iPod, receiving input wirelessly from servers that have been storing live performances for a long time. The disc is somehow able to detect its owner's musical preferences, then download a subset of material from the servers for playback."

"That sounds impossible," she said, despite efforts to remain neutral.

"Well, just think how magical an iPod would appear to someone a thousand years ago."

"So you're saying the disc is something designed and built by . . ." She had difficulty mouthing the words.

"Yes, an advanced civilization. And I think it was designed to look like a phonograph record so humans could comprehend it – so we'd have some idea how to interact with it. But choosing a shape like an LP means the designer was viewing our world from a very specific time period, early in the twentieth century."

"How do you mean?"

"Lateral-cut disc recordings were developed in the first decade of the twentieth century, starting out at five inches in diameter and quickly expanding to twelve. They soon became more popular than Edison cylinders."

Evan selected an old cassette tape from a box, and held it up as a talking point. "Magnetic tape first appeared in Germany in the thirties, but it wasn't a routine format for music until the late forties." He threw the tape back.

Finally, he picked up a conventional LP and waved it as a prop. "Any extraterrestrial culture viewing Earth during the early twentieth century would have seen a flat, round disc as our most common and reliable tool for distributing music. I'll bet that's when the Record first appeared."

Setting the LP aside, he walked closer to her. "But long before dropping off the Record, they must have hidden special devices capable of storing all possible live music, going back centuries or more. I can't imagine how they actually captured the sounds in the first place, or where these devices might be hidden."

"Evan, if all this music you hear is authentic, then how does the Record works? What's it made of?"

"There's still a lot I don't understand, but I'll tell you what I've learned so far from my work at Imperial." He took a seat next to her on the sofa. "I recruited a couple of faculty members and a few students from labs specializing in nanotechnology, but of course I didn't tell them where I got the disc. I said it was a joint MIT-industry collaboration, and that I couldn't share any background. I don't think they believed me, but they were happy enough just to participate in something so mysterious."

He paused, searching for the best way to summarize months of work. “We started by looking at the surface layers. Scanning probe microscopy told us about the physical and chemical properties, while atomic force microscopy showed us structural features. Raman spectroscopy gave hints about the types of molecules used in the disc. X-ray and gamma-ray imaging showed layers deeper inside. To make a long story short, it’s an incredibly complicated mixture of organic-based electronics, organic-metal interfaces, and biopolymer-based scaffolds – designs that are hundreds, maybe thousands of years beyond our current steps into nanotechnology.”

Jeanette was trying desperately to absorb everything. “A lot of jazz has already been recorded. By us, I mean. Does this Record-server system really add so much?”

“It provides much higher quality versions of everything, and most importantly, fills in countless live events that were never formally recorded by humans.”

“You keep mentioning the quality.”

“Yes; consider the history of sound recording. Before 1925, recordings were made by physically channeling the sound vibrations through a large horn to a stylus that cut grooves directly into a spinning wax disc. The quality of those acoustic recordings was horrible – harsh and inaccurate. Finally, around 1925, sound could be converted to electronic signals using microphones, and sent to a stylus for cutting the master disc. The recording quality improved, but was still rough by modern standards. The audio quality I hear from the Record is always perfect. At first, it was hard to believe I was hearing historical events, and not modern-day re-enactments."

"Then how can you be sure you're really hearing the original performances?"

"It's a combination of several things. Sometimes band members introduce themselves, or someone else does. Sometimes background sounds help to identify the time and place. Occasionally, conventional recordings of the same live event are available for comparison, especially from the forties onward.

"But in the end, these examples weren't enough. In January, I felt I should visit cities where jazz developed, to check known collections and libraries, hunt down famous musicians or their families, and talk to recording company employees. I pretended to represent the owner of a recently discovered music vault. I never showed the Record itself to anyone, of course; I took copies of my digital recordings for experts to hear. Also, I deliberately added distortion to the audio files I was going to play, so they'd sound 'older' and not shock listeners with their perfection. Several sound engineers at small record labels helped me compare my files to their own vault holdings."

Evan carried over several binders of notes from his trip across America. It reminded Jeanette of someone preparing to share photos of a summer vacation. She could sense his enthusiasm, and was now less concerned about any delusions. He sat down close beside her, his body touching hers slightly, but neither pulled away in a self-conscious reaction; the contact felt natural and welcome.

"New Orleans was my first stop, since jazz began there. Rhythms, harmonies, and melodies from the black slave experience mixed with European and American folk music to give a special sound. The earliest styles were piano ragtime and marching band funeral music. I visited archives at New Orleans and Tulane universities, checked the city's Oral History Project, and contacted small music societies. I looked around for any documentation to confirm what I was hearing on the Record.

"Here's an example. The king of early jazz was Charles 'Buddy' Bolden. His band never recorded, mainly because he'd burned out by 1910, before the technology existed. However, from the Record's outer edge I've heard a group introducing itself as Bolden's. Their style of playing, and the background sounds, make the performance seem authentic, based on everything we know about those times. I've also heard material by Freddie Keppard's band; he actually declined to record when given the chance in 1917. As a result, the first formal jazz recording in America involved an all-*white* band, The Dixieland Jazz Band.

"Another famous group was led by Joe 'King' Oliver, a cornet player. His band included Sidney Bechet on sax/clarinet and Louis Armstrong on trumpet. In 1923, Oliver's Creole Jazz Band became the first black jazz band to formally record, using that awful acoustical transfer method. But whenever this band appears on the Record, the sound quality is flawless.

"A lot of music happened in Storyville, the 'red-light' district. Piano jazz was nightly entertainment, and one of the best at it was Jelly Roll Morton, who combined ragtime and blues. I'm convinced I've heard Morton playing in a bordello using the Record, since I've compared the style to his original paper piano scrolls. Anyway, in 1917, the government raided and shut down the district, forcing many musicians to move to northern cities like Chicago or New York. Some went overseas."

Evan opened another binder. "Chicago was the next stop on my road trip, though not a pleasant place to be in winter. I visited libraries at the University of Chicago, as well as private collections. Morton cut many of his recordings there in the mid-twenties, with his group called the Red Hot Peppers, and I've listened to them play live on the Record. Oliver's band also went to Chicago, where they did quite well. By 1925, Louis Armstrong left Oliver's band to start his own group called the Hot Five, to explore scat singing and horn improvisation. Supposedly the Hot Five never played live. However, on the Record, I've heard one of their performances – they stated it would be their only live gig."

The largest binder now appeared in Evan's hands. "Then it was on to New York City, where a major jazz scene existed in the twenties. I dropped by the National Jazz Museum of Harlem to see a newly discovered collection of records – thousands of rare, unreleased material from the late thirties, which helped my research a lot.

"New York is where composer and band leader Duke Ellington got started, mainly at the Cotton Club, which catered to all-white audiences. The only known human recording of a Cotton Club performance surfaced ten years ago when a 1931 German radio broadcast was discovered; that helped to confirm a similar event on the Record.

"In a class of his own was Art Tatum, a self-taught piano virtuoso. By the thirties, he was so famous that classical artists like Horowitz, Gershwin, Rachmaninoff, and Rubenstein would visit the clubs to watch his performances. One episode at the Onyx Club shows up on the Record, with Rubenstein's presence acknowledged by Tatum at the set's end. On the guitar side of things, I heard a jam session by Charlie Christian at Minton's Club from the late thirties; he practically introduced electric guitar to jazz, and later joined Benny Goodman's band.

"During the forties, new styles came out – freer flowing lines, with experimental harmonies and more improvisation. All this was eventually called 'bebop,' though not by the musicians themselves. Like I said, it became easier for people to make live recordings, which helps me to identify the Record's versions. For example, thanks to some crude tapes of a Charlie Parker gig at the Three Deuces in 1948, I was able to confirm the session when I heard it on the Record. And some poor quality recordings of Thelonius Monk on piano with John Coltrane on sax at New York's Five Spot Café in 1957 helped me identify those sessions on the Record."

Evan set aside the New York binder, and gestured with his hands. "I've heard rare events from the west coast too. Ray Charles in Seattle in the late forties; the Dave Brubeck Quartet from the early fifties in San Francisco; and a rare session in San Francisco where guitarist Wes Montgomery played with John Coltrane's group at a 1961 Jazz Workshop, which was never formally recorded.

"Finally, I ended up in Kansas City, just as my cash was running out. There, FBI agents approached me at my hotel. Atkins had reported me as a missing person, and they tracked me down from a few credit card transactions I was forced to make. But I had bigger problems than Atkins. Some recording company executives had grown suspicious, assuming I'd stolen historical recordings, or was working for European labels that don't pay royalties on old recordings and release them cheap in Europe. In short, a lot of lawyers became interested in my activities. However, the FBI couldn't hold me – there were no formal charges.

"I decided to return to Europe to complete my work, and a stay in Paris was critical. As I mentioned before, the French were wild about jazz from the earliest days. For many black musicians, Paris was a chance to leave behind the racism of America and head to a major center of art and entertainment. Just think how exciting it must have been in the twenties, with so many nightclubs in Paris featuring jazz bands.

"I'm close to finishing all the research I need, and Paris will be the perfect place to reveal the Record." He looked fondly at Jeanette, who was now half asleep. It was understandable; jazz was not her passion. He wished he could share exciting accounts of Bach and Beethoven. His wristwatch showed midnight, and the noise of traffic outside had dwindled to the buzz of an occasional passing motorbike. He offered his comfortable couch, and she gladly stretched out rather than trek back to her hotel.

She fell asleep almost immediately, and Evan covered her gently with a spare blanket. He sat and gazed from a chair across the room, feeling like a fool for virtually ignoring this woman in recent years. Yet here she was in Paris, with him – what were the chances of that? Could he convince her to follow him on this strange quest? Would they have to give up their careers to decode the Record? Would they become a couple? It was all too much to ponder in one night. He wandered off to the rear bedroom and slept.

Chapter Eight

Jeanette awoke to considerable confusion as she took in the unfamiliar surroundings. It was early Monday morning in Paris, of that she was fairly certain. Then she remembered sleeping overnight on Evan's couch. He had just returned from a local bakery with pastries – now neatly arranged on a plate – and was brewing coffee in the kitchen. She dragged herself to the small dining table, still trying to process the previous night's incredible tale. He marched in with two freshly prepared cups of espresso, greeting her in a chipper voice, which she found mildly annoying at this hour. After taking a few sips, she asked him for more details about the Record, and then waited for the caffeine to take hold.

"From atomic force microscopy, the surface isn't really smooth, but looks like a thick carpet of fibers. Each fiber is actually a nanosized sphere attached to a long stalk. I was able to isolate some of these nanospheres, since they break off easily. A friend took the samples to Hamburg, Germany and exposed them to X-rays from a free electron laser, or FEL, which gave us diffraction data. FEL is a new method to analyze tiny samples of crystallized molecules; it's being used now to determine the three-dimensional structure of proteins. However, I didn't get around to processing the X-ray data yet.

"Deeper inside the disc, there seem to be diamond lattices that might be serving as hardware for quantum computers. This is something humans have only just begun to explore, by trapping an individual atom inside a nanocage and reading out the atom's quantum state, such as electron spin, as a 'qubit.' That's the quantum equivalent of a silicon-based computer bit. One lab in my department has made progress with fullerene – a round shell of interconnected carbon atoms – to enclose a nitrogen atom. The fullerenes are then inserted into a diamond lattice. So far, only simple quantum calculations are possible; we're way behind whatever's happening in the disc.

"We also found that the Record is slightly radioactive," he said in a more reserved tone. Jeanette recoiled instinctively and stopped chewing her croissant. "But it's very low level," he quickly added. "The radiation is generated from deep inside – probably an inner layer serving as a power source. The disc's outer shell blocks this type of radiation, which is mainly alpha decay."

Opening a spreadsheet file on his computer, he studied the screen for several seconds. "From the radiation energy levels, a physicist friend identified several interesting elements. One is thorium. It's found in the earth's crust at about the same level as lead. He detected three radioisotopes of thorium in the Record: 229, 230, and 232; they all decay through alpha emission.

"The most interesting thorium isotope is 229. This atom's nucleus has a very low energy excited state, which gives it the potential, more than any other known atom, for applications in high-density energy storage, super-accurate atomic clocks, and even stable quantum computers. I've seen several published papers testing these ideas; just imagine what a few thousand years of additional research might give you.

"Thorium 230 and 232 are very stable, and we're not sure what purpose they serve. However, when thorium-232 is exposed to neutrons, it can convert into uranium-233, which is fissile and has been used as fuel in nuclear reactors – with reduced nuclear waste. Similar power generation may occur inside the disc, if there's a way to activate thorium-232; perhaps with a neutron source that we can't detect.

"Next up, we found uranium-234, a naturally occurring isotope that's also an alpha emitter, but it's not fissile either and couldn't serve as a nuclear fuel, unless it too absorbs a neutron to become uranium-235, a standard reactor fuel.

"Finally, there's the element Americium, which doesn't even exist naturally on Earth, but must be created artificially inside reactors and particle accelerators, as was first done in 1944 at Berkeley. It's extremely rare and expensive, but is still used today in commercial smoke detectors, though in tiny amounts of course. There's a nuclear isomer of Americium in the Record called 242m that can undergo nuclear fission with only one percent of the mass needed by uranium. For example, 242m could serve as fissionable material even in the form of a thin, metallic film. There's research looking into applications of 242m as a nuclear battery, or even –

get this – as fuel for interplanetary space ships using nuclear propulsion."

He looked up, emphasizing the point, and then continued reading his notes. "It all relies on the fission products of 242m, which can either propel a spaceship directly in deep space, or heat up a gas or fluid to power a generator. Maybe we're being given a hint of how they move through the galaxy.

"Actually, both the Russians and NASA have considered nuclear-powered rockets for interplanetary travel, though not using Americium, which is much too rare to be practical. According to the Russians, a journey to Mars using nuclear propulsion would take only six weeks instead of the eight months with conventional chemicals." He finally pushed the laptop back, resting his eyes.

"There's one more thing I haven't mentioned," Evan said hesitantly. "The disc has the potential to produce incredible energies. It actually prevented us from doing any invasive work at Imperial. Electromagnetic emission levels went off the charts when the disc was put under physical stress. That might explain a spherical bubble I found under the London Eye, surrounding the Record."

Jeanette kept glancing back at the Record, so Evan reiterated. "Again, there's only a trace of background radioactivity when the disc is at rest." An expression of weariness suddenly crossed his face. "I can see years of work ahead, and I can't do it alone. But at least I can argue that the music isn't playback of human-made recordings – it's not the latest iPod."

Evan excused himself and left for a back room to freshen up. Jeanette walked around the flat, swinging her arms in circles to loosen up, thinking through all the science. She unexpectedly found herself standing in front of the turntable. Staring at the disc, she observed nothing more than she had the night before, but after Evan's description, it now had a surreal presence – like an idealized 'black body,' absorbing all incident light. Simultaneously, it embodied something monstrous, like the black crystals from an old science fiction film that grew upward hundreds of feet, only to come crashing down upon cities.

But mostly it was a breathtaking exhibit, as wondrous as The Rosetta Stone had been when she visited the British Museum at age ten. Her right arm rose without conscious effort, and she saw her hand reaching out toward the disc, as if some powerful magnet were pulling it forward. One more step brought her index finger within inches. She had an overwhelming urge to simply touch it, like a childhood compulsion to place one's hand in a fire. Seconds became hours; she was a slowly moving statue.

"No!" Evan's voice exploded behind her as he returned. Jeanette jerked her hand back, slamming her elbow against a stack of electronic gear. Grimacing, she knelt down in pain as he rushed over.

"Do you know what you could have done?" he shouted.

Instantly regretting his outburst, he helped her up. "I'm sorry I yelled. But the Record's content changes according to its owner, and I've invested so much time in its jazz mode. I don't know how easily I could get it back."

"So just touching the Record makes it play a different kind of music?" she asked, still rubbing her elbow.

"I think that's part of it, based on Nigel's account of hearing classical music, and me hearing jazz. There's also some kind of fine-tuning the first time you hear the disc. But it's more than just different music, Jeanette. It's something that affects the owner in an emotional sense. Nigel noticed the same thing."

Evan guided her back to the couch, taking her bruised arm and stroking it tenderly. "For example, from the Record, I've heard jazz or blues played primarily on electric guitar or piano. As you know, those are what I play and enjoy hearing most. Naturally, some performances involve horns, especially on the early stuff, but not as much as you'd expect if the disc sampled jazz randomly. In other words, the Record is personalized. It's a potential tap into every live jazz performance ever given, as long as there's something special for *me*. Even the 'microphone position,' if you could call it that, is biased toward my favorite instruments."

"It's like a personal gift," she half asked, half stated.

"Exactly. Whenever I receive a gift tailored to please me, it means something. It's some kind of message. And if someone wanted to send a message that didn't rely on any particular language, yet would have maximum impact, what better way than music custom-designed to stir the emotions of each person?"

"Well, if you're being sent a message, what is it?"

"I have no idea. Nigel debated this for years, without reaching any conclusions. He did say that the Record influenced him in a positive sense, creatively. At the same time, he thinks it was responsible for bizarre sensations, perhaps hallucinations. He was reluctant to talk or write about those aspects."

Several minutes elapsed in silence, and Evan appeared lost in thought. "You seem worried," she said. "Is there something you haven't told me?"

"I'm facing bigger issues than a hidden message in a magical record. Some of my lab notes were stolen near the end of my stay at Imperial. They summarize the disc's general properties without giving away too many specifics. It must have been a co-worker who realized something very unusual was being studied, although no one knew the whole story except me. Think about it. This disc would be priceless to anyone looking for a technological edge – private companies, governments, or military powers. Fortunately, I still have the most detailed lab results on a laptop and a few storage disks. The only other person who knew of my work was Atkins; I talked with him briefly in December by phone."

She mulled over his concerns. “Some of the biggest winners with this technology would be pharmaceutical companies. New drug delivery methods would let them reformulate existing drugs, expand into new drug markets, and extend their patents. In fact, drug delivery offers higher margins than almost any other use of nanomaterials right now – certainly a lot more than you get from paint or sunscreens.”

“All the more reason to get the Record into the public domain,” said Evan, “so no one can monopolize it.” He walked into the audio room and returned with the disc, now protected by its original metal box. Heading toward the back, he gestured for her to follow. “Let me show you something – my little construction project after moving in.”

In the bedroom, he opened the folding doors of a large storage closet. Spanning its width was an assortment of shirts and jackets on hangers, which consumed most of the closet’s volume. Pushing all these to the left, he exposed the right sidewall, covered by wood paneling. He jiggled the corners, and to her surprise, the entire panel lifted out as one piece, revealing a tall but narrow chamber extending back several yards.

“There’s an empty space running behind my bedroom wall, which I can access through this closet – I heard a hollow sound when rapping on the wall. I’m not sure why it’s there, but this building is over a hundred years old, and was probably remodeled several times. Anyway, now I’ve got a hiding place for the Record and other valuables whenever I go out."

Holding up the metal box, he spoke with even greater pride. "There's one more precaution I've taken. When I was at Imperial, I redesigned this box to have a false bottom, and under that I installed a tracking device – just in case someone runs off with it." He placed the box inside the chamber, and then reseated the closet's sidewall.

It was now mid-morning, and Jeanette prepared to leave. "Well, thanks for breakfast, and a very interesting story. I need to get back and visit my relatives; probably for most of the day. But why don't we walk around Paris tomorrow?" She took out a business card and wrote down the name of her hotel. "I'll stop by at nine in the morning, okay?"

Evan agreed. He would take a much-needed break from the scholarly crusade that had consumed him since last summer.

Chapter Nine

Pick a district at random, wander without a care, and let yourself become lost; you will always discover something interesting in Paris. Such was the strategy of Jeanette's father, and she hoped to follow it today. Arriving at Evan's flat on a beautiful Tuesday morning, she was slightly disappointed by his request to start specifically at Musée d'Orsay. However, after two hours of viewing impressionist paintings, and a tasty lunch at the museum café, they began a leisurely stroll along Rue de Bac. The strategy paid off once they spotted Deyrolle, the unique taxidermy shop Jeanette had not seen since childhood.

"*C'est intéressant*!" she said, yanking Evan off the sidewalk. What at first seemed like an appliance store transformed as they climbed a large staircase to the second level. Stretching out before them was a series of rooms crowded with stuffed animals of various shapes, sizes, and poses, alongside display cases full of small creatures, shells, dried plants, and other curiosities. The store had been a fixture since 1881, and resembled a long-forgotten wing of the Smithsonian. Entering the last and largest room, Evan was astounded to find a vast collection of mounted insects and butterflies, many of which were for sale.

Jeanette gazed about, wide-eyed, but then frowned and walked up to Evan, speaking in a hushed voice. "Do you suppose the beings who made the Record view us this way, as specimens to be mounted and displayed?" Evan did not answer, but continued viewing the spectacle.

Despite initial reluctance, he purchased a small butterfly with bright-blue, reflective wings. With a wink he told Jeanette, "The iridescence, or change in color at different angles, is caused by light reflecting off nanoscale crystals in the wings." She rolled her eyes.

They left the store and walked a few blocks south into a district of narrow streets and lighter traffic, eventually stopping at one of the ubiquitous cafés with tables spilling out onto the sidewalk. Evan ordered a few treats and, "*Deux cafés au lait, s'il vous plaît,*" to impress Jeanette with his improving pronunciation. They relaxed and studied passersby, as mandated by Paris café etiquette.

"It's nice to be out doing normal things, and forget about the Record for a while," he said.

"I agree. Sorry to bring up the subject back at Deyrolle."

"That's okay. You had a good point," he said, finishing off a treat. "Did you spend much time in Paris when you were young?"

"We would all come over once a year, at least until I started college. After my mother died, my father lost interest in regular travel. But those early trips were wonderful. He loved watching me as I experienced each attraction for the first time."

"How did your parents meet?" Evan asked.

"Both were studying medicine at the University of Paris. My father grew up in France, but my mother left Vietnam in 1975. Despite some previous training, she had to redo most of med school for western credit. They got married and moved to Canada in the late seventies, just before I was born. She never went into practice, though; only my father did. What about yours?"

"My mother studied music in Edinburgh, then moved to London, where my father was an engineer at University College. As an interracial couple, they faced some challenges, but felt pretty safe in central London – there it was 'hip' to be mixed. He ended up at a small firm; she became a private music teacher."

A woman passing in front of them tugged at her young daughter's hand, urging her to hurry by using a common nickname. *"Venir petite puce!"* The girl only resisted, giggling.

Jeanette laughed and turned to Evan. "That mother said, 'Come along little flea.' My father had a nickname for me on our trips to Paris – '*Trinette,*' which means 'little innocent.'"

Evan grinned with recognition. "That's also the name of a popular song by French jazz legend Claude Bolling."

"So what about your name? Any special meaning?" she asked.

"Well, my dad told me he was distantly related to Arthur 'Blind' Blake, who played blues guitar in Chicago in the twenties. But I'm hoping my ancestor is actually Eubie Blake, a ragtime pianist born in 1883, who lived to be one hundred years old; those would be good genes to have."

Jeanette watched a young couple walk by, arm in arm, chatting happily. She shot an affectionate glance at Evan, but he was deep in thought. Finally he looked up. "Your last name reminds me of a short story by Jorge Luis Borges about a man named Pierre Menard, who sets out to rewrite the novel *Don Quixote*, or at least part of it, almost 300 years after Cervantes. It turns out that Menard's text is exactly the same, yet it sparks a very different response in readers once the historical context of the two authors is contrasted. Borges is asking, does a piece of literature have any absolute significance, or is its meaning wholly defined through the reader's interpretation?"

"The Record is like that, isn't it?" she asked, the topic being unavoidable. "The meaning of the disc depends on the owner's emotional response to music." She gulped down her last sip of coffee, and then continued. "In the end, is the Record just a device for our listening pleasure, and nothing more? Or could it be a tool for them to study us?"

"That's an interesting idea. To study us?"

She set the cup down and propped her chin on one fist. "Maybe they're curious to know why music matters so much to us."

"I've certainly wondered that," he said. "Music in some form is found in all cultures and throughout history, even though there's no obvious need for it."

"Well," she said, "some types of music, like singing and rhythmic dancing, were probably important in prehistory for social bonding and knowledge transfer, giving certain groups an advantage, and that's a cultural selection process. Also, Darwin felt that musical ability might provide a sign of biological fitness to attract the opposite sex, which would be passed on through a sexual selection process."

Just as she finished speaking, their waiter walked up and presented the bill, while humming a tune and staring at Jeanette. The couple laughed, much to his bewilderment.

"What will you do when all this is over?" she asked. "Once you've publicized the Record? Go back to your job? Use the disc as a research project?"

"I'm not sure. I suppose I could donate it to some institution, if they'd guarantee its safety and public access. As for breaking the news, I've already decided on Paris. I think it's appropriate, since jazz allowed me to verify the Record's content. Maybe I'll present my evidence at Curie University, which is close to my apartment."

He pulled out his phone – now fully charged – to check text messages, and then looked up with excitement. "Oh! I wish I'd seen this earlier. One of those men at my place Sunday night, Jean-Paul, has a nephew with a collection of rare records. It might help me to answer a few remaining questions, but I'd need to stop by today, since they're leaving town tomorrow on vacation. He lives in Saint-Denis. Is that far?"

"It's a suburb just a few miles north of Paris. You should be able to take the metro there directly.

Here, look at this map." She held up her smartphone. "His address is close to a station."

"If I head over now for a quick look, I can make it back in time for dinner. If there's nothing useful, then I'll just wrap up with the documentation I have now. Want to come along?"

Jeanette was saturated. "I think I'll pass."

"At least wait at my place, and we'll eat somewhere close later," he said.

They took the metro back to his apartment. Once inside, he grabbed a laptop and began to exit, but then stopped and walked into the audio room. Sound flowed through the speakers. "I'm leaving you with some music *direct* from the Record, not just one of my digital files. It's jazz of course – sounds to me like something from the forties. Even I can't predict what will play. Anyway, you can adjust the volume with this remote, and you don't have to worry about resetting the tonearm when it finishes."

He walked close to her, speaking softly. "I had fun today."

"Me too," she said with a smile.

"I'm glad you're here. I thought about us getting together more often back in Boston, but I was always distracted. Right now, you're one of the few people I can trust."

"Well, I'm still not sure what's going on, but I'd like to help you figure it out."

"Good. I'll see you in a couple of hours. Please make yourself at home." Unexpectedly, he took a step forward and embraced her. Pulling back slightly, he kissed her. It was long and passionate, and just what each wanted at that moment. As they parted company and waved goodbye, their world seemed full of new potential.

Evan was only half a block away when he saw them again – two young men loitering in a doorway, apparently just chatting and smoking. Yet they had been there when he and Jeanette left his apartment that morning and, as before, they glanced his way a bit longer than expected for residents of a large city. Each wore the same jeans and T-shirt combination exhibited earlier, and each fumbled with a cell phone. Somehow they didn't strike Evan as either maintenance workers or students from a local university. Most notably, they seemed anxious in the place they were standing – as if it was not their actual residence. Evan tried to shake it off. *I'm reading way too much into this*, he concluded. Perhaps *he* was the odd one here – an obvious foreigner who had shown up in *their* neighborhood, thus arousing suspicion.

Nevertheless, some deep instinct told him to stop, turn around, and head back to his apartment, pretending he had forgotten something. Things were different now that Jeanette had entered his life. Yet his stride remained unbroken, as a pedantic ego drove him onward to complete this one small task.

Immediately after taking a seat on the metro, Evan began daydreaming about the public announcement he would deliver, perhaps through a seminar with media coverage. Would this be the moment that defined his 'huge impact' on the world? Understandably, the news would be greeted with skepticism until all the details could be shared and his claims verified. Regardless, how should he begin his speech?

He pictured a large auditorium. A photo of the Record was projected onto a huge screen, with the disc occupying most of the frame for maximum effect. He approached the microphone and cleared his throat. A pin could be heard if dropped. A steady, confident voice emerged from the podium.

Ladies and gentlemen, you are looking at the first evidence of intelligent life beyond Earth. No, that was too similar to a line from a novel he had once read. He cleared his mind as much as possible without losing track of the passing subway stations. Then the perfect introduction came to him. It was something Nigel might have written.

For millennia, music has been one of the most direct ways of connecting with the human soul – of grabbing one's attention and influencing basic emotions and desires. And though music takes many different forms, its power is not diminished by a person's race or culture. I believe this miracle has been exploited by an intelligent life form beyond our solar system, in order to send a message. What this telegram says, I have not determined, but it was certainly tailored for the human dimension of reality.

Ever since the ancient Greeks, many have proposed that the order and motion of the universe generate a special harmony, referred to as 'the music of the spheres.' Well, we finally have a chance to experience this harmony, and it is literally through audible music. Let me show you how.

PART II

DESIRE FOR POSSESSION

Chapter Ten

His code name was Jacques, at least this month. He had risen rapidly through the ranks to oversee one sector of a highly sophisticated crime ring in France, dealing with the theft and sale of intellectual property, novel technology, computer software or hardware, and other bounties of cybercrime. Yet to most, he was a well-respected, if painfully introverted, computer systems analyst working at a small consulting firm in *La Defense*, the large business district west of Paris. He blended seamlessly with countless other clean-cut, twenty-something professionals who pursued dreams of running their own businesses. However, Jacques harbored an atypically rough edge. He had struggled most of his youth, hindered by poverty and tossed between foster homes, even living on the street for a couple of years. But all that was long behind him, before he chanced upon a sponsor who sent him to respectable schools, which in turn allowed him to hone his natural skills at computer technology. While outwardly patient, he secretly viewed the shortest path to success as the only viable one. His real name mattered little anymore.

The illicit empire to which he belonged featured nearly autonomous cells scattered throughout the region. Each was assigned a bland label that changed frequently to avoid any memorable footprint in cyberspace. This structure had been Jacques' brainstorm, earning him a leadership role. Currently his own team, consisting of handpicked friends of unquestioning loyalty, was denoted F1602 and based in Paris. Most of them, like Jacques, hid in plain sight at professional day jobs. They used a complex array of encrypted and encoded communications to coordinate with analogous teams across Europe, at least when they willingly cooperated. Jacques was still required to report to a high-level set of 'managers' in powerful positions at large corporations or in government, who completed transactions through international contacts and access to secret bank accounts. But these upper-tier proceedings were of little concern to Jacques; his final share of the profits offered a far greater income than he could have ever envisaged just a few years ago.

The first four months of 2016 had been unusually exciting. The search was on for a special object, rumored to be in Europe and first seen in London, which promised unparalleled opportunities for revenue. Details were vague, but he guessed it was a new substrate for computer chips, or a novel type of solar cell, based on sketchy descriptions filtering in. Most importantly, it was a prize for which interested parties would pay handsomely. Jacques sensed that this particular case warranted a bit more research, if only to escalate the international bidding war to come.

In May came a lucky break. He learned where the owner of this object resided – Paris! It was imperative to act quickly, but with caution. Given the unprecedented situation, and nonstop buzz in underground communication circles, there would be other players involved in the same pursuit. A thorough, quiet, and clever search, without dramatic confrontation, was always the best approach in his line of work. Therefore, a trap must be set.

Today, the owner had taken the bait and vacated his apartment, where the prize was almost certainly hidden. Jacques ordered his team to execute a prearranged plan, and then returned to the formulation of strategies for the item's liquidation. He was, after all, a businessman first; others could work out the petty infractions needed for acquisition.

It was late afternoon when Evan arrived at St. Denis metro station and walked several blocks toward an address provided earlier. Over the housetops he could see the enormous Stade de France, the country's national stadium, used for football and rugby. In the other direction, he spotted the majestic Cathedral Basilica of Saint Denis, named after the first bishop of Paris and patron saint of France. The district had even been the site of a Gallo-Roman village.

Once at his destination, he knocked on the door and was greeted by Jean-Paul, who seemed unusually anxious. Upon entering, Evan was invited to sit, and the nephew was summoned from a back room. Just as Evan noticed a stack of DVDs on the table, two young men entered the front door from behind, while two more appeared in the hallway. At first he assumed they were simply the nephew's friends. But after a menacing circle formed around him, and Jean-Paul began mumbling apologies, it became clear that Evan had been tricked. Jean-Paul was now tearing up, and Evan was momentarily more concerned for the older man.

A fifth young man finally entered – apparently the real nephew. Glaring unsympathetically at his uncle, he spoke in English for Evan's benefit. "Uncle, why are you so sad when we're planning a party?"

The nephew stepped forward and plopped down in the other armchair angled toward a flat-screen television. He glanced over casually at Evan. "Monsieur Blake, thanks for stopping by to watch movies with us."

"I thought I was here to see old records," Evan said, despite knowing the invitation to be a ruse.

"I'm afraid you're wrong. Instead, I've gathered several interesting French films. I studied Cinema in college, and would like to share some highlights – many of which you've no doubt seen. I'd guess there are about twelve hours' worth, so we'd better get started."

"Uh, no thanks, maybe next time." Evan rose a few inches, not really expecting to get far. Sure enough, strong hands pushed him back roughly into the chair. Although no weapons were displayed, their intentions were clear enough – to hold him here while they searched his apartment. He chastised himself for letting down his guard at the last minute.

His mind began racing. Even if Jean-Paul had disclosed the existence of rare recordings, could these people know anything about the Record? And what about Jeanette? What if they found her? Would they hurt her? Should he mention that she's an occupant, yet knows nothing? Almost anything he said might backfire and make things worse for her. So he chose to say nothing, and simply look for opportunities to escape. They had taken his phone, and the chances of calling the police from a bedroom seemed remote. Perhaps the bathroom had an open window?

As if the nephew could overhear these deliberations, he leaned over and muttered, "Report any of this, and we'll kill you."

I was waiting for that line, Evan thought to himself. *It's probably straight from one of those French films*.

Sifting through the DVDs, the nephew made his choice. "Let's start with my favorites from the eighties, *Jean de Florette* and *Manon des Sources*. Have you seen these? Ah, my heart throbs for Emmanuelle Béart. I could watch her all night. And you?"

"Sure. Or Juliette Binoche, or Catherine Deneuve," Evan said, surprised to hear himself participating in the absurd conversation.

"Splendid! We'll be moving into French New Wave a bit later on; for example, Godard's 1960 masterpiece, *Breathless*. It inspired me to pursue a life of crime." He laughed at his own joke.

The nephew snarled for someone to start a movie, although the two men at the door remained firmly planted. Jean-Paul was no longer present, and Evan hoped he would come to no harm. The charade continued. "I'll get some popcorn started in the microwave. Would you like anything to drink? I'll see what my uncle has available; never anything good, I'm afraid."

Thus began the most bizarre evening in Evan's memory: several men and their hostage, watching films spanning several decades of French cinema. The movies had no subtitles, but he cared little. A terrible feeling of defeat overcame him, yet he refused to display any sign of frustration. He focused on a single task – to memorize their faces. One day he would exact revenge.

The living room of Evan's apartment glowed in the natural light of early evening as Jeanette read contently. However, after several hours she grew concerned – Evan had neither called nor answered his phone. Feeling hungry, she prepared a light snack from the kitchen, hoping this would not spoil her appetite for dinner. At one point, she considered venturing out alone to eat, but intuitively sensed a need to stay inside.

Feeling unusually tired, she lay down for a short nap on his couch, now an old friend. Around ten, she awoke to noises outside. The music had stopped, and the interior lights were off. Someone was jiggling the front door knob, yet it did not sound like Evan. When the manipulations became more aggressive, she concluded a burglary was in progress. Creeping away from the door in bare feet, she avoided a squeaky floorboard that had announced itself earlier. Her mobile phone was somewhere in the kitchen, but a search now seemed too risky.

Only one course of action was tenable – seeking shelter in the hiding place Evan had constructed. But as she turned to go, an image blasted into her head. The Record! It was still resting on the turntable, as accessible as fresh fruit in the marketplace.

She ran into the audio room, lit only by tiny LEDs on the racks of equipment, and stopped short of the turntable – but only for a second. Lifting the disc off its platter with her bare hands, she raced toward the back bedroom, fully aware of her violation of Evan's trust; it was necessary under the circumstances.

Despite the darkness, she located his closet with the removable sidewall, and was relieved at the absence of scraping noises while lifting out the large wooden panel. Stepping into an even blacker abyss, she reseated the board behind her by means of two strategically placed inner handles. She stumbled once in the darkness, but avoided falling. The chamber itself was the size of a long, spacious storage closet, and she felt her way along toward its back recesses, inadvertently kicking a few boxes. The ceiling sloped down to only a few feet in height at the rear. She groped around to find an empty spot to sit, hoping that this section was free of spiders.

Outside, she could hear the front door forced open and several persons enter. Moving systematically from room to room, they yanked things down and threw them about. The group seemed to be looking for something – but what? The Record? Echoing inside her head was Evan's statement about the incredible wealth awaiting its owner. But surely so few knew about it; perhaps this was just a routine burglary. However, one fact was hard to ignore. Evan had been conveniently called away. The intruders were probably expecting an empty apartment.

The wave of commotion surged onward as they neared the back rooms. She remained as still as possible despite a pounding heartbeat and uncontrollable trembling. Rather than struggle to locate a stable perch for the disc, she resigned herself to hold it. She shut her eyes and bowed her head, clearing her thoughts, as if this would magically remove any trace of the hidden panel. Several disturbing memories raced through her mind. As a child, she and her family had once packed into a hallway closet during a rare spring tornado in Montreal. The same uncertainty now surfaced regarding what she would find after leaving her shelter.

Finally, the trespassers reached the main bedroom. Drawers were pulled out forcibly and dropped to the floor. French language was audible, but not interpretable until the very end when someone called off the search. Footsteps receded, and her surroundings became quiet. However, she refused to exit prematurely, in case the calmness was a trick; the artifact she nurtured was too important.

Stretching her arm out cautiously, she detected several folded blankets stacked nearby. Spreading one out onto the small clearing, she lay down, still cradling the Record. She had an odd desire to hold it now, this curious thing that had bonded her and Evan. Contrary to her expectations, no unpleasant sensations arose from touching it. Her imagination flashed through several scenarios, then exhaustion pushed her over the edge and into a deep sleep. After a vortex of disturbing visions and sounds, a haze lifted. Jeanette was standing at the rear of a large concert hall.

Chapter Eleven

It was the most magnificent auditorium Jeanette had ever seen. An elaborate, beamed ceiling unfolded high above, and the wide, dark-walnut stage was adorned with black-velvet curtains. A lavish, twenty-foot chandelier hung at the center, crafted from countless prisms of fine crystal set in a frame of highly polished brass. Wood paneling along the sides of the hall showcased intricate carvings of flowers, and offered a rich scent of fresh oak. The grandeur of everything suggested an extravagant period from Europe's past.

At first, she merely stood and strained her neck to look around, but soon felt compelled to venture down the gently sloping aisle, covered in thick, burgundy carpeting. All the seats were occupied with indistinct shapes, like ghosts sitting motionless. As she continued forward, she glanced down at her body and recognized the purple satin dress – one of her favorites for formal occasions. Reaching the tenth row, her preferred location in music halls, she noticed an empty chair close to the aisle. After sitting, she became aware of the orchestra, patiently awaiting their leader. Had they been there all along? When the conductor appeared, the audience remained silent. Mounting the podium, the maestro raised his baton, and music flooded the hall. Then she saw a grand piano. Was it sitting there before? The pianist was not recognizable, but his style of clothing, long hair, and manner of playing all hinted at an earlier era. Regardless, this was going to be a piano concerto, and one of her favorites.

She pondered the inner struggles of young Brahms as he composed his first piano concerto. The work was several years in the making, and first performed in 1858 to mixed reviews, mostly negative. Ironically, Brahms' integration of piano and orchestra was considered lacking in keyboard virtuosity, and thus out of step with the period's more extroverted styles. But to her, it encompassed the passions and desires of youth like nothing else she knew. Every measure was familiar; she had once studied the piano score.

The apparitions around her remained motionless, much to her relief. Absent were the coughs and program-rustling that accompanied most live concerts. If this was a dream, it was fantastically vivid. She leaned back in awe, engaged as never before with a musical performance.

At the end, a brief silence allowed reverberation of the final notes, which she always appreciated. The audience then erupted in wild cheering and applause – but only through sound; she did not actually see the ghosts moving. She yelled, "Bravo!" while clapping herself. The pianist stood and took a long bow. As he rose, he seemed to stare directly at her.

Several minutes passed and the hall grew quiet again, with the pianist remaining on stage and returning to his bench. Jeanette wondered whether she should leave, but her options were limited. The surrounding apparitions had merged together into a strange matrix that trapped her in the chair; she simply could not stand up. Over the next few hours, she was treated to a series of her favorite piano concertos. Only occasionally did she ponder the elapsed time, or how the musicians could play continuously without a break.

After a final ovation, the apparitions stood up and vanished. The stage cleared, and the theater became dark. Jeanette felt herself sinking deeper into the warm seat and losing consciousness. But it was a welcome euphoria. Whatever had happened, wherever this place was, she felt safe, overwhelmed by the impossible.

Shortly after dawn, Evan ran the two blocks from the metro station to his home, debating whether to call local police. He was horrified to see the condition of his apartment. Turning on lights and peering about for lingering intruders, he whispered Jeanette's name as he tiptoed into each room. The Record was clearly gone, but it seemed a trivial matter at this point. A wave of nausea hit him at the thought of her lying injured somewhere, or being held against her will. He did not think he could endure the loss of someone so special again.

Making his way toward the bedroom closet, he hoped against hope that she had remembered the secret chamber. However, the removable panel looked perfectly positioned. Could she really have closed it so well from the inside? After pausing to take a deep breath, he pulled the panel back. Once his eyes adjusted to the dark, he could see Jeanette lying at the rear. She began to stir, and then sat up.

Never had the sight of someone simply moving brought such relief.

He entered the space part way, trying to help her out, since she seemed only able to crawl. Jeanette set the Record gently aside before moving forward. After more light defined the chamber, she took his hands, and they exited the closet together. She was gasping for air and unable to speak coherently. They sat on the floor for several minutes, with her cuddled in his arms.

Evan spoke softly in her ear. “I was so worried about you. I’m sorry I’ve dragged you into this. It’s all my fault, leaving you here alone.”

“What . . . happened?” she said between breaths.

“It was a trick. I was held at Jean-Paul’s. They were after the Record, I think, since they took it, along with my LPs. But they left other things behind – even some cash and a watch, for Christ’s sake.”

“Evan, I *saved* the Record. I took it inside.”

“That’s great, Jeanette. Thanks. But what matters now is how you *feel*.”

“I’m sorry, but I had to touch it. I had to–”

“I don’t care. Are *you* okay?”

“I’ll tell you in a minute,” she said, trying to stand up. “I think I’ve been in there all night. What time is it?”

“Almost seven.” He helped her to the edge of the bed, where they sat together. She was staring ahead with glassy eyes. Evan took her hand in his, studying her and wondering whether to call for an ambulance.

Jeanette pointed at the window, her arm wavering. Morning sunlight was streaming into the bedroom, illuminating one wall with a splash of orange. “Do you see that light? It’s like something I saw yesterday in a Degas painting. It’s wonderful.” She turned and gazed at him with a silly grin. “Everything looks so wonderful . . .”

“I’m really getting worried about you. I never dreamed someone would have to hide in that closet for so long. There might be toxic fumes inside the walls. Look, let’s go to the emergency room at Pitié-Salpêtrière Hospital. It’s not far.”

“No! That’s where Princess Diana died almost twenty years ago, and also Josephine Baker in 1975. I won’t join the list.”

“It’s also where many famous people have been treated and released.”

“I’m fine, Evan.” She straightened her back with considerable effort. “My thoughts are clear now. While I was asleep last night, I heard . . . no, I dreamed . . . oh, I don’t know. I *experienced* a concert. I can remember every bit of it. I’ve never had such a realistic dream, though. I think it had something to do with the Record.”

After a moment of intense thought, her eyes widened and shot over toward his. “Yes, that’s it! I was holding the Record while I slept. It *did* something to me.” She began laughing and stood up, twirling her arms ecstatically. “It’s amazing!”

Evan wondered if she had ingested some sort of hallucinogenic drug, accidentally or otherwise.

Jeanette remained in an emotional whirlwind, and began weeping while she apologized again for 'changing' the Record to her musical preferences. Panic coursed through Evan as he considered potential injury from such close proximity to the Record. *Radiation perhaps*? If there was permanent damage, it was ultimately his responsibility; he had asked her to stay, told her about the closet, and failed to store the disc properly.

Finally she stood up in front of him, almost lecturing, and pointed a finger at the closet. "Evan, are you listening? I didn't have to *play* the Record. I just *held* it! Anyone can use that disc, even without stereo equipment!" She stopped and sat down, silent, as the implications of this latest finding sank in.

Suddenly she was up again. "Quick! We must get the Record out of here, before they return! Come on – let's pack up. We can head over to my hotel." She rushed into the living room.

Evan evaluated his belongings. The closet contained backup disks for his laptops; he had refused to risk any sort of external server for such priceless information. The audio gear could stay for now; the thieves were clearly not after such commodities. He could arrange for everything to be boxed and shipped to London later. While he gathered a few personal items, he could hear Jeanette in the next room, alternatively humming, crying, and laughing, though the outbursts gradually subsided over the next hour.

With the Record restored to its original box, which in turn was nested in a rolling suitcase, they stepped out into a cool Wednesday morning and glanced around suspiciously. As they walked arm-in-arm down a narrow street toward Luxembourg Gardens, the city now seemed a very different place – a vast labyrinth with a ferocious Minotaur lurking about. Evan tried to assess the overall situation. His trust in the small team of musicians had been violated, and Jeanette was afflicted in some strange way because of it. Also, he might have to rationalize his stay in Paris to local police, assuming the break-in was registered, although he had no intention of reporting it.

By mid-morning they had reached her hotel, and instead of the anonymity enjoyed by most tourists, they faced scrutiny from Jeanette's cousin Pierre, manning the front desk. She introduced Evan and simply told the truth; he was a colleague whose apartment had been burglarized, and thus needed a room. Pierre checked his books and spotted a last-minute cancelation, allowing Evan to be accommodated.

After placing items in his room, Evan contemplated sleeping with the Record himself, in order to test its powers. Within an hour, however, Jeanette called and asked him to stop by her room, merely one floor above. When he knocked, she opened the door and ushered him in without delay, scanning the corridor for nosey relatives. Evan was still watching her with concern.

Yet she appeared at ease. “Since we arrived, I’ve stabilized. I don’t think I’ve been harmed. We’ve simply discovered another way for the Record to create a musical experience, though I suspect my own mind provided the visual part.”

“Well, let’s get some rest and plan our next move. I suggest we hang around here today. There’s no way they could trace us to this hotel. Still, we should put the Record in a safe, if the hotel has one.”

“Yes, I’m sure they do,” she said. Both were standing, and when she walked closer, he realized she had just finished a shower, and wore only a cotton bathrobe. Her long, wet hair cascaded behind, and her face was flushed from the warm water. “I think something incredible took place last night, and I’m not sorry it happened.”

She continued to look up at him, although he was only a few inches taller, and then rested her head on his chest. He wrapped his arms around her, and an envelope of warmth and sensual longing consumed them. As they began to kiss, he untied her robe and slipped his hands inside, finding a soft, receptive landscape. Her robe dropped to the floor, and she began undressing him. They remained in her room the rest of the day.

Chapter Twelve

From their hotel window, an unbroken canvas of treetops defined one edge of Luxembourg Park, the colors growing richer as a cloudless Thursday morning dawned. Evan sat up in bed with a start and surveyed the room for signs of intruders. He turned to Jeanette, lying beside him, and then leaned back in relief. But as they relaxed in bed with arms intertwined, the reality of their strange predicament came rushing back like frigid water.

"We have to get out of this city," he said. "Maybe there's someplace in London we can stay. I need more time before going public."

She glanced over, now alert, wondering about his reasons for a delay. Then her face lit up. "Evan, I have an idea. I was planning to visit my aunt in Lyon this weekend. Let's go together, and let her hold the Record. It may do something for her. Music therapy can be useful for Parkinson's patients, although that's usually music coming from the *outside*. What I experienced was something generated *inside*."

"Jeanette, that sounds risky. We don't know what happened to you. Remember how disoriented you were at first?"

"I realize it's a long shot, but if there's any positive effect, or some medical benefit, just think how powerful your description of the Record will be."

Clearly 'no' was not going to work. "Let's at least talk about it more."

"Fine with me," she said, pulling him down toward her.

The couple showed up for a late breakfast in the hotel café after most guests had departed for business or touring. Still playing the role of casual friends, they ignored the stares of her relatives, who studied them with great curiosity. Back in her room, various strategies were discussed. Evan agreed to shave off his beard in the hope of changing his appearance slightly. As for luggage, he felt it was important to transport the Record in its original metal box, which would only fit inside his largest suitcase. They continued sorting through research materials Evan had salvaged, deciding what should remain in the hotel safe while they traveled to Lyon. She held up one of his optical disks used for data storage. "Evan, isn't this the X-ray data you never processed?"

"Yes, why?"

"I used to work on this sort of thing. I'd like to check it out."

"Sure, bring it along. Maybe we'll have time in Lyon."

Shortly before noon, the room's outdated telephone startled them with a loud clang. Jeanette answered hesitantly and stared at Evan while she listened. After she hung up, panic crept into her voice. "Pierre says there's a policeman downstairs. Could this be another trick?"

Evan raced down several flights of stairs to the lobby, stopping short on the final step, still out of sight. He peered cautiously around the corner and observed a man in a well-worn suit relaxing in the reception area, sipping the complementary coffee. Jeanette suddenly appeared behind Evan, almost frightening him off the stairs. She whispered in his ear that he might need a translator. Evan decided to take a chance, stepped out, and approached the man confidently. Jeanette also came into view, but stayed closer to the front desk.

"*Bonjour. Je suis Evan Blake*," Evan said.

The man rose slowly, seemingly bored, and pulled out a small wallet with photo identification. He replied in English. "Mr. Blake, I am from the Paris office of Interpol. Your building manager notified local police yesterday of a break-in at your apartment. Then the police contacted us. My supervisor sent me to request that you stop by our headquarters. Here is the address. Ask for Gerard Lambert when you arrive."

Evan stared at the paper in disbelief; the central office was in Lyon.

The agent sensed his confusion. "Mr. Blake, you are not under arrest. We are asking for your help with an important matter. Lyon is only a couple of hours away by TGV, or high-speed train."

Evan shook off his daze. "Yes, but how did you find me?"

The agent held up Jeanette's business card, the one she had left in Evan's apartment with her hotel written on the back. "The police found this and gave it to us."

"Oh. I see," said Evan, his embarrassment mixed with relief that the burglars had not scavenged it during their search.

Jeanette walked up. "Should I come?" she seemed to ask of both men.

"It's up to you," the agent said with a yawn, and shuffled out of the hotel.

The couple looked at each other, and then at Pierre behind the front desk, who pretended not to notice all the excitement. Since he knew little English, Jeanette told him this was a routine investigation into the burglary. After returning upstairs, the couple decided to leave Paris immediately; people were beginning to learn of their location.

Seeing Lyon spring into view on a sunny afternoon was as magical as the approach to Paris itself. Capital of the Rhône-Alpes region, its history could be traced to the original Roman town of Lugdunum. Lyon was also a major business center and gastronomical mecca. Two nearly parallel rivers, the Rhône and Saone, formed a narrow peninsula that defined the city's bustling center. It reminded Jeanette of an imaginary connection between Ile de la Cite and Ile St. Louis on the Seine in Paris.

Jeanette's aunt was living in a special care facility next to the Pierre Wertheimer Neurological Hospital, which housed a major CNS research center. Jeanette knew of a small boarding house nearby where she had stayed in the past, and from which they could access the facility during its weekend visiting hours. Tomorrow, Friday, they would put in an appearance at Interpol. However, today was just for them.

After checking into their modest lodgings, they took a taxi to explore the city. First up was the well-preserved Roman theater on Fourvière Hill, an area with numerous churches, and once the city's religious center. Next was a mandatory walk through 'Old Lyon,' a spectacular Renaissance district rivaling Venice, and accented by narrow cobblestone streets lined with shops. Later they enjoyed local dishes in a traditional restaurant called a *bouchon.* Jeanette was more adventurous regarding the cuisine, while Evan did his best to avoid any dish with the word *cervelle*, or brain, settling instead for sausage-based alternatives. Their day finished with a warm evening stroll to the sounds of modern music from the *Nuits sonores*, one of Europe's largest electronic music festivals, held each May. Evan was always invigorated after hearing young musicians explore new styles. He yearned to participate in the groundbreaking jazz sessions of the forties. But he knew he already had the next best thing: a virtual time machine called the Record.

Later that night, after Jeanette had fallen asleep, Evan crept over to his large suitcase and removed the metal box. One final experiment was needed in order to seal his appreciation for the Record. He carried the disc back to bed and held it in his arms, facing away from Jeanette. Feeling a tinge of guilt, as if he had invited another lover to join him, he tried to conjure images of a grown man cradling a stuffed animal. Then he waited. Not surprisingly, given his anticipation, it took longer than usual to fall asleep.

A spotlight sliced through the darkness, revealing a stage inside a large nightclub packed with tables. Evan coughed as clouds of cigarette smoke wafted by, but found some relief after sipping the beer suddenly placed before him. He was alone, though other tables were occupied with two or three patrons. The audience members were indistinct, like cardboard cutouts of people – some painted white, some black. Returning his gaze to the stage, he was surprised to see a pianist, guitarist, and drummer at the rear; he had not noticed them before. The sound of the trio warming up was soothing. A drone of conversations hummed all around, yet he could not make out complete sentences – only enough to confirm the language as English.

The show's host marched out in a style of dress from the forties. He walked up to a large microphone mounted on a stand, and tapped it for a sound check. There was a loud thump, and Evan started. The host welcomed his audience to Café Society in New York City, and announced the show's lineup, consisting of prominent female jazz singers.

Evan searched his memory. The establishment had opened in 1938 in Greenwich Village as the country's first racially integrated club. It was founded by former shoe salesman and jazz fan, Barney Josephson, who dubbed his joint facetiously 'the wrong place for the right people.' Soon afterward, Barney opened a second club in the basement of a large building, where Evan guessed he was now sitting. The walls were decorated with satiric murals poking fun at the world of 'high society.' Both clubs were hugely popular, and yet, only ten years later, Barney was forced to sell them under a cloud of criticism related to his brother's leftist political leanings.

The show finally got underway. One after another, some of Evan's favorite singers materialized, each performing a few ballads or jazz classics, accompanied by the small trio of instrumentalists. He was not shocked to see a young Billie Holiday deliver her unique and poignant interpretation of *Strange Fruit*, the anti-lynching protest poem set to music. He was thrilled by the boogie-woogie and bebop innovations of pianist and composer Mary Lou Williams, often cited as jazz's greatest female musician. This was followed with bewitching numbers from Sarah Vaughn, Ella Fitzgerald, Dinah Washington, and Lena Horne; all had sung at Café Society.

Then there was a pause. Evan considered standing up to leave, but the entities around him remained fixed – perhaps in anticipation? The stage cleared magically, and the host returned, whispering excitedly. A very special treat was now in store, he explained. Despite the jazz venue, a famous soprano had dropped in to bless them with a song or two. Evan was perplexed, until he spied the figure emerging from the shadows. Unlike his positive reaction to the previous singers, anxiety surfaced and escalated quickly to dread. Finally, Rosina stood ablaze in the spotlight, basking in warm applause and affectionate shouts from the audience. From somewhere offstage, a small orchestra began to play, and Rosina took a deep breath. Evan wanted to listen, more than anything, but a sharp pain surged up from deep inside and flooded his entire being. He screamed, yet no sound emerged.

His eyes opened and he was in bed. Apparently he had not cried out, for Jeanette was still sleeping soundly. Rising, he found himself in a cold sweat, but certainly not as disoriented as she had been after her session. He speculated that this was because of his previous exposure to the disc, which he hastily repackaged. Sitting in the calm predawn hours, he reflected on what had just transpired. The dramatic end to his 'adventure' was not really so shocking; he had been unwilling to hear Rosina's recordings ever since her death.

The overall experience was exactly as Jeanette had described – like an incredibly vivid dream, but far more tangible than any human dream should be. He felt as if he had just returned from the actual club. There were few mental cues to mark the last few hours as an illusion. One of those cues was the music itself – clearly a courtesy of the Record.

Evan stood up and stared at his suitcase once more. If nothing else were to come of this strange device, he concluded, he could at least travel the world promoting its hallucinogenic properties, like some modern-day Timothy Leary. He returned to bed, and slept without dreams.

Chapter Thirteen

The five-story headquarters of Interpol sat midway between the Rhône and Lyon's majestic Parc de la Tête d'Or. Given its resemblance to a modern corporate office, Evan and Jeanette checked the plaque outside twice to confirm they were really standing outside Europe's top crime-solving institution. Once inside, their initial impressions were maintained as they traversed a trendy, sky-lit atrium filled with potted plants, and offering panoramic views of the river.

An escort guided them through a maze of cubicles separated by four-foot-tall partitions, which offered little privacy for the occupants. Everyone seemed very busy on this Friday morning. In a nook somewhat larger than the rest they were introduced to Special Agent Gerard Lambert. In his mid-forties, with a close-trimmed scalp and goatee, he wore a leather sport coat topped off with a wrinkled, loose-fitting tie. His frazzled appearance suggested he was juggling several cases at once. An exchange of pleasantries ensued between Jeanette and the charmed Gerard, which to Evan's mind lasted a bit longer than necessary.

When an incoming phone call distracted Gerard, Jeanette translated their initial chat. He had complained that Interpol functioned around the clock, unlike twenty years ago when things were more relaxed and regular work hours were augmented with lavish lunches. Interpol had dramatically increased its scope and efficiency of international monitoring, all while operating on a relatively modest budget.

Gerard now turned his attention to Evan, graciously switching to English. He shook Evan's hand while holding a coffee cup in the other, and gestured toward two austere metal chairs jammed in front of his cluttered desk. Dirty cups were scattered among multiple stacks of papers and file folders, and from the center of the chaos emerged a computer monitor, like a Mayan pyramid rising up from the jungle.

"So, we finally get a peek at the famous Professor Blake," Gerard said, looking at no one in particular.

Evan tried to show no reaction. "Are you disappointed?"

Gerard ignored the question. "Thank you for coming in, Dr. Blake. I head a task force investigating the theft and sale of intellectual property. This includes cybercrime, and even pharmaceutical crime such as counterfeit drugs. All this 'high-tech crime' has become a lucrative business in recent years, especially in Europe, given our recession. In fact, it now competes with more traditional commodities such as illegal drugs, weapons, stolen art, and even human beings. In the last few years, it's become more organized and coordinated – almost like the Mafia. It's no longer just small-scale hackers. We've also seen the involvement of people in top positions of companies or governments, who direct operations and cash flows. Meanwhile, the 'ground forces' are quite fluid, constantly restructuring to avoid detection."

Evan sensed he was in way over his head. Normally he would just walk away, but given the existence of the Record, this was no longer a normal world.

Pulling out a manila folder labeled with Evan's name, Gerard opened it and looked through the first few pages. He continued in monotone. "Our computers picked up your name from a routine scan of local crimes. Your Paris apartment was robbed this week and reported by the building owner, though not by yourself. Several individuals were later caught in a sting operation trying to sell musical recordings to a European record label, which raised the possibility of pirated material. When confronted, they were found with other goods bearing your name, presumably stolen in Paris. These items included data storage disks and records. Now, usually my division doesn't bother with such 'low level' activity, but two of the suspects were already linked to a high-profile crime circle involved in company break-ins. Do you have any idea why they would target you?"

Evan decided it was best not to share anything regarding the Record. He debated whether to even reveal the thefts of his lab notes at Imperial, almost certainly the source of a leak, unless Rollins or Atkins were responsible, which seemed unlikely. At this point, Evan trusted no one except Jeanette, who sat quietly nearby playing the role of innocent girlfriend.

"I do have some very rare recordings of early musical performances," Evan said. "I can't reveal their origin except to say that I obtained them legally. I realize the market for old recordings is active now, especially in Europe, but it's hard to believe that organized crime would get involved."

"True; such a thing should be of marginal interest, but some people are desperate for any new contraband." Gerard frowned slightly while leafing through the rest of the folder's documents. "It seems to me that there's a level of interest in your activities going far beyond rare recordings. In fact, in a number of intercepted communications over the last few months, along with statements from those in custody, your name appears *several* times. You, or things in your possession, have generated unprecedented discussion throughout the entire high-tech crime community. I've never seen anything like it. Do you have any idea how all this came about?"

"No, not really," Evan said. He hoped the language barrier would mask his insincerity.

"We've also seen the word 'nanotechnology' tied to your name. Could you enlighten me?"

"That just reflects my field of research at MIT. Many people share my interests. I don't see why I would be singled out." However, the drill was now getting close to the nerve. Evan could see what Gerard was doing – repeating the same question in different ways, trying to find a trapdoor into his mind. Evan looked at Jeanette, worried that she would be the next target of this process. She noticed his concern, and excused herself to search for a restroom.

Gerard then leaned closer to Evan. "There's something else, Dr. Blake. The day after the robbery, Paris police were watching your apartment, and confronted a Russian citizen who seemed to be 'casing' the place. He was in France legally, but had only recently entered the country. His paperwork supported his claim to be a bureaucrat with diplomatic privileges. However, his reason for visiting Paris was vague. He was not held, and I have no reason to suspect him as the burglar. Here's a picture from his passport." Gerard swung the monitor around for Evan to see. The name was Alexander Ulyanov, and the photo showed a middle-aged man with a neatly trimmed beard. Evan rubbed his own chin, wishing he had retained some facial hair.

"But I think you'd better worry more about the French group focusing on you," Gerard stated coldly. He fixed his gaze solidly on Evan for the first time. "Make no mistake, Dr. Blake. These criminals will not hesitate to injure or kill anyone who gets in their way, and you were lucky to escape the Paris incident unharmed. You do realize, I hope, that you're putting Ms. Menard in danger as well."

Don't I know it! Evan was thinking. He felt a rush of vulnerability like never before. Multiple parties were interested in him, and it had reached a global scale. The theft at Imperial, two incidents in

Paris, and now a mysterious Russian – not to mention a wildcard in Boston named Atkins. On top of all that, the FBI and Interpol had him on their radar screens.

Jeanette returned and mentioned their need to depart soon, citing the planned visit with her aunt, while conveniently omitting the fact that this was scheduled for the next day. With all the formal courtesies, Gerard bade them farewell, but watched closely as they left his post. He knew Evan was hiding something. At the same time, Evan's appearance was incredibly fortuitous. The professor might serve as bait to lure the most clever and elusive elements of the modern crime scene. However, Gerard had serious doubts whether Evan would survive, if faced with such ruthless opponents. He grudgingly placed a phone call, asking a local detective to watch over the couple while they were in Lyon. It might be worthwhile keeping the bait alive as long as possible.

In one of the many cubicles nearby sat Yuri, representing the Russian Federation at Interpol. He had worked in the high-tech crime division for only a few months, with Gerard as his supervisor. Although Gerard had not discussed the Blake case in detail, many here knew that Evan was of great interest to Interpol. One of Yuri's current assignments was to conduct an investigation of Alexander Ulyanov. What no one knew was that Yuri also reported to Alexander, in a very discreet manner – by leaking requested information. At the top of the current wish list was the location of Evan Blake, and Yuri was pleased to have just emailed, via encoded messages, an update on Evan's whereabouts, along with facts regarding the French organization pursuing the professor. Yuri did not know the reasons for Alexander's interest in Evan, only that the request had been given highest priority. Over the next few months, Yuri would continue his 'official investigation' of Alexander for Interpol, accumulating just enough superficial data to make his final report look thoroughly researched.

On the same day as Evan's visit to Interpol, Jacques moved his F1602 team to Lyon, in the guise of a business venture related to his company's expansion. He was fuming over the lost opportunity to snatch the object in Paris, and now he had to worry about potential competition from an analogous French crime team based in Lyon. But Jacques knew he had the upper hand, since he alone had traced the couple's travel – through the use of Jeanette's credit cards. Her name had first appeared on a business card found in Evan's apartment, which the thieves had wisely left behind, seemingly undisturbed. Still, the sudden appearance of this woman was puzzling.

Jacques sat alone in a Lyon café and appraised the situation. His men had followed their general instructions, holding Blake while acquiring all LPs, computers, and optical disks from the apartment, but they had failed to scrutinize their loot closely enough to realize that nothing truly novel was present. Worse, two of them had attempted to sell audio CDs with historic tracks to a French record label, and had been reported to authorities, nearly exposing F1602.

The next time around, Jacques brooded, there would be no subtle tricks; he would simply acquire the couple and all their possessions at one time. Furthermore, everything except the primary objective was expendable. No traces of evidence would be left behind.

The only other matter of business was a proposal by one of Jacques' high-level managers; a man who facilitated illicit transactions from deep within the French government. Jacques had met this man only once in person, but relied on him in numerous ways; for information about companies, patents, and regulations; assistance with exports across international borders; even money laundering. Recently there had been a call for better coordination between Europe and Russia in terms of technology-related crime, since the latter was a lucrative market for the stolen contraband. Jacques' manager was negotiating with a sophisticated crime organization inside Russia, one with important ties to that country's government. Jacques had been asked to include a couple of its members during his current exploits. It was an unwelcome distraction, since he preferred working with a close-knit local crew, especially on such a critical project as Evan Blake. But it was a compromise he accepted in order to maintain a good relationship with his French manager. Plus, Russia just might end up as the highest bidder, once Blake's little treasure appeared on the auction block.

Chapter Fourteen

The special care facility in Lyon was devoted to patients with Parkinson's or Alzheimer's disease, along with a few stroke victims. Jeanette's aunt, Rachel Menard, had been allotted a small private room, but she required nearly constant care. On this particular Saturday morning, visitors included music therapist Adrienne Sinclair, who had trained at the Institute for Music and Neurologic Function in New York before relocating to France. Jeanette was generally familiar with music therapy, as described in publications by Oliver Sacks – one of the Institute's founders – but she was eager to talk with Adrienne and learn more. The two arranged a meeting, which included Evan.

"My aunt shows little response when music is played in a group setting. I think it may be the selection. Today I brought an old record with some of her favorite music." Considering it was *the* Record, Jeanette knew that her last statement was probably correct, although nothing was guaranteed in these circumstances.

Adrienne looked bewildered, but for unexpected reasons. "I don't know if there *is* a phonograph player in this building. They usually play music from CDs or a computer. I'll have to check with facilities." Jeanette bit her tongue to avoid saying that a turntable would not be necessary.

Adrienne then presented an overview. "For patients with neurological conditions, listening to music sometimes relieves restrictions on movement and speech. It can also help to restore past memories and emotions. For Parkinson's patients, who have difficulty initiating or continuing movement, we've seen how music can free them to dance or even sing, although the effects are short-term, and treatment must be repeated almost daily. But that's preferable to pharmaceutical therapy, which can lead to drug tolerance."

Before she continued, they watched a short video on Adrienne's laptop of typical results. "We're not sure why music triggers the appropriate neural circuits, but rhythmic music usually works best. It's as though we can get around the blocked pathways through some 'back door.' Many patients are able to sing long before they can talk, especially in recovering stroke victims. Also impressive are the results with Alzheimer's, where improvements in awareness and sociability are possible."

Adrienne picked up and reviewed Rachel's chart. "Let's see; age seventy-two; symptoms beginning around sixty. In your aunt's case, exposure to a variety of music has led to a few self-initiated limb movements, but it never really came together to the point where she could proactively walk around. As you know, she can be led about, and can perform many basic functions, if someone helps get her started. But she freezes again when left alone. So, if you have some new music today, by all means give it a try."

The phone on her desk rang, and Adrienne thanked someone for locating a turntable in the basement; it would be brought up to Rachel's room.

Evan and Jeanette walked toward a corner of the main wing where Rachel was sitting in a cushioned armchair. She wore a colorful cotton dress and comfortable slippers, and her long, gray hair was tied back with a turquoise-studded brooch that Jeanette had sent years ago. Her eyes moved slightly to follow Jeanette's approach. The head nurse reminded them of Rachel's rest schedule; a nap would occur later in the afternoon.

After the nurse left, Jeanette knelt beside her aunt, speaking enthusiastically in French on a variety of topics. Jeanette glanced back at Evan as if to say, 'This is my normal visitation routine.'

She also formally introduced Evan, who said, "*Bonjour, Madame Menard,*" out of politeness, although Rachel continued to stare straight ahead.

Finally, Jeanette mentioned that she had brought a little gift, and took the thin cardboard box from Evan. Holding the disc by its paper sleeve, she let it slip out onto Rachel's lap, then repositioned her aunt's passive hands on top. Rachel was able to move her hands slightly around the circumference, and then looked over at her niece. Jeanette elaborated. "My aunt understands most of what's going on, so she's probably expecting us to put this on a record player. I'll tell her we can listen to it later."

Over the next couple of hours, Jeanette brushed and arranged Rachel's hair, read magazines aloud to her, and chatted briefly with neighboring patients and staff. They had no idea how much time was required for the disc to take effect; it was like a clinical trial for some new drug. Evan sat back and watched raptly, like someone anticipating the start of a fireworks display. A staff member walked by and chuckled, noting that a record was best heard using a turntable. Jeanette replied that the LP was a favorite of Rachel's, recently discovered in an attic, and they simply wanted her to hold it first.

By mid-afternoon, the head nurse approached and reminded them of Rachel's naptime, which meant lying undisturbed in her private room. This scenario sounded more promising as an application of the Record. Jeanette helped her aunt to stand, and the nurse assisted Rachel with walking. Evan and Jeanette followed a few yards behind. Rachel held the Record tightly in her folded arms.

"It's interesting how fluid her movements are once she's underway," said Evan.

"She loved ballroom dancing as a young woman," said Jeanette. "All that potential is now trapped inside. It tears me apart inside every time I visit."

Once they entered Rachel's room, Jeanette spoke to the nurse in French. "My aunt wants to hold this record while she sleeps, since it means so much to her."

"Now dear, you can't really know that. We have specific rules, and it would be too dangerous to leave a breakable object with Rachel during her nap. She sometimes has convulsive movements."

"Please. There are signs I can read. I'll stay in the room to watch."

"Well, I suppose. But I'll be back soon to check on things. Rachel is special to me too, you know. I've taken care of her personally for many years."

The nurse pointed at Evan. "Your friend will have to leave, though, since he's not a relative."

Evan guessed what the nurse had said. "No problem. There's a cafeteria downstairs, and I brought some reading material. I'll make sure my cell phone is turned on. *Au revoir*."

Jeanette settled into an armchair next to Rachel's bed and read magazines, glancing over occasionally. At one point she almost rose to halt the experiment, but then remembered all the musical magic that the Record could instill. *It's worth a try.*

After an hour, Evan received a call from Jeanette, asking him to rush back. She sounded excited and out-of-breath. He ran up a flight of stairs, but tiptoed quietly down the corridor of private suites, knowing he was in violation of visiting hours. Creeping into Rachel's room, he saw Jeanette standing next to an empty bed. Then he realized his view was partially blocked by the open door. Closing it carefully, he was shocked to witness Rachel standing up and taking small, slow, rhythmic steps. She was sleepwalking while cradling the Record. Her eyes were nearly closed, and a slight smile accompanied nearly inaudible humming. Jeanette was beaming, and they watched the little performance in amazement. Although Rachel's footwork remained limited to a tiny area, they stood nearby to prevent any collisions or a fall.

Neither Evan nor Jeanette could recall bodily movement from a session with the Record; each had woken in a sleeping posture.

Only ten minutes later, the head nurse re-entered and gazed with astonishment at the transformation. Apparently Rachel had never stood during any therapy session, yet here she was, dancing away even in the 'absence of music.' Confused and suddenly concerned, the nurse rushed off to notify Adrienne. For Evan and Jeanette, there was only one course of action. It was best to end the show before the music therapist arrived, so she would not launch a case study of this 'modern miracle.'

They guided Rachel to the edge of her bed, and with great reluctance Jeanette began tugging on the Record. Rachel's eyes darted about, and her grip only strengthened, in contrast to the earlier lethargy. Evan could see a look of anguish building on Jeanette's face as she continued to pull without success. He wondered if there was any risk in disrupting a Record-induced dream before it reached a natural conclusion.

Spirited footsteps echoed outside as the nurse and Adrienne marched down the hallway toward the room. Jeanette took a deep breath, braced herself, and yanked the Record away in one motion. As the disc left Rachel's hands, she froze almost immediately. Seconds later, Adrienne entered, and the only activity visible in the room was Jeanette beginning to weep softly.

“Did you have a chance to play your record?” Adrienne asked.

Jeanette could not speak – she was too distraught over the interruption. Evan stepped forward, prepared to lie. “No, the turntable wasn’t working. But we’d like to come back and try again in the near future.”

“Oh, sorry to hear that. Well, next time just bring the music on a CD or memory card, or just email us the music files. You could leave that record here, of course.”

The nurse walked closer to Rachel, studying her face, and spoke in a loud voice. “I guess you’ve enjoyed your niece’s visit today. I can tell something has made you very happy. Now try to rest.”

They helped Rachel into bed, where she appeared to doze off. Evan put his arm around Jeanette and spoke in a whisper. “We’ll come back with the Record someday, I promise.” She acknowledged him with a slight nod.

As Adrienne turned to leave, she asked, “By the way, what was your aunt’s favorite music? I’ll try to be more specific with the tracks I play at our next session.”

“Strauss waltzes,” said Jeanette.

At that moment, across town, Alexander Ulyanov stepped off a train from Paris along with a small entourage of young Russian men. Behind them rolled identical black suitcases, and their long black raincoats seemed out of place on a sunny afternoon. They walked through the station with the air of a fine-tuned military unit. Most of them were, in fact, former Russian military personnel, including *Spetsnaz*, or Special Forces. Alexander was the obvious leader, judging from his age and the way he interacted with everyone, yet the relationships remained informal, and they addressed him as Alex. Several on the team boasted engineering backgrounds, like Alex, but today they were serving as a security detail.

Alex worked for a tiny, nearly unknown department in the Russian government. It was a remnant of the massive Soviet bureaucracy, and of little concern to more recent administrations preoccupied with the fragile economy. This highly specialized division, part academic pursuit and part military application, had focused on a single topic for decades: the analysis of a very special disc.

He sat with his team in a small restaurant at the station, addressing them quietly in Russian while summarizing their current assignment. The target was a French 'gang' known as F1602, who had tracked down the disc in Paris, yet botched a burglary attempt on Tuesday night. This information had come from Alex's Russian contact at Interpol. And since Blake was in Lyon – another tidbit from Interpol – F1602 would strike again, but more aggressively. That was fine; it was better to let the French do the dirty work. However, Alex would be nearby this time, to insure a proper resolution to the whole affair.

The plan was for two members of his group to join F1602 posing as representatives of Russian organized crime. It was all in the spirit of 'international cooperation,' supposedly arranged at high levels and on late notice – a test of underworld camaraderie prior to future collaborations. The leader of F1602 had fallen for the sham. Alex ordered his two actors to go along with any scheme the French concocted; the remaining Russian team would then intercede and wrap things up.

Alex finished the briefing by reminding them of their primary mission – to return a priceless treasure to its rightful home in Russia. They would not be leaving France without it.

Chapter Fifteen

The last day in Lyon was full of uncertainty. A return to London seemed logical, but it was potentially as treacherous as Paris. Evan and Jeanette discussed their options indoors while a steady Sunday rain discouraged further sightseeing.

Jeanette began a serious examination of Evan's traveling collection of research material. She transferred files from his backup disks to her computer, along with software allowing her to process the raw data he had obtained last fall. That data included an X-ray diffraction analysis of the nanospheres blanketing the Record's surface. In Evan's experiment, a beam of powerful X-rays had been focused on an isolated sample. Some of this radiation was scattered by the sample, generating a pattern of small spots on a detector plate. The intensity and spacing of these spots contained information about the structure of molecules forming each nanosphere. It was a technique for which Jeanette had received formal training, called X-ray crystallography.

As she stared at one pattern of spots, not yet knowing what secrets would emerge, the historical significance of the moment struck her. Eighty years earlier, Nobel laureate Dorothy Crowfoot Hodgkin, working with Professor J. D. Bernal in England, had viewed the first X-ray picture of a crystallized protein, not yet knowing that molecule's three-dimensional structure. Their work launched the field of structural biology, in which the atomic-scale architecture of a biological molecule like an enzyme is used to explain its function. Jeanette also thought of Rosalind Franklin, who in the fifties generated and analyzed X-ray diffraction photographs of fibrous DNA, which helped Watson and Crick to infer the structure of the double helix.

By late afternoon, Jeanette had finished, and sat staring at a computer graphics display of colorful images known as an electron density map. The results appeared as twisted tubes, constructed graphically of fine wire mesh, and wrapped around each other like a family of worms. The surface of each tube represented the electron cloud defining a molecule's shape. It was still necessary for someone to interpret these shapes, so she used interactive tools to build atomic structures that fit inside the tubes.

After another hour of work, she turned to Evan and spoke, triumphant; "You know those little nanospheres on stalks, projecting from the Record's surface? Well, they contain DNA."

He responded without looking up from his book. "Of course, I'm not surprised. The Record's no doubt been contaminated from years of human contact, and God knows what other creatures."

"No, Evan, it's more than that. The spheres have an inner core of highly *organized* DNA. Remember, X-rays are scattered coherently only when they pass through an *ordered* lattice of molecules, like a crystal. Any contaminating DNA from the environment would be stuck on at *random* orientations, and wouldn't be visible in this experiment." He stopped reading.

She turned back and scrutinized the images again. "For this density map, the best fitting atomic model is a double helix with two strands of sugar-phosphate polymer, and with paired bases in between. The overall dimensions match DNA."

Evan now walked over and peered at the screen in astonishment. "Can you read the sequence of bases? Could it be human DNA?"

"I'm not sure; the resolution of the X-ray data isn't high enough," she said in frustration, pointing out features of the image. "These pancake-like blobs represent the bases, but the shapes aren't well defined. I can't distinguish between adenine and guanine, or between cytosine and thymine. At this point, I couldn't even rule out a novel base, beyond what's found in human DNA or RNA. You should definitely send out more nanospheres for another round of analysis."

He scaled back the image and studied the overall molecular packing. It consisted of many stacked sheets, each sheet formed by a tight-knit array of double-helical strands. "They seem to be using 'DNA origami' to build the scaffolding inside each nanosphere – but at a very advanced level compared to us."

"Isn't that something you've been tinkering with?"

"You're right. DNA is a great material for building nanoscale objects. A long, single-strand molecule of DNA can be designed to fold up into almost any two or three-dimensional shape you want, through internal base pairing, along with some help from short 'staple' strands. The idea was conceived by Ned Seeman at New York University almost forty years ago, and now there's a whole field called DNA nanotechnology. You probably saw the 'smiley face' and 'world map' created out of DNA, and viewed with atomic force microscopy, published back in 2006."

He sat down next to her and drew some pictures on scrap paper. "In my lab we've made extremely small electronic circuits by attaching gold particles to a flat, pre-formed DNA template. The ultimate goal is to make computer chips much smaller than anything currently possible. Other labs are building functional objects from DNA – devices that walk, detect their surroundings, act as tweezers, and perform simple computations. There's even a tiny box made from DNA with a hinged lid, called a DNA nanorobot – something right up your alley. The DNA self-assembles into a clam-like container less than 100 nanometers across, and holds a payload like a drug or antibody. When the container senses a particular cell surface, it opens up and delivers the payload."

"Nanorobots are entering clinical trials soon; I was hoping to summarize the results for my class next semester."

Evan could not take his eyes off the display. "I wouldn't be surprised if DNA is serving as a scaffold for other parts of the disc, too. It all makes sense now, thinking back on the spectroscopic results from last year, which showed that biopolymers are involved."

Hunger finally overcame curiosity, and they wandered off to a small local café to reflect on their findings. After returning to their room, they arranged for a ride to the train station early the next morning. Then it was off to bed.

But Jeanette could not sleep. Today's discovery was linked to some memory just out of reach. Eventually drifting away at midnight, she dreamed of experiments she had witnessed at graduate school in Toronto. One summer evening she visited a friend in a neighboring lab as he arranged several cages of mice. To her amusement, he was feeding them bits of strawberry gelatin. When she joked about the mice enjoying a decadent lifestyle, he explained how the gelatin was actually spiked with nanoparticles containing DNA. Not just random DNA, but a gene encoding a specific protein. The mice rushed over to lap up the tasty treat, unaware that an orally-administered gene would soon be incorporated into their cells, leading to the expression of a measurable test protein. It was fascinating to watch how readily the creatures could be recruited for human purposes. Her friend smiled and stated, "Gene therapy made simple!" The comment had haunted her for weeks.

Jeanette's eyes opened wide, and she bolted upright. Turning to Evan, who was sleeping beside her, she began shaking him. "Evan! I just thought of something."

He rolled over, still half asleep. "Huh? Is something wrong?"

"What if the DNA inside those nanospheres isn't just a structural scaffold? What if it's a *package* waiting for delivery? You said yourself they break off easily. Maybe the DNA encodes genes, and is meant for transfer into human cells, like gene therapy."

Evan sat up slowly, rubbing his eyes, unable to wake as quickly as she needed. "Do you really think that's possible?" he asked.

"Gene transfer is something humans can accomplish *now*. Imagine what an advanced civilization could do."

"Well, you lost me there."

"Consider the transfer of a gene into a cell to treat some deficiency, like the absence of a critical protein. This is usually done using modified viruses as the delivery vehicle. One application is Parkinson's disease, where the brain neurotransmitter dopamine is lacking. In human patients, viral gene therapy can be used to introduce the DNA for enzymes that will increase the level of dopamine and relieve symptoms – but only temporarily."

"Yes. I've heard about this."

"That's a start, but most labs are trying to get away from viral packaging, since a virus will sometimes insert DNA incorrectly, or cause a dangerous immune response. Non-viral packaging for genes is now the trend. Materials like charged polymers, peptides, calcium compounds, organically modified silica, and chitosan all form nanoparticles when mixed with DNA. Chitosan comes from chitin – the exoskeleton of crustaceans like shrimp and crabs. One group in my department has been engineering such nanoparticles to cross the blood-brain barrier, and reach specific cells in the brain. So far, they can deliver genes into the brains of living mice without toxic effects."

"So, you mean one purpose of the nanospheres might be non-viral gene delivery in order to alter us in some way?"

"Yes, and things could get even worse. If the spheres *are* sophisticated enough to function as a retrovirus like HIV, and can actually integrate foreign DNA into our genomes, then the modification might be permanent. And if the change affects *all* our cells, including reproductive cells, then . . ." She was unable to complete the sentence.

Evan finished for her. "Then the changes would be inheritable." The magnitude of his words weighed upon them for several seconds.

Her voice began to quaver. "Don't you see Evan? It's the perfect ploy. The Record lures you in, using your favorite music, and then impregnates you with particles containing genes of their own design, for God knows what purpose." She started trembling. "Shit! What's happened to us? And what have I done to my aunt?"

He took her hands. "Now look, we won't know for sure what's going on until we get back to a lab and analyze the disc. A lot of experiments are needed, and you'll be the best person for the job."

She was still distraught, so Evan tried another tack. "Don't forget, Nigel owned the disc for almost ten years, and he didn't turn into an alien."

"I think it may be more subtle than that," she said, frowning. "Anyway, didn't Nigel tell you about strange sensations after long-term exposure to the Record?" She stared out of the window, simply wanting to leave this place. "We need to get back to London and talk to Nigel. Maybe he'll agree to have some medical tests done on himself."

Evan attempted to ground her with practical considerations. "Okay, let's think through what kind of experiments would be needed. How could you tell whether the nanospheres had entered the human body?"

"Well, maybe they can be traced through physical properties, like radioactivity or bound metals. Also, we could search for foreign DNA that's been incorporated into various tissues, or for expression of new proteins." She calmed down as she focused.

"If these things really are getting inside our bodies by design," he said, "could it be related to the message in the music?" Neither had an answer, and both fell silent. With this puzzle, it was always one step forward, two steps back. Yet one thing had become clear. Unraveling the Record's mystery was no longer a mere option, but a necessity for their future well-being.

Chapter Sixteen

Eager to leave Lyon, Evan and Jeanette rose at dawn, packed, and ate a light breakfast at their hotel. As they stood outside on the sidewalk of the narrow, nearly vacant street and waited for a taxi, they smiled at one another in a consoling manner; the burden of sheltering this secret would soon be over. A Peugeot taxi arrived and the driver popped the trunk from inside. His delay at stepping out distracted them from seeing a black van pull up behind. Its doors flew open and four men jumped out; they charged forward and surrounded the couple. For an instant, Evan assumed these strangers were Interpol agents sent for their protection. However, the men's aggressive nature quickly dispelled any such hope.

Pushed violently into the van and onto a middle-row bench seat, Jeanette tried to scream, but a hand slapped over her mouth. Evan noticed their luggage being thrown into the van just before his vision was obscured by means of a cloth hood pulled over his head. His hands were yanked behind and bound with tie-wrap. Curses from Jeanette indicated she had received the same treatment. The entire episode took less than twenty seconds. The taxi driver, clearly an accomplice to the kidnapping, scanned the scene for witnesses, and then drove off.

As the van sped away, Evan managed to shout, "Jeanette, are you okay?"

She replied with a muffled voice. "I think so." Each then received a slap on the head from the two kidnappers sitting behind them. Hands probed their pockets. Evan's wallet and Jeanette's mobile phone were confiscated. The hoods prevented them from seeing an inconspicuous car parked in a side alley, occupied by the private investigator hired to watch over them. He had been shot dead with a silenced pistol only a few moments before the van's arrival.

Evan could detect the van driving on a smooth highway for at least thirty minutes, followed by a slightly rougher road – probably a two-lane blacktop – another half an hour. He also heard a few words of Russian exchanged between the two men in the front seat. Finally he noticed a bumpy road – likely gravel – lasting several minutes until the van reached a full stop. Evan again fantasized a simulated kidnapping designed by Interpol, but then dismissed the thought as a denial mechanism.

They were led somewhere inside and planted in metal chairs back-to-back. After the hoods were removed, they found themselves sitting at the center of an old, abandoned warehouse. A partial view through dirty windows revealed overgrown vegetation, suggesting a remote location. The four men once again formed a circle around the couple, discouraging any attempts to flee. No effort was made to ease the discomfort of their hands, now jammed against the backs of their chairs.

The warehouse was empty except for a few rusty desks scattered around the perimeter, where several men worked on computers, paying little attention to the show at center stage. Evan could also see his luggage being searched. He assumed this place was a makeshift headquarters for some clandestine group – probably linked to those who had robbed his apartment. The men on the periphery were in shadows, but Evan recognized at least two of them from the episode at Jean-Paul's. Jeanette tossed her hair back and glared at everyone, though after several minutes she relaxed and concentrated on the conversations in French drifting over from the busy workers.

Evan's main concern at this point was the removal of the hoods. Being allowed to see the kidnappers' faces was not a good sign. A sense of dread began building in him, but he tried to remain calm. Eventually, a man left the small crowd and approached. "Dr. Blake, Dr. Menard, you may call me Jacques," he said in English, with a strong French accent. The steel box was marched out like a trophy, and placed on a small table next to them. Jacques opened it and looked inside, but did not remove the Record for closer inspection. Evan waited for Jacques to continue, but distractions kept arising, as other men walked up and whispered, or pointed out something on a laptop.

Evan's patience ran out. "What are we doing here?" he said loudly.

"Oh, I'm sure you've guessed," Jacques replied. "I arranged the search of your apartment, as well as your delay at St. Denis. I run an organization that deals in the acquisition of novel technology and related software." Glancing around the warehouse, he waved his hand in a circle. "These are unusual accommodations for us, but I thought it necessary today, given the value of your package."

With an air of pride, Jacques went on to provide a high-level overview of his organization and its accomplishments. He could have been a friendly representative from some financial institution pitching an investment portfolio. Evan became increasingly worried as Jacques shared more and more sensitive information.

Picking up several printouts, Jacques scanned the lists of numbers. "I've had bids from around the globe, even before this little prize was in my hands." He touched the top of the box, as if to confirm it was really sitting beside him. "Let's see; government officials from, as you would say, 'third world countries,' a few military leaders, several industrial representatives, and so on. We're getting up into the six-figure range now. It's really quite amazing."

Evan thought back to his stolen lab notebook. How would it be interpreted, if read by someone outside his field? At the moment, it was hard to remember exactly what he had written down. Was there really enough material to enable such a successful promotional campaign?

Jacques shot a stern look at two of the kidnappers who had shuffled off to the side, avoiding contact with the others. He spoke in a booming voice so they would overhear. "Oddly, I haven't received any bids from Russian officials, but we do have two Russians with us today. They were part of your welcome committee, and have recently joined our Lyon efforts. They have excellent credentials in this business, and I'm trusting them to bring me news from their comrades."

Why am I not surprised to find Russians here? Evan asked himself. Yet neither man's face matched the photo shared by Gerard at Interpol.

"Once you arrived in Lyon," Jacques resumed, "it was just a matter of time before we picked you up and brought you here. Why, you might ask? Well, it's very simple. I would like to increase the value of this package. You have personally studied it in more detail than anyone else, unless Dr. Menard has helped with your research." Evan was sickened to hear her name dragged into this mess.

Jacques continued. "We have notes and files related to the device, of course, but it would be better if we knew more about its construction and potential uses. I have access to some labs where you could continue whatever analysis you wish – to expand your knowledge. We would compensate you financially. In other words, you increase the value of our commodity, and you share in the profits. You essentially become a member of our team for a few months, get very rich, and then go back to your previous life."

The Frenchman almost seemed serious about the proposal. Evan viewed it as nothing but a one-way ticket, with no better outcome than the current situation. Jeanette was muttering "No," repeatedly, in a defiant but barely audible voice. Her bravery was incredibly moving to Evan. He knew that little time remained to think things through, yet he was at a loss to invent some clever scheme to free them. Could he really trust these people to release Jeanette if he offered to stay behind and help with research? Aches and pains racked his body now, distracting his focus.

Finally, he reached his limit. “Listen, you already have more than enough information to interest anyone. I won’t be able to provide anything else. I’ve quit the analysis. It’s all yours.” He didn’t really believe that, but it sounded convincing. To his great relief, he had not documented their discovery of DNA, nor would it be obvious from Jeanette’s computer files due to their formatting.

Jacques was silent, and it was hard to gauge his reaction. Suddenly Jean-Paul’s nephew emerged from the shadows. “Nice to see you again, Professor.” Turning to Jacques, he said, “One of his laptops has a double password system. I’m sure we could bypass it eventually, but it would be easier if he just told us.”

Jacques glared at the nephew. “Then take care of it yourself!” He picked up the box with the Record and carried it to the side of the room, clearly discouraged in his efforts to recruit Evan.

The nephew seemed taken aback, but then realized this was *carte blanche* to get the information. He pulled out a pistol and walked over to Jeanette’s side, staying far enough out so that Evan could follow the weapon while turning his head. The pistol was pointed at Jeanette’s face, and the nephew spoke as threateningly as he could. It was his big moment on stage. “I will count to three. You will give me the passwords, or I will kill her.” Jeanette cursed at the man, which Evan felt was not the wisest move. The count began. “One . . .” But he didn’t even need to reach ‘two.’ Evan was taking no chances, and spouted off the desired passwords.

The nephew walked closer to Jeanette. “Don’t move.” He placed the muzzle of the gun against her head, and fondled her with the other hand. He spoke so Evan could overhear. “I’ll bet you’re a hot one, eh? Maybe I’ll just take you into the back room where we can have some fun.”

Again Jeanette spewed words in French, probably a string of colorful profanities, enraging her tormentor. Evan was impressed with her ability to say things that got under the skin of French men. He would have to ask her about that later, if there was a future.

“Bitch! I’ll kill you anyway!” The nephew aimed the pistol using rigid, outstretched arms.

By now Jacques had returned to the center, and called out to the younger man. “Enough! Go back to work on the computer files.” Jacques clearly retained authority over the others; it was not a democracy. Despite his intervention, Jacques was not teeming with newfound mercy. “Last chance, Professor. Do you want to help us with the device or not?”

“You have my answer,” Evan said, his face rigid.

Then, as casually as Jacques had begun, he concluded. “So be it. Take them away.” He wandered over to a distant table and continued examining Evan's laptop. The passwords had already been implemented.

Evan and Jeanette's hoods were restored, and the couple was led back to the van, with the same group of men serving as escorts. Fortunately, the nephew was not among them. As another drive got underway, Evan sensed a reversal of the mechanical cues he had experienced previously: A bumpy gravel road, followed by a smoother asphalt road. But then something went terribly wrong. The van was lurching along a new route, if it was a road at all, and this continued for some time. He could hear branches scraping the side of the vehicle, as if they were negotiating an overgrown trail. Finally, the van came to a violent halt. Curses in French spewed from behind, aimed at the Russian driver.

Once again doors flew open, and they were pulled out onto what felt like an uneven dirt surface, covered with small twigs. No city noises were evident; only the rustling of trees. Evan guessed they were in an outlying wooded area. Both were shoved harshly and told to move ahead, their hoods still in place. They stumbled through crunching leaves, uncertain whether a tree trunk might suddenly appear in their path. After brushing against each other once, they tried to stay close. Neither vocalized any concern – it might only confirm the reality of their situation.

A command to stop was issued in English, but with a Russian accent. Evan heard the footsteps of two people approaching; a brief verbal exchange between them confirmed they were the Russians, probably assigned the task of execution as proof of their loyalty.

Evan knew that only seconds remained, yet the Russians were hesitating, perhaps to accommodate the couple's last wishes. The two Frenchmen, much farther away and likely at the van, were yelling in French to hurry up; apparently the Russians neither understood nor cared.

Evan and Jeanette pressed together back-to-back. Their tied hands met and gripped tightly together. No one ordered them to separate.

What does one say at the end? Evan reflected. "Jeanette, I'm sorry about all this. You know how I feel about you."

"It's okay, Evan. I feel the same. I think we'll see each other again, somehow."

Evan refused to say goodbye; he wanted this to be a nightmare from which he would soon wake. The next sounds were hammers cocking on two handguns, located only a few feet away. The clicks echoed through the woods.

Jeanette whispered something in Vietnamese. Evan knew these were the last words he would ever hear. Beautiful words – a beautiful voice – an immortal voice.

Each pistol fired once.

Chapter Seventeen

I think, therefore I am, was Jeanette's next realization.

For Evan, it was less academic. *So this is what it feels like to be shot in the head – there is no pain.*

Each became aware of standing upright. Their existence had somehow endured. The sensation of each other's fingertips persisted, along with a slight breeze on their bare arms, and the sound of leaves rustling in the wind. All these proofs of consciousness washed over them in a single second. The only discomfort came from their wrist ties.

The next sound to reach their ears was even more startling, as another two rounds thundered through the forest. Both jumped in reaction. But this time, Evan knew the blasts were farther away.

A crunching of leaves on the forest floor signaled footsteps approaching yet again. Evan had never been more uncertain of his fate. He grabbed Jeanette's hands tightly, and held his breath.

Despite the overcast day, they were blinded as the two masks disappeared in a single jerk. Their wrist ties were cut immediately afterward, all orchestrated by the younger Russian. Evan and Jeanette turned their heads slightly to look at one another. Neither appeared to be harmed. Swiveling around to examine the scene between themselves and the van, Evan saw the older Russian standing over the Frenchmen, who lay on the ground near the van. They were not moving.

Evan's eyes met those of the younger Russian, who burst out in a jovial manner. "Yes, Professor, you are being rescued!" Evan surmised that the Russians had walked up, pointed their weapons at the couple, and then whirled around to fire upon the Frenchmen with frightening precision. A second volley had insured the desired conclusion.

Evan and Jeanette gazed at each other, embraced for a moment, and then both promptly fell to the ground and threw up.

Back at the van, the two Russians were smoking, chatting, and laughing, as if out on a Sunday picnic. The older one spoke on his mobile phone in Russian, and they signaled for Evan and Jeanette to return to the vehicle.

The couple instinctively hesitated. Was this another trick? Had everything been staged in order to scare them, so they would cooperate when given a second chance at the warehouse? Would two people really have been sacrificed to maximize the drama? Evan was convinced the Frenchmen were dead, given the ghastly appearance of their head wounds; it looked too real to be a Hollywood special effect.

Evan and Jeanette could read each other's thoughts. Both were considering a dash, and both had reached the same conclusion: *What chance do we really have? We can't outrun these guys.* With extreme reluctance they hobbled toward the van, trying not to stare at the two bodies nearly blocking their path.

"Now what?" Evan asked the Russians, feeling numb.

"Now we go back to warehouse," the younger man said in a thick accent. "It has been secured, and you will meet our boss."

Apparently another set of players was in control. Evan questioned whether his future was any rosier. He hesitated at the van's door.

"Please, Professor. Hurry up," the young Russian said. "More Frenchmen may be nearby. Also, I don't like this forest. I prefer city."

As they climbed into the van, he spoke again. "There is no shame you got sick. It always happens when people almost die, but then survive." Evan wondered how often this man had witnessed such an event. They sat in the van's midsection, behind the Russians, but this time no restrictions were placed on their movement.

While the older Russian drove, the younger one turned around and began a casual conversation. Apparently this was just an ordinary drive in the countryside for him. "My name is Viktor. My friend here is Oleg, but he does not speak English." The driver glanced briefly in the mirror and acknowledged them with a nod, all the while barreling down the bumpy dirt road.

"You are lucky," Viktor explained. "We pretended to join F1602 only two days ago, after we learned you went to Lyon. We knew they would come after you."

Evan and Jeanette were holding on to each other like young children riding home after a terrifying amusement park ride. The drone of Viktor's cheerful voice was surreal, yet somehow comforting.

"It is very touching scene, to see you like this. When I watched you in the forest together, I almost cried. It was my pleasure to kill those Frenchmen. On my team we do not kill innocent civilians – especially pretty women."

Viktor turned toward the front and lit a cigarette, pointing out something frantically to the driver. They seemed to be arguing over a fork in the road, but quickly resolved the issue while checking a map on Viktor's smartphone.

Viktor turned back again, his arm stretched out along the top of the front seat, eager for more discussion. "I sometimes watch those TV shows where people sing and judges rate them. You know these shows, yes?"

"What?" Evan could barely focus on a topic so remote from their current situation. "Oh, yes, I think so."

"I have pretty good voice. I can sing well, but I have to sing in Russian. Still, how does one get audition? Does that happen in your home town, back in America?"

"Well, maybe. I'm not quite sure. But if you get us out of this mess, Viktor, I will definitely send you more information."

"Excellent!" Viktor said with a big smile, apparently in complete trust. He returned to a more subdued conversation with Oleg.

Jeanette had become very quiet, perhaps from shock, as she curled up next to Evan. At that moment Evan became resolved, with a grim determination surpassing any other decision in his life, to escape at the next possible opportunity.

The van eventually arrived at the warehouse and pulled up alongside two black SUVs. *Do villains ever choose a color besides black?* Evan wondered. As they walked closer, Evan could see bullet holes in the warehouse windows, which he did not recall from his previous stay, though that had involved only an interior view.

Stepping through the door into the warehouse again was nearly impossible. It was like forcing oneself through an invisible glass barrier. The urge to turn and run was overwhelming, even though their new hosts did not appear as threatening as the last. However, they did finally enter without coercion, and were greeted with a very different scene. The cast now consisted of several men in paramilitary clothing, mulling over the same equipment and computers used by F1602 just hours before.

Evan noted calm conversations in Russian all around him. As the couple was escorted further inside, he noticed one Frenchman on the floor off to the side, apparently dead. It was the nephew. Despite Evan's experiences in St. Denis and this warehouse, he would have preferred to see Jacques lying there instead.

Viktor was watching Evan's eyes closely, and seemed eager to elaborate, using almost apologetic tones. "My team stormed this warehouse, and drove most of them off. They were allowed to flee as long as they didn't carry anything away. But that one, over there, stayed to fight, and was regrettably killed. It was never our intention to start a battle. We would rather avoid anything that draws attention in a foreign country."

A tall, older Russian man with a graying beard looked up at Evan and walked over in a confident manner. Evan instantly recognized him as Alexander from the passport photo shared at Interpol. This moment seemed destined. The man gestured for them to sit in the same metal chairs used for the previous interrogation. However, the atmosphere was now benign – at least on the surface.

"Hello, Dr. Blake and Dr. Menard. Please, call me Alex. We have no intention of harming you, and we'll drive you to a train station shortly." Alex's English was tinged with a British accent, suggesting he had spent considerable time in the UK. Evan made a mental note to check on this later.

"I'm sorry for what you just experienced, but we were lucky to intervene at all. I placed some of my men in factions of this crime organization as 'moles,' so we could intercept the disc if it fell into their hands, which was almost certain after you moved to Paris."

Evan could see items related to the Record being scrutinized. While the final outcome for the couple was still uncertain, at least this time they were offered cold drinks from a small refrigerator, which had been stocked generously by the French team.

“Who are you, exactly?” Evan asked. “I mean, your little group here.”

“In the strictest sense, we work for the Russian government, but it’s a very small branch.” Alex pointed to the metal box resting on a table across the room. “I’ve been looking many years for that disc. It first disappeared from Russia – its original home – in 1989. I always suspected it had fallen into the hands of Nigel Thompson, given his rise to fame in the music world over the last dozen years; that’s usually how it works. However, we didn’t find it in his apartment during a search in 2009, and I assumed it had been hidden away indefinitely. Then, late last year, black market circles began humming about something of incredible value, in the possession of one Evan Blake. This was a red flag for us, though no one else knew the full story. Finally, we heard news of a burglary and people trying to sell rare, old recordings – another footprint of the disc. We tracked you to Lyon, and then inserted two men into F1602. Just in time, I’d say.”

Alex scanned through one of Evan’s notebooks, though not the one stolen from Imperial. “I see you’ve uncovered a great many things. Much of this we know already, although we never got very far with the nanotech aspects.”

Once again, Evan was relieved he had not written anything related to DNA content. Apparently this was something the Russians had not discovered, or were not admitting. He almost expected another insane offer to travel to a foreign lab and continue research, but the topic did not arise.

"We appreciate this device more than you might think, and have taken full advantage of its musical properties," said Alex.

Jeanette jumped in, for some reason eager to share her own observations. "We found that music is accessible by simply holding the disc." Alex showed no reaction, suggesting he already knew this fact.

Alex slid his chair closer, and spoke in a quieter voice. "When you walk out of here, you'll no longer have any evidence related to the disc, and thus no one will believe your story. Therefore, I'll share some history. At this point, you're practically colleagues in its study." He glanced around to verify the absence of eavesdroppers.

"The disc arrived in Russia early in the twentieth century," he said.

The couple looked at one another knowingly, and Evan interrupted with scarcely hidden pride. "I've always suspected that, since it resembles the most advanced form of musical storage we had back then."

"Yes, very good. We made the same inference."

"Where exactly in Russia was it found?" Jeanette asked.

"At the Tunguska site in central Siberia," Alex said.

"You mean the large explosion that occurred in 1908?" Evan asked.

"Indeed. Tunguska remains the largest impact event in recorded history, with an estimated energy of ten to fifteen megatons, or about one thousand times the power of the Hiroshima bomb. It destroyed eight hundred square miles of forest, an area slightly larger than metropolitan London. Soon afterward, skies throughout Europe lit up for several nights. If the impact had occurred just four hours later, St. Petersburg would have been destroyed, given the earth's rotation."

"Oh please," Jeanette said, "don't start in with stories of crashed alien spacecraft or wayward black holes."

"No, nothing like that. We believe Tunguska was a completely natural event, caused by the air burst and disintegration of a fragment from a comet or asteroid. So far, the debate between these two possibilities has not been settled. However, the date of June thirtieth did coincide with a close approach of Comet Encke, and a meteor shower was in progress, so a fragment from that comet is a good candidate. But let me tell you a bit more history."

Chapter Eighteen

Like actors in some early Soviet *avant-garde* theater production, the three occupied simple metal chairs clustered in the middle of an empty, corrugated-metal warehouse, with natural illumination filtering down from skylights high above. Evan and Jeanette leaned forward as Alex chronicled the Record.

"As you know, there was turmoil in Russia between 1905 and the mid-twenties, with civil war and revolution; thus, very little effort was expended to chart remote regions of Asia. Finally, in 1927, Russian geologist Leonid Kulik received funding from the Soviet government to explore the Tunguska region, in the hope that the event involved a metallic asteroid – a potentially rich source of iron for use in the booming Soviet industry. No one had ever laid eyes on the site except local Evenki tribes. The natives guided Kulik's team, but with reluctance, since they believed an angry god had caused the event.

"The research team was surprised at the lack of an obvious crater, seeing instead a vast area of scorched and flattened trees. Interestingly, within a couple of miles of the epicenter, the trees were still upright, though stripped of limbs and bark, since an airburst had occurred directly above. Several other expeditions were launched during the next decade, but no significant iron deposits were ever found. Over the years since, detailed studies of soil and trees in the area have supported a comet or rocky asteroid theory. The region was opened to international scientists only in 1991.

"A potential crater arising from an asteroid fragment may exist in the form of nearby Lake Cheko, according to a group at the University of Bologna in Italy. However, a Russian group from our Troitsk Innovation and Nuclear Research Institute, using ground-penetrating radar at the Suslov funnel, found what may be a piece of ice from the nucleus of a comet – remember, there is a permafrost in Siberia. As you can see, there are still unresolved issues."

Alex adjusted his chair's position yet again, and his voice became even softer. "So far, everything I've told you is public information. Now let's go beyond that.

"In 1938, Kulik conducted an aerial photo survey of the devastation. He noticed something odd from the images, and teams were sent in to investigate. Near the epicenter the soil was disturbed in an artificial manner. Buried underground was a metallic, ellipsoidal pod, about four feet long, and clearly not of human origin. From analysis of the area, they deduced it was placed there shortly after the impact event. The pod contained our little disc, which was whisked away to Moscow for further analysis. Unfortunately, that time period corresponded with Stalin's Great Purge – a mass repression against his own people, in which thousands were executed. When Stalin learned about the disc, he called it the Soviet Union's greatest treasure, and a way to assure world domination, even though its potential application was by no means obvious. The technology was beyond comprehension; no one knew where to begin.

"Over the decades, scientists privy to the secret concluded that while Tunguska was a natural event, our visitors chose the site precisely because it would become the focus of world attention. Furthermore, given its remoteness, any investigation would be led by top scientists committed to an arduous journey. Yet the destination was not as difficult to reach as, say, the South Pole, since the Trans-Siberian Railway had just been completed."

Thus far, Alex's account seemed plausible, but Evan sensed this was only the tip of the iceberg.

Alex finished his drink and continued. "Obviously, the disc's designers didn't fully appreciate our politics, which delayed discovery for thirty years, and prevented widespread dissemination of information. And they were clearly too optimistic about the potential for world cooperation, even *if* everyone had been informed. But their basic strategy was sound. The eyes of the world were drawn to the Tunguska event from the beginning. Research at the site was vigorous and continues to this day. The explosion generated enormous interest for years, and has been a source of inspiration for many facets of popular culture. Our visitors took advantage of a natural signpost on earth, but their thoughtful donation was sequestered by a selfish few."

Evan inwardly questioned whether the disc was really a 'thoughtful donation,' now that he and Jeanette had uncovered its DNA content. The need for thorough analysis screamed out more loudly than ever. For the moment, however, he focused on extracting information from Alex. "Speaking of the selfish few, what was done with the disc over the years?"

"Its ability to generate music was soon discovered, and it became largely a tool for that purpose. However, in the 1950s many scientists became interested in its radioactive signature, for potential space and weapons applications. Yet no one knew how to extract tangible materials, or even formulas, from the object.

"So, the most interesting application remained music. The disc inspired classical musicians to become better performers and composers. Have you ever wondered about the disproportionately large number of talented Russian musicians in the twentieth century? Culture and training were part of it, of course, but a select few were allowed to interact with the disc. It became, for musicians, something akin to the use of steroids among athletes. You can imagine the competition for access to such a device."

"Did famous composers like Prokofiev and Shostakovich use the disc? Does that partially account for their creativity?" Jeanette asked.

"Not necessarily. While those two were granted limited access at the beginning of their careers, they quickly fell out of favor with the political establishment under Stalin, and were prohibited from further contact. They soared to great heights based on natural genius."

Alex slid his chair back a few inches and straightened his back; he was near a stopping point. "In short, what you might call a 'secret society' arose to allocate disc usage; sometimes for musical development, sometimes for scientific research. But this society soon became a fringe element of our culture, and today only a handful of officials know the whole story. The device is considered more of a curiosity now. Still, any technological advantages it might offer, however slight, are motivation for continued secrecy."

"What happens now?" Evan asked, suddenly realizing that he had uttered the same phrase a few hours earlier, after narrowly escaping death.

"All your research materials will stay with us, but you may retrieve your personal belongings. We can transport you anywhere you want to go." The men in the warehouse had finished packing, and were already loading the vehicles outside.

Viktor approached, wheeling their suitcases; everything had been thoroughly searched. When one small bag spilled its contents onto the floor, Evan knelt down to help Jeanette pick up the items. While squatting, he glanced over at the dead Frenchman and noticed something lying on the floor under a large desk next to the body. It appeared to be a handgun that had slid across and come to rest directly beneath the desk's file cabinet, thus remaining hidden from view. He made a mental note, and his heart began pounding as he sorted through possible courses of action, assuming he could muster enough courage.

The crew hauled out the last boxes of material, owned ever so briefly by F1602. Soon, two cars could be heard driving away, leaving Viktor, Oleg, and Alex to deal with the most important contraband – the Record. Alex motioned for Viktor to take the couple back to the van.

Evan fully believed that they would be taken to a train station, yet was determined to see the Record leave France with him instead of Alex. The van would have to be hijacked somehow. As he walked toward the door, he charted a path that would bring him alongside the large desk.

The next chain of events was so unexpected that the Russians were caught completely off-guard. Evan fell to the floor, reached under the desk, and with a clear mental map to guide his hand, grabbed the pistol. Jumping up, he pointed it at Alex, who stood only ten feet away. To Evan, the pistol had a rather plastic, molded appearance, and he desperately hoped that he was holding a real weapon and not a toy.

Viktor and Oleg, almost out of the warehouse, stopped and spun around. Well-trained responses kicked in, and they quickly removed their own pistols, although the shock of Evan's performance had slightly delayed their normal reaction time. Alex raised his hand, signaling them to freeze.

"The disc goes with me, or else I shoot Alex," said Evan, speaking loudly so that everyone would hear. However, it sounded like someone else's voice, and the world around him became surreal. He was in a Wild West scene, standing on a dusty street, facing down the sheriff.

"Threatening me will not stop my men from shooting you," Alex said with unnerving calmness. "They know I'm prepared to sacrifice myself if necessary." Alex then revealed a pistol he kept in a holster on his side, hidden under his jacket, and raised it slowly toward Evan.

Jeanette's face was painted with horror. She looked back and forth at the two weapons, as if watching a tennis match, and then fixed her eyes on Evan. All she could do was utter a soft plea. "Evan, please don't."

Evan was not listening. He was set on one goal, and his determination clouded all other considerations. But at least the voice was beginning to sound more like his. "It's not right. Something like this belongs to everyone – not to any one country or company. I was ready to announce it. People need to know that an extraterrestrial artifact exists."

Alex replied in a matter-of-fact style. "My actions are not purely from choice. I ultimately report to those at very high levels. To return without the disc, once its presence in Europe has been established, would mean serious consequences for my team."

Evan was beginning to sweat, but showed no sign of backing down. "No, there's too much at stake, and I've put too much work into it – as much as any of your people."

"We can agree; a lot is at stake," Alex said. "But you don't have the full picture. I'm afraid I have no sympathy for your desire to profit from the disc's discovery."

"Don't patronize me!" Evan shouted. "This is not about profit. We'll need open study if we're ever going to decode it. That can't happen if it's buried in Russia again."

"Well then, we have an interesting situation. Are you really prepared to die for this cause?"

After several minutes of deafening silence, Evan knew his bluff had been called. He felt the first real touch of fear, although it was different from his experience in the forest. This time, his fate rested in his own hands – literally. His grip began trembling, and it was obvious he had much less experience, if any, with such a perilous confrontation. Despite extreme frustration, he decided to stand down. He lowered his weapon, and then set it on the floor. Oleg ran over to pick it up, while Jeanette emitted an audible sigh.

"I think your motivations are admirable," said Alex, still pointing his pistol, "assuming you speak the truth about wanting to share. Such a day will come, I assure you, but not right now."

Alex re-holstered his weapon. Oleg and Viktor positioned themselves behind Evan and Jeanette while escorting them to the van. The ride was now exceedingly awkward, with Viktor remaining silent, visibly disappointed in his new friend. As promised, the couple was delivered to the Lyon train station, and even provided with travel money. An hour later, they sat in a station café, planning their next move.

Evan was devastated. In the struggle for possession of the earth's most valuable relic, he had just lost the first battle. "I guess I wasn't meant to play this kind of game."

"Evan, have you already forgotten? We almost died today. Let's just think about what we have now." She took his hand in hers, and they sat peacefully, watching passersby.

After several minutes of reflection, she leaned over and spoke in a whisper. "Evan, there's something I need to tell you. You were holding a Glock pistol. It fires when you pull the trigger; there's no safety. Alex had a Czech CZ-75, and I could see that his safety lever was *engaged*, though I'm sure he's experienced enough to shoot quickly anyway. But I don't think he *wanted* to harm you, and he assumed you wouldn't shoot him. In other words, the whole stand-off was as much a gamble for him as it was for you."

Evan looked at her in amazement. "How do you know so much about handguns?"

"My uncle was on the police force in Montreal. When I was a teenager, he took me to the shooting range often, and taught me how to fire different kinds of guns," she stated nonchalantly while munching on a cookie.

"Oh, *I see*," said Evan, nearly rolling his eyes. "Well, next time I'll just toss over the gun and let *you* handle things."

"Fine with me," she said with a grin.

After they called Nigel and explained their situation, he insisted that they come to London immediately, where he would meet them and provide accommodation. From Evan's perspective, this was not the end, but merely the next phase of the adventure, for he had every intention of following the Record's trail, and at least one means of doing so.

Chapter Nineteen

The tired couple stepped off a train in London's St. Pancras station, looking like refugees from a war zone. As they trudged toward the exit, Nigel made his appearance, elegant and unfazed. He welcomed each warmly, saying he could hardly imagine what they had experienced in just over a week.

Because of his professional successes, Nigel now owned three flats in London, which he used to house visiting musical celebrities. Today's guests deserved not only VIP treatment but seclusion as well. He ushered them into a private limousine waiting at the curb.

"Do you always travel this way, Nigel?" Jeanette asked.

"No, not really, but I have it available when necessary, and this is certainly one of those times."

The limousine pulled up in front of a luxury apartment building in Mayfair, containing a lavishly furnished flat. "Stay here as long as you'd like," he said. "There's a computer inside you can use for any research."

After a tour of the flat was complete, all three sat down in the living room and opened a bottle of wine. Evan and Jeanette described their encounter with the French and Russian teams, but not all their technical findings about the disc.

Nigel sat quietly while listening to their account, then spoke. "At least this explains the break-in at *my* place in 2009. It was the Russians looking for the Record, which of course I'd already buried under the Eye. Well, whatever; they definitely have it back now. Do you think they've taken it to St. Petersburg?"

"I may have a way of finding out, but it's only a slim chance," said Evan.

Jeanette's face brightened as she remembered his modification. "So you'll be able to locate the box anywhere in the world?"

Nigel looked puzzled, and Evan explained. "Inside the metal box, I installed a tracking device that links to all the earth's major satellite systems – GPS, Russian GLONASS, and Iridium low orbit. There's an application I can download to pinpoint the signal. But before you get your hopes up, remember whom we're dealing with. Alex and his people will probably check the box and disable any electronics, or simply find a new container for the Record."

After a long pause, Nigel addressed Evan. "I realize you're upset about losing the evidence, but at least you spent almost a year with the Record. I was wondering if you noticed any . . . long-term effects?"

"Nothing I could put into words," Evan said.

Jeanette queried Nigel hesitantly. "Evan told me you were reluctant to write about your own symptoms, in case readers thought you were . . ."

"Mad? Well, I've certainly had those concerns," Nigel said, looking down. "Some very bizarre sensations occurred during *my* time with the disc, though they faded after I buried it. Still, a few things persist to this day."

Evan tried to reach out. "Nigel, we're all in this together."

He looked up abruptly. "You mean, Jeanette too?"

"Yes, I touched it," she said. "And I found that just holding the Record, at least during sleep, induces some kind of musical experience."

"Oh, I see. I'm sorry you were affected," Nigel said.

"No, it's okay. It was incredible," she replied.

"I guess I never tried holding the Record. But I touched it a lot, and I was close to it physically for almost a decade. I'm convinced it can interact with you from a distance, once it synchronizes to your presence."

"Could you tell us about those bizarre sensations?" Jeanette asked.

"I'll start with some examples from early on. Sometimes, while listening to music and looking at the rain, I saw each drop glowing with a different fluorescent color. Other times, music could evoke a taste or smell matching the mood of the melody, if that makes any sense. Occasionally, a non-musical sound, like a loud bird call or thunder clap, could trigger a burst of music inside my head so realistic that – for an instant – I thought someone was playing a musical instrument in my flat."

"So far what you've described is called synesthesia," said Jeanette. "Connections formed between normally separate brain activities. It's been well documented – for example, by Oliver Sacks. It can show up in a few people per thousand."

Nigel took a long sip of wine and then continued. "Later experiences are even harder to describe. Some selections of music – especially complex, modern pieces – could generate a new idea or concept, or induce visions of three-dimensional objects. I shared one of these concepts with a mathematician. He looked at my drawing of an ellipse inside of a triangle with amazement, and said it was an illustration of Marden's Theorem, which relates geometrical figures to the roots of polynomial expressions. Another time, I had a vision of a rotating star cluster, like in a spiral galaxy, and panicked when stars at the edge moved as fast as those near the center. Later, a physicist said my 'observation' was the current motivation for updating theories of gravity, whether by revising general relativity, or by introducing 'dark matter.'"

After his confessions, Nigel looked even more worried. "Do you think listening to the Record over such a long time changed me in some way?"

"Possibly, but we're not sure," Evan said, glancing at Jeanette. Her expression advised him to proceed with caution. "Nigel, there's something we haven't mentioned yet, because it's very speculative."

Evan delayed, so Jeanette stepped in. "There's DNA in the Record. It seems to have a structural role, but conceivably it could enter our bodies. And if it works like gene therapy, then anyone touching the disc might become altered in some way. The effect would probably be proportional to the length of exposure, and might not show up for quite a while. Until I can do specific experiments, it's all a hypothesis. Obviously, research is impossible without the disc. However, we might be able to examine *you* in order to find out."

"So foreign DNA gets injected into us. Terrific!" Nigel said sarcastically, tossing his hands into the air with exasperation. "Any idea what happens next?"

Jeanette remained the calm, objective teacher. "We already know that the Record's audio properties are customized – it interacts with each person's brain in a tailored way. Perhaps *all* the disc's features work together. Maybe DNA is guided to regions of the brain that are activated when we listen to music, allowing those particular neurons to be modified. This would be similar to targeted gene therapy, which is doable today. Of course, the Record could target many different places in the brain at once."

The two men stared at each other, impressed with the novelty of her theory. Finally Nigel asked, "Why do you say 'many different places' would be modified?"

"That comes from brain scans using functional MRI. *Several* areas are activated when we listen to music. Not surprisingly, some of these overlap speech and language centers. But music also activates sites of higher-level thought and organization, along with primitive emotion and reward centers. Still, there seem to be unique pathways in the brain that exist solely for music. For example, processing of pitch information in speech and music are separate. When brain damage reduces a person's ability to hear speech intonation, it rarely disrupts the perception of melody."

Nigel stood and stretched his legs, walking around the room several times before returning to his chair. After sitting, he poured another tall glass of wine. "But such a clever device, this Record – to do what, ultimately? Why expend so much effort to modify a few humans?"

"We've wondered the same thing," said Evan. "Maybe their goal *was* to select only a few people. I think Alex might know – all the more reason to find him."

"What makes you think he'll tell you?" Nigel asked.

"I don't know, just a hunch. But even if we can trace the Record, Alex might be elsewhere. It may be guarded by someone much less sympathetic to our curiosity."

After an hour had passed, Nigel rose to make his exit. "Here are my direct phone numbers," he said, writing on a piece of scrap paper. "Please let me know if you get more information." He left them with wishes for a rapid recovery from their stressful trip.

Evan and Jeanette collapsed on the couch, and spent the remainder of the day resting. They risked only a couple of brief excursions outside their flat. London seemed safer than the Continent, but they knew this could change dramatically if they reacquired the Record.

The next day, Evan had an update to share. He called Nigel while staring at an Internet map of the tracking results. “Nigel, the Record, or at least the box, is in central Moscow.”

“Well, that makes sense,” Nigel said. “Just where a bureaucrat like Alex would end up. It’s probably stuffed away in a safe at some high security installation – maybe even under the Kremlin. We’ll definitely never see it again.”

After he hung up, Evan turned to Jeanette. “I think it’s time we head home and try to shore things up. I may not have a job or even career opportunities when I get back.” Jeanette said nothing, but simply leaned against him.

Another day passed, and Nigel received a second call from Evan. “I have some interesting news on box tracking. The current location is Krasnoyarsk, in southern Siberia. I did some research – that’s the third largest city in Siberia, with a million people. Several large industries and a number of universities are located there.”

“Hmm. Perhaps a place where research could be done, while remaining outside the mainstream,” said Nigel.

“Possibly. A number of Soviet industries were moved there for safety during the War.”

On the final full day in London, the tracking results were updated yet again. This time, Nigel stopped by for a visit. “The box has another location,” Evan said. “It’s very close to the original Tunguska impact site, in a town named Vanavara.”

Nigel looked at the map. “Good Lord, that’s an isolated spot.”

"Yes, but I've seen websites offering trips to the Tunguska epicenter starting from Vanavara, which is about forty miles away."

"It's strange, though," Nigel said. "Why would they move the Record there? Maybe it's a trap – sending the empty metal box somewhere to see if you'll follow. This is starting to look suspicious, Evan, especially since Alex told you that Tunguska story."

Jeanette joined in. "Yes. Maybe Alex wants to lure you there, and then hold you prisoner to do more research. At this point you probably know more about the disc than any Russian scientist."

"But why that location, at the source itself?" Evan asked. "Surely there's no research facility out there. Look at the satellite maps."

"It's hard to tell what the Russians have built at any given spot," Nigel said. "It could be underground. Again, Alex knows that this region might attract you."

"Or maybe Alex just grabs you at Vanavara and flies you to another city, then tortures you for more information," Jeanette said, her expression growing more concerned.

"*Or*, maybe this is a *friendly* invitation," Evan countered.

"A terrible place for a party," Nigel responded.

"I know it sounds hopelessly optimistic," Evan said, "but I think Alex has planned all this, and I don't think his intention is to abduct me. He could have done that earlier."

Jeanette made one final appeal. “But if you go there of your own free will, your disappearance is easier to cover up. He doesn’t have to drag you kicking and screaming across the border. I don’t like the looks of it.”

“Well, the whole idea is moot anyway. I’d have to jump through hoops to get a visa and explain my business in such a remote area. Let’s just go home.”

The limousine to Heathrow arrived at their flat early the next morning, with Nigel on board. At the airport, he came inside to see them off. As the three sat in a bar sharing a final round of drinks, the conversation faded, and each became lost in private thoughts.

Evan broke the silence with unexpected zeal. “I’ve made a decision. I’m going to find some way to get over there. To Siberia, I mean – either as a tourist or guest lecturer. And it needs to happen this summer.” He sat up straight and stared at Nigel. “I have one question for you.”

“You’re going to ask me if I’d like to come along?”

“You’re a mind reader,” said Evan.

“Naturally,” Nigel replied. “My brain has been upgraded by aliens, remember?” He paused, and then answered Evan’s question soberly. “Let’s just hope you’re reading Alex correctly.”

The men turned their gaze to Jeanette, who feigned bewilderment for several seconds, and then burst out, “I’m in!” She lifted her wine glass, eyeing the two, and asked, “To Oz?”

The pun was clear, and they lifted their glasses in return. “To Oz,” Nigel replied. “We’re off to see the Wizard.”

PART III

THE JOURNEY EAST

Chapter Twenty

A cool breeze blew across the brick patio, despite a thick enclosure of manicured shrubs and flowering plants. The cozy oasis, meticulously prepared by Susan Henderson, was tucked behind her small home in Cambridge. Jeanette sat at a marble-top table sipping iced tea, awaiting Evan's arrival. The couple had been invited to dinner on this pleasant Saturday evening in late June.

Carrying out a plate of cheese and crackers from the kitchen, Susan queried Jeanette about a movie they had seen together earlier in the day, but Jeanette was lost in thought and did not respond. That was happening a lot lately. Right then, Jeanette was remembering her first week back at the lab, when she had walked around in a daze, unable to focus on routine issues facing the group.

Since Jeanette's return to Boston, the two women had spoken on several occasions, but the conversations had always involved highly edited versions of the European adventure. Jeanette had clearly experienced a life-changing event, yet was unwilling to reveal any details to her friends. She had also flown to Montreal to visit her father, and for the first time, felt reluctant to share facts about a trip to Paris, which saddened her greatly. Finally, disturbing dreams interrupted her sleep now, necessitating the occasional use of prescription sleeping pills.

Susan squeezed Jeanette's shoulder as she walked past, taking a seat nearby and listening to the wind chimes. Evan arrived at seven-thirty, and Jeanette became more animated in his presence. After enjoying an Asian stir-fry dinner, they all retired to the patio, where the darkness was broken by several candles flickering inside colored glass containers. Over the course of the next hour, the couple finally divulged their account of the Record. However, they omitted their brush with death. Jeanette knew that Susan's reaction would be to call Interpol the very next day and file a complaint.

Susan turned to Evan and lowered her voice, as though they were standing in a campus hallway. "You haven't told me much about Atkins, or your return to work."

"For a while, I was suspicious of Richard. You see, last fall I told him I was studying an object with unusual material properties, though of course I didn't call it extraterrestrial. He's now admitted to sharing this with representatives from a conglomerate of industries that provides research funding to universities. Richard was boasting how his department could soon offer a huge breakthrough in nanotechnology, based on my recent discovery, but only if MIT received money upfront to support the analysis. It was irresponsible, but I don't believe he ordered my work at Imperial to be plundered and distributed. Someone from that meeting must have informed their European colleagues, which fueled a desire to know more. Scraps of data from my stolen notebooks then encouraged criminals to search for me specifically." Evan glanced at Jeanette, who was shaking her head sideways, reminding him that Susan should not be told of the kidnapping.

Evan then shifted to a perkier mode. “But my faculty position remains intact. Richard even argued with the board of trustees for some flexibility in my return. I think he was embarrassed about releasing the information. I assured him I would bring the new technology to MIT, but only if some company didn’t stamp it as proprietary, and if the university didn’t try to patent it. So, basically, he and I are doing each other a favor. In the end, I was able to negotiate another month of downtime, which I may need,” he said, grinning at Jeanette. She smiled back.

As an anthropologist, Susan was watching their interplay. “Jeanette mentioned she might take off again in July. Is there something you two aren’t telling me?”

Evan broke the silence that followed. “We know where the Record is. At least, the tracking device associated with it. My instincts tell me the signal is an invitation. Jeanette doesn’t share my optimism, but I’m working on her.”

“Where is it, then?” Susan asked.

“This will sound strange; central Siberia.”

“My God, surely you’re not going there? Wait, *how* are you going there?”

“The first step was applying for a visa. In the past, this involved a letter of invitation, but that requirement was dropped in 2012. Still, I wanted my trip to look business-related, so I got myself invited to the Siberian Federal University in

Krasnoyarsk, as a guest speaker in their Nanotechnology Department. The visas came easily after that. Jeanette will travel along as my 'wife.'"

But Evan knew the process had involved considerable uncertainty. Alex could have used his government connections to block their entry. However, the approvals had sailed through, boosting Evan's optimism regarding the quest.

"So you think the Record is in Krasnoyarsk?" Susan asked.

"No, not quite. We still have to fly a couple of hours to a little town north of there, called Vanavara. We could probably go as tourists, since people visit to see the Tunguska impact site. But we don't want to advertise our movements too openly."

Susan frowned at his last statement, so Evan quickly continued, before she could probe. "We learned that an Italian research group from the University of Bologna organizes expeditions to the Tunguska region every few summers. They're going next month to search for evidence of impact at a lake just a few miles from the epicenter. They use a cargo plane from Italy to Krasnoyarsk, followed by a Russian cargo helicopter to Vanavara. I think they'll let us ride along on the helicopter trip."

Again, it all sounded simple, but the arrangements had been complex and incredibly fortuitous. Nigel, who often conducted symphonies in Italy, was acquainted with the head of Bologna University's Music Department. Through this connection, he convinced the Tunguska expedition leader, Enrico

Facchini, that his team would benefit from the inclusion of two more scientists – an engineer and a biologist. It helped that Enrico, a huge opera fan, remembered Rosina's 2008 performance, and had been told of her connection to Evan. Despite the tentative plan, Evan still wanted to meet Enrico prior to the trip. Flying into Vanavara with the Italians was important – it would allow stealth, since Evan had not listed the town on his itinerary for the visa application.

An even bigger issue was the return, since presumably Evan would be smuggling out Russia's greatest secret in the form of a small metal box. A commercial airline departure might involve searches, especially if Evan's name appeared on a watch list, courtesy of Alex. However, the box was something that would readily disappear among tons of gear aboard a cargo plane headed back to Italy. And while the Italians might be surprised to see Evan choosing to leave Krasnoyarsk on a cramped cargo flight, he was prepared to show the disc to Enrico if necessary, as his ticket home. Assuming the disc was in Vanavara at all, Evan reminded himself.

Jeanette filled in the rest. "Nigel is quite famous in Russia, and was able to arrange a conference with other composers in Moscow. He thinks he can break away and join us in Krasnoyarsk on the pretext of sightseeing. I don't know all the details, but he has friends in important positions." Jeanette also stopped short of telling Susan that their ultimate goal was to remove the Record from Russia.

After everyone had finished dessert and coffee, the conversation returned to the Record, and Jeanette directed a question at Susan. "We've always wondered, what's the oldest music you might hear using the device?"

Susan thought for a moment. "Well, in German caves, archeologists have found bird bone flutes dated at thirty to forty thousand years old. Another recent discovery was a Chinese flute nine thousand years old; when played today it produces a pentatonic scale – essentially like modern Chinese music."

"It's amazing how people just trying to survive would take the time and energy to make musical instruments and play them," said Jeanette.

"Couldn't a flute have been discovered by accident," Evan suggested, "and then refined through trial and error to sound more pleasant? Or maybe they were deliberately trying to replicate sounds they already knew from the human voice?"

"Voice – that's it," said Susan. "Singing is certainly the oldest 'music' you'd hear on the Record. It's a byproduct of the evolutionary steps that enabled speech. And speech has been around, in some form, for at least two hundred thousand years."

Susan set her coffee down, preparing to elaborate. "The ability to sing in specific tones may have arisen by chance, and pursued simply because it sounded nice, but there could be adaptive reasons for its persistence. Some even propose that primitive singing evolved into language, since humans could probably utter tones before they had distinct sets of words. In any case, it's likely that singing and speech co-evolved. So, just hand the Record to a professional singer, and he or she will hear the most primitive musical events in human history."

Susan paused, adding, "Oh, sorry, Evan. I forgot about Rosina."

"Don't worry. I understood what you meant," he replied.

"Did you ever hear Rosina singing on the Record?" Susan asked Evan.

"Once – almost, but the experience ended early. The Record only generates music that has a positive effect on the listener, and it's been painful for me to hear her voice in recent years."

Susan then changed the subject, and described some of her past travels around the world. But as the evening wore on, her demeanor grew sullen, until Jeanette finally asked, "Is there something wrong, Susan?"

Susan struggled to form the words, as if she were asking an impossible favor. Finally it came out. "I want to come with you – to see this thing. Maybe I can help with the decoding. I sense the Record is tied in deeply with the human story, even if it arrived only a century ago."

It was a compelling argument. Evan and Jeanette looked at each other, and both nodded. "We'll have to check with the Italian team,"

Jeanette said, "and you'll need to apply for a visa quickly. In fact, you'll probably have to process everything at the Russian consulate in New York in person."

"This is fantastic!" said Susan, her eyes lighting up. "I've always wanted to explore Siberia. The closest I've come is visiting native Evenki tribes in southern Mongolia about twenty years ago. I'd really like to see the related Russian cultures first-hand." The excitement in her voice was contagious. It struck Jeanette that her friend, sporting a short hairstyle, athletic build, and deep tan, fit the profile of a hardy explorer better than herself. Bringing Susan along would be a blast.

They began studying maps of Siberia, and Susan checked a transportation website. "Do you realize Krasnoyarsk is a major stop along the Trans-Siberian railway? Why don't we just make a vacation of it, and take the train from Moscow to Krasnoyarsk? It's only three days, according to this schedule." The idea was appealing – a relaxing voyage through one of Asia's most picturesque regions. Susan turned to Evan, explaining further. "It's a perfect time for me to go. My husband's an archeologist, and he's away on a dig in Turkey for a couple of months."

Evan studied the route, mumbling to himself, "One of the stops before Krasnoyarsk is a city called Novosibirsk." A look of recognition crossed his face, but he said nothing else.

Since Susan had experienced many different habitats, Jeanette asked, “What’s the weather like in Siberia this time of year?”

“The place you’re going can be quite warm in the summer, and you’ll even find swamps, marshes, and mosquitos, if you can believe it. That’s because the top layer of ice melts, but the water can’t drain away with all the permafrost below.” Then, addressing no one in particular, she added, “Two things that really scare me – swamps and mosquitos.”

The couple thanked Susan for a wonderful evening, and as they exited into the balmy night, Jeanette turned and giggled. “You’ll make the perfect Lion for our trip!” Susan was left standing in the doorway with a puzzled expression.

Chapter Twenty-One

Stepping off the plane in Milan was more difficult than Evan had anticipated. It was all too reminiscent of that day, eight years ago, when he had arrived here with Rosina, also en route to Bologna. It was her triumphant return to Italy, following a breakthrough in America and two album releases. A horde of local reporters had surrounded her while Evan stood back and looked on with pride. The Italians took their classical artists very seriously, he remembered.

But there was little time for anguish now. Evan, Jeanette, and Susan were allotting only three days to Italy before a plane would whisk them off to Moscow. They hoped to meet the Bologna team and confirm their invitation to join the expedition. Few noticed the motley trio of Boston professors as they trudged through the Milan airport. Evan assumed they were of little interest to hostile parties, now that the Record was back in Russia.

Transportation to Bologna remained unresolved. Jeanette was leaning toward a high-speed train, while Evan could barely take his eyes off websites advertising Ferrari rentals. But as Jeanette and Susan noted, someone would end up jammed into the back seat – if such a space existed at all. He settled instead for a small Fiat, which appeared equally lacking in rear-passenger legroom.

Such considerations were soon forgotten as they got underway. The hilly countryside of northern Italy was spectacular under a brilliant blue sky. In some ways, it reminded Evan of drives through New England; however, the unique architecture of each passing town was a constant reminder of a very different history. Along the way, Susan suggested a detour through Cremona, a landmark town for music in Europe. They were not disappointed. Dramatic sights within its central square included the twelfth-century cathedral and octagonal Baptistery, both of Romanesque-Gothic design, along with Europe's second tallest brick bell tower, housing the world's largest astronomical clock.

Their tight schedule forced them to focus on Cremona's Stradivarius Museum, particularly in the town where violins were first made. The museum featured many drawings and models, as well as instruments manufactured by Stradivarius. Susan whispered that she hoped to someday hear these violins being played on the Record. They also learned of other workshops producing superb stringed instruments, with names like Amati and Guarneri. Although the town hosted a number of festivals of Renaissance and Baroque music throughout the year, no performances were scheduled for this afternoon. As they drove away with some regret, Evan noted that, ironically, Cremona was the sister city of Krasnoyarsk.

The approach to Bologna was even more breathtaking. A sea of terracotta tiles spread out before them, contrasting markedly with the surrounding dark-green hills. Evan negotiated their car through the busy city center and found a hotel near the university, their ultimate destination. As a bonus, they received a text message from Nigel. He was planning to fly in and greet them that evening, and would stay to help with the introductions.

Roaming about in the afternoon, they were dazzled by the city's medieval street plan, historic towers, and warmly colored buildings. Much was built under porticoes, which looked suitable for a sudden shower – apparently a common occurrence. The vibrant social atmosphere resulted from a large student population and the abundance of cafés and trattorias dotting the streets and plazas. Bologna's claim as the culinary capital of Italy seemed warranted as they explored the enormous central marketplace, featuring endless arrays of fresh cheeses, meats, fruits, vegetables, dairy and baked goods. Jeanette promised herself to return someday with Evan, under more normal circumstances.

When evening approached, they returned to their hotel and found Nigel waiting in the lobby. It was an emotional reunion for all, including Susan, who appeared as star-struck as Jeanette had been in London. The four strolled to a nearby restaurant recommended by Nigel, and enjoyed local pasta dishes. Everything was washed down with fruity Sangiovese wine.

Over dinner, Nigel inquired about their plans. "Are you ready for the big Trans-Siberian journey? I've always wanted to do that, but never traveled far enough eastward on my Russian tours. I was scheduled to conduct at the Opera Theater in Novosibirsk a few years ago, but it got canceled."

Nigel and Evan locked eyes for an instant; the men seemed to share some private knowledge.

"Evan's planned a layover in that city, but he won't tell me why," said Susan.

"It's the map, right?" Nigel addressed Evan, ignoring Susan. Evan did not answer, and Susan shot a look of frustration at Jeanette.

"I'll explain later, Susan," Jeanette said. "It's probably nothing."

Logistics were discussed next. In two days, everyone would return to Milan, with Nigel flying on to Moscow for a series of concerts and workshops. The others would also fly to Moscow but immediately board a train. Nigel planned to meet them in Krasnoyarsk a week later, and then all would hop over to Vanavara, courtesy of the Italians. That last assumption would be confirmed tomorrow.

In the morning, the four travelers wandered onto the main campus of the University of Bologna, the world's oldest university, established in 1088. Their first stop was the Department of Music and Performing Arts. Despite the summer season, a large crowd of students had gathered in anticipation of Nigel's arrival. It was analogous to the reception for a rock star, with young people pressing forward to request autographs and take pictures.

Evan was happy for his friend, but uncomfortable with the publicity. He gestured for Jeanette to remain on the sidelines with him. It was best if their images did not appear in any local news broadcast.

Soon a stocky, balding, round-faced man walked over and introduced himself as Enrico Facchini, coordinator of the Tunguska expeditions. He offered to rescue the trio from the madness of Nigel's reception, and escorted them to a quiet courtyard several buildings away. They ordered coffee and cookies from a nearby vendor, and then relaxed in colorful Adirondack-style wooden chairs.

"I hear you're interested in joining our expedition to the Tunguska site," Enrico said. "What sorts of experiments were you considering?"

An awkward silence followed. Apparently, the initial communication had not been clear. The Boston trio only wanted to stay in Vanavara, not travel to the actual impact site out in the wilderness. Yet Evan did not want to jeopardize this opportunity by appearing parasitic or deceptive. He struggled to find a way. "Well, we thought we could help with analysis of any samples you bring back to town from the site." Next he tried to stall. "Perhaps you could bring us up to date on your research."

"As you know," Enrico said, "this has been an ongoing project for twenty-five years. Our previous expeditions found evidence that Lake Cheko, northwest of the epicenter, is actually a crater formed by a small fragment from the original cosmic body. The lake has a curious funnel-like morphology, and appears younger than 1908, based on radiometric dating of sediment cores from the bottom, as well as the absence of aquatic plant pollens in the older sediments. From initial seismic analysis, there's a magnetic-density anomaly about ten meters below the bottom. In the last few years we've begun georadar, magnetometry, and video surveys of the bottom, and even started drilling at the lake's center. This trip will involve more of those efforts."

"And could you remind me of the transportation arrangements?"

"We'll be hiring two Russian MI-26 cargo helicopters at Krasnoyarsk; one will go to the lake, where a base of operations exists; and the other to Vanavara, where lab work can be performed. Each helicopter holds about thirty people and twelve tons of equipment. There should be enough room for you . . . three, it seems now."

Evan's brain was still spinning. Enrico was pleasant and helpful, which made it painful to push their charade too blatantly. Complicating matters, Susan had been introduced without warning, and no one had even mentioned Nigel as a potential passenger. Yet obtaining the disc was paramount, and superseded any guilt over telling a few white lies. Evan was sure Enrico would understand later.

Evan proposed several contributions that he and Jeanette could make from their respective fields, even though it all sounded slightly contrived. Regarding Susan, they had to admit that her primary motivation was interaction with local Evenki tribes. Finally, he mentioned that Nigel wished to visit Vanavara as a tourist. In the end, Enrico appeared willing to accommodate this odd team of professors who had never worked in geology or astrophysics, perhaps solely as a favor to Nigel.

Enrico continued his description. “A couple of small buildings in Vanavara have been converted into labs for analyzing core samples, plant specimens, and the like. I’m sure you could help with some experiments there. We occasionally borrow electronic equipment from a small military base at the edge of town, which has a low but constant staffing level. I don’t know its purpose, but they’re usually quite friendly.” Evan and Jeanette exchanged a quick glance. The base sounded promising as a location for the metal box.

Enrico then changed the subject. “Your wife was Rosina Bianchi, correct? I remember her performance in 2008; it was remarkable. I used to be on the organizing committee for the festivals, because of my longtime interest in opera. We were devastated to hear of her passing. Did you two have any children?”

“No,” Evan answered quietly. The word lingered in the courtyard.

Finally, the group said *arrivederci* and began walking away, leaving Enrico to finish his coffee. Suddenly, Evan stopped and returned alone, speaking this time with as much sincerity as he could muster. “You and I both know there’s more to my request than I’ve admitted. All I can say right now is that it involves a discovery greater than anything you can imagine. I promise that you’ll be included, somehow.” Evan paused for effect, and then said, “We both want answers to what happened at Tunguska.”

Enrico stared at Evan, expressionless, giving the slightest indication of a nod. Then he looked back down at his cup. Evan desperately wanted to say, ‘Just wait until I show you a *true* cosmic body.’

The next morning, the trio bid Nigel farewell at the Milan airport. Parting was even more emotional than the reunion had been two days earlier, since the next segment of their journey was totally unpredictable.

Nigel flashed a smile at everyone. “If for some reason we can’t meet in Krasnoyarsk, then go on to Vanavara without me. I’ll find some way to reach the town on my own. Hell, tourists are flocking there constantly to see alien space ships, right?”

Evan studied Nigel carefully. “Are you sure you want to go through with this? Instead of just staying in Moscow and enjoying some nice music?”

Nigel sighed. “Doing this draws a full circle for me. I can’t run away from it anymore.” He turned and left them with a friendly wave.

The back corner of a Paris café provided a welcome refuge for Rene Louvel, his face lit by the blue glow of a laptop as he worked feverishly on a presentation. It was a proposal for an integrated computer hardware-software package that his consulting firm would pitch to several Russian companies seeking to upgrade factories, following endorsement of the ‘EU-Russia modernization’ program. Rene’s idea was to target manufacturing plants of interior Russian cities, where reform was most needed. The strategy promised to be quite lucrative in terms of future contracts. His company's management was eager to support travel to facilities in Siberia over the summer, and his first stop would be Krasnoyarsk, to visit the large aluminum plant.

Rene completed his task, pushed the laptop away, and studied his reflection in a mirrored wall nearby. Almost thirty years old, he had been very successful in many ways, but one unfinished task overshadowed all other considerations. It involved acquiring the single item that would guarantee him spectacular wealth and a lifetime of leisure. It had once been in his grasp, only to be snatched away within hours. Another thing he no longer owned, but cared for much less, was the code name Jacques. Last but not least, Rene had lost three teammates in the Lyon episode. Things were personal now, and God help anyone who got in his way.

July had gone spectacularly well, with Rene receiving unsolicited information regarding Evan Blake's travel plans to Krasnoyarsk. There could be only one reason Blake would journey to such a remote spot in Russia, and it had nothing to do with the seminar now posted on the Siberian Federal University website. Clearly Evan had located the disc. Rene's tip was second-hand; the source remained hidden deep within international power circles. He assumed it was one of the bidders from May.

Much planning was still needed, due to uncertainties over cooperation between Blake and the Russians. They had, after all, rescued and released him. For the upcoming mission, Rene had recruited a trusted partner who neither Blake nor Menard would recognize. The presence of Menard was actually a bonus; she would make the perfect tool for convincing Blake to hand over the prize. Rene knew of their rail travel from Moscow, but puzzled over the one-day layover in Novosibirsk, as revealed by two sets of train tickets. Perhaps Blake had deliberately added the stop to distract anyone in pursuit. Rene dismissed it as unimportant. The final chapter would be written in Krasnoyarsk, and within two weeks. He celebrated his anticipated victory by ordering a glass of wine and carrying it outside to soak up the sounds of the city. There was music in the air.

Chapter Twenty-Two

A rush of doubt nearly toppled Evan backward as he took his first step onto the Trans-Siberian Railway car in Moscow's busy central terminal. Was the whole trip just a hopeless, selfish pursuit of glory? The likelihood of finding the disc, much less getting it out of Russia, suddenly seemed infinitesimal. Also, there was no guarantee that the consequences for humanity would be positive – the disc's true purpose had yet to be determined. Finally, he was exposing Jeanette and Susan to unnecessary risks on such an open-ended journey.

His impasse was broken when Jeanette yelled down from inside the passenger car. "Evan, hurry up – the train's leaving in ten minutes!" She turned back to Susan and continued a discussion of their cabins. Evan cleared his thoughts and finished the climb. People were counting on him down the road, so for better or worse, he had to focus on logistics. He followed the women along a narrow corridor as they located adjacent first-class compartments, each featuring two fold-down berths.

During the planning phase, they had learned that no single 'Trans-Siberian Express' existed. Rather, there was an assortment of trains and routes across Siberia, ranging from 'domestic' trains with local stops, to a handful of direct cruise trains targeting Vladivostok and cities in China. The trio chose a 'Rossiya' domestic train, which allowed partial trips, but was nevertheless favored for its higher-quality, faster service. The bright blue and red-striped exterior complemented its recently refurbished interior, and one car offered a restaurant with a bar.

As the train eased forward, Evan marveled at the concept of a double-track system electrified all the way to Vladivostok, a destination requiring one full week's travel. The Railway's western routes had been completed by the end of the nineteenth century, but the journey across Asia on a single train became possible only in 1904. The trip to Krasnoyarsk consumed about half the total line, yet remained a staggering 4000 kilometers.

Despite relatively comfortable cabins, they spent most of their first day in the small bar and lounge area, where a number of Russians were eager to hear stories from America. Their anxiety about being recognized gradually subsided as they settled in to watch the changing landscape. Classic images flowed past like pages from a Russian coffee table picture book.

That evening, they wandered into the dining car, bringing with them low expectations of the cuisine. However, while the menu was not extensive, it provided tasty basics like schnitzel and potatoes, soups and salads, and even Russian champagne. Once darkness fell and the crowd dispersed, they discussed cities ahead. Susan knew of the layover in Novosibirsk, but remained clueless regarding the reasons for its choice.

Evan finally explained. "Last year, not long after I found the Record, I discovered something unusual about its protective paper wrapper. The sleeve was very old and hand-made – probably by the Leningrad shopkeeper who gave Nigel the Record. One night, after I accidentally ripped one edge, I noticed something written on the *inside* surface. After opening it up completely, I saw a hand-drawn floor plan for a large building. Nigel had never known about this; I showed him a photocopy later.

"Next to the drawing were Russian words, which I asked a friend to translate. Apparently it's a schematic for the basement of the Ballet and Opera Theater in Novosibirsk, showing several galleries, like a museum. The map is dated 1951, and one exhibit is distinctly marked. I have no idea whether such a museum exists now, but this was too interesting to pass up. I was going to tell you once we got underway. Again, it may mean nothing."

"What's so special about that theater?" asked Susan.

"It's the largest in Russia, even larger than the Bolshoi in Moscow, and now the most technically advanced. It took a decade to build, from 1933 to 1944, with the first performance in 1945. During the war, a number of treasures were moved from Moscow and stored secretly behind the walls of the unopened theater, including Peter the Great's throne, Pushkin's manuscripts, and many paintings. After the war, most of these things were returned, but a small collection remained on display. We have a map for the museum as it existed in 1951, and there's something the shopkeeper wanted Record owners to see."

"Do you still have the photocopy?" Susan asked.

"Yes, it survived all the mayhem of our last trip, and it's with me now. But remember, a lot can happen in sixty-five years." Silence engulfed the room as their imaginations filled in various scenarios. By midnight, they had surrendered to the cramped, fold-down beds, with their only consolation coming from the gently swaying rhythm of their vessel.

The second day began with a hearty breakfast of eggs and bacon. Evan and Susan struggled through the meal in a grumpy mood – they had not slept well in the unfamiliar bedding. Jeanette, however, was in good spirits. "I slept fine," she said, "thanks to some sleeping pills I brought along. You're welcome to try one, but they're pretty powerful, at least on the first dose." She turned back to the window, pointing out features of the passing view. Hilly forests defined the lower elevations of the Ural Mountains; the complete range stretched away for hundreds of miles to the north and south. This morning they would also see Perm and Yekaterinburg, the latter best known as the city where Tsar Nicholas II and his family had been executed in 1918.

After lunch, Evan and Susan each commandeered one compartment for a nap, while Jeanette explored the train more fully. In the lounge, she initiated a conversation with a college-aged Parisian couple on their summer vacation. They mentioned a Frenchman traveling alone, who seldom appeared, and ate meals in his cabin. His description as large, tall, and thirty-something was a relief for Jeanette, since this image did not match anyone she remembered from Lyon.

Shortly afterwards, she spotted a man fitting the sketch perfectly. He ordered a beer at the bar, and was preparing to return to his cabin when Jeanette walked over and craned up to see his face. "*Bonjour monsieur, êtes-vous de la France*?"

The man returned a stunned look, and then avoided her eyes while answering in French. "Yes, I'm on a business trip to Irkutsk. Well, I'm very tired, and need to rest. Enjoy your day." He walked away more spryly than she had expected for someone of his size. Jeanette tried to keep her suspicions in check, but decided to mention the encounter to the others.

As evening approached, the land flattened out into the steppes of Western Siberia – seemingly endless plains covered with luxurious vegetation and birch groves. Extensive agriculture was evident thanks to the rich, fertile soil. Another thousand kilometers remained before they reached Omsk, itself only halfway to Novosibirsk. During their second night on the train, Jeanette chose not to take a sleeping pill; she wanted to remain alert, despite the strong lock on her compartment door.

On the third day, the train pulled into Novosibirsk station and Siberia's largest city. The trio took all their belongings and departed, as did many other passengers. Standing at the rear of the platform until the train had pulled away, they watched in vain for the tall French man. Despite the dense crowd, they were confident he would have stood out.

Here was a city begging for exploration, with ample cultural and entertainment opportunities. In Soviet times, Novosibirsk had been nicknamed 'The Chicago of Siberia,' based on its rapid growth and industrial development. Tour books now touted it for its easy-going feel and burgeoning café culture.

Their taxi pulled up alongside the colossal Ballet and Opera Theater, adorned with Parthenon-like columns and featuring an enormous central dome, ninety feet wide and a hundred feet high. The dome was self-supporting, without any girders or columns. The theater's interior was vast, and nearly empty given the absence of any performance that day. They made their way down a large marble staircase to a lower level, where a small museum was advertised using only a tiny sign. No one manned the entry gate, so they waved at a guard strolling leisurely in the distance. Eventually, a staff member was summoned, and an elderly woman named Valentina appeared. A local resident, she had worked at the museum, in one capacity or another, for over sixty years. Her English was surprisingly good, and she began by noting how her first name and age matched those of pioneering female cosmonaut, Valentina Tereshkova. Jeanette found the woman immensely charming from the start.

They showed Valentina the photocopy, which she scrutinized for several minutes, apparently as fascinated with the historical map as they had been.

"My goodness, this takes me back to my earliest days as a guide here, when we had a lot more available for viewing. Yes, I do know this particular location," she said, pointing to the marked spot on the map. "It's a remote corner, rarely visited. Come along and I'll show you." She led them down a large corridor that accessed several spacious galleries, filled mainly with paintings. The tapping of their shoes on the smooth marble floor echoed loudly in the cool, cavernous space. Eventually they reached a dead-end that lacked exhibits.

Valentina stopped and spoke enthusiastically. "Many years ago, we had a display here called 'Miaskovsky's Speculation' – just a modest-sized glass case with some papers inside. It had been transferred here during the war, and was shown to the public for about a decade following the composer's death in 1950. Do you know much about Nikolai Miaskovsky?"

Jeanette answered diplomatically. "We could use a refresher, I'm sure."

"Well, he was a great Soviet composer who wrote twenty-seven symphonies, along with many other works. He originally studied under Rimsky-Korsakov, and then became a teacher at the Moscow Conservatory in 1921. He was also a good friend of Prokofiev. In the thirties, his symphonies were very popular in Western Europe, and even the United States. In 1941 he was evacuated, along with other famous composers like Prokofiev and Khachaturian, to the northern Caucasus region, for safety. This was a rather eccentric period in

Miaskovsky's life, when he wrote a musical score that supposedly represented a lost work of Beethoven."

Valentina continued as if the display were sitting nearby. "In 1799, at age twenty-eight, Beethoven wrote his String Quartet in G, Opus 18, Number 2. But a year later, he revised the work, writing a completely new slow movement, and the original score was lost forever. The first version was played only a few times, probably for Prince Lobkowitz, the supporting patron who contracted several quartets. Anyway, Miaskovsky offered to the world a manuscript of what the original adagio might have sounded like. Would you like to see it?"

They were stunned. "But . . . it's no longer here," said Evan.

"Oh, I never said that! The display was moved to our archive area decades ago. Not enough interest in it, I suppose. I can take you in for a peek. Just don't tell any other staff members!"

She guided them to an inconspicuous side door, where they entered a large storeroom cluttered with wooden crates, sculptures, paintings, and tapestries. Evan could scarcely imagine such an impromptu private tour at the Met or Louvre, especially for complete strangers. Near the back they saw a rectangular glass display case, measuring roughly two feet per side and a few inches high, resting on a sturdy wooden stand. The lighting consisted of a few buzzing fluorescent bulbs strung high above, and a small window passing only a hint of sunlight.

However, Valentina carried a flashlight with her, something that Evan had not noticed until now.

She pointed out the display's unique features. "The composer assembled this case with the help of an unknown friend during the war years. As you can see, the glass is reinforced around the edges with a welded metal frame for strength. Apparently Miaskovsky wanted this to be a time capsule of sorts; to be opened someday to verify his claims. There is, of course, no way to prove whether this score is anything close to the lost writings of Beethoven."

"Still, for something so unusual to be hidden away from public view just seems wrong," said Susan.

"Well, one thing to remember is this: In 1947 Miaskovsky was singled out, along with Shostakovich, Khachaturian and Prokofiev, as a principal offender in writing music with 'anti-Soviet,' 'anti-proletarian,' and 'formalist' tendencies. Such an about-face, eh? That's Soviet politics for you! Miaskovsky was lucky to have his score displayed at all. It happened only after widespread sentimental reaction to his death."

Jeanette jerked her head sideways, motioning Evan away from the display. They pretended to admire a statue nearby while Susan asked Valentina more questions. Jeanette whispered that fragments of the original quartet had been discovered in the seventies. Then, in 2011, a music professor pieced them together into something performable, and probably close to the original. Thus, it *would* be possible to check Miaskovsky's proposal, written decades before the fragments were uncovered. If his proposal was accurate, then he probably *did* hear a 1799 recital – using the Record, of course. As a top Soviet composer, he might have been allowed to examine the disc shortly after its discovery in 1938.

"Has this manuscript ever been copied, or stored digitally?" Evan asked, as he returned to the display.

"Probably not," Valentina said, hesitantly.

"Do you mind if I take a picture?"

"Well, as long as you don't publish it somewhere."

Wiping off layers of dust with a nearby rag, Evan took several photographs through the glass. Peering inside, he studied the yellowing manuscript. It was indeed a four-stave score, with about twenty measures visible on the first page. His eyes were then drawn to one side of the display. The manuscript rested on, but did not fully cover, a square paper sleeve, from which a round black edge peeked out. Anyone else would have seen an old phonograph record positioned under the score as a visual backdrop. But Evan had a different reaction. He moved his head closer and closer, trying to make out the details, while adrenaline began to surge through his body.

Borrowing Valentina's flashlight, he illuminated the single inch of exposed material. His pulse quickened further. The LP was very thick – too thick – and its featureless, matte-black surface sounded alarms in his head. It took all of his will not to lift the case and shake it, in order to slide the LP out of its sleeve. He stood up straight and backed away, feeling faint, and quite certain he had just viewed a copy of the Record.

From afar, Jeanette read his face, and walked silently to his side. He jumped slightly as she touched his shoulder, and then he pointed to the case. After bending over and straining to look inside, Jeanette's jaw dropped as well. Susan distracted Valentina with further questions, leading her off into a distance corner.

"But Evan, are you sure?" Jeanette whispered. "Maybe phonograph records made in the early forties just look strange."

"Not this strange," he said.

Evan's thoughts now veered in a more sinister direction. Was there any way they could remove this case from the museum, perhaps using a side door or fire exit? Why not just break the glass and extract the disc? They would have to tie and gag poor Valentina, leaving her in the storeroom. Could they divert the guard who lazily patrolled the basement area, or tie him up too? He finally just sighed. It was all too exhausting to contemplate, and he was tired of dramatic confrontations. Also, he knew Jeanette would not agree to any scheme that endangered their host.

When Evan thanked Valentina for her time, Jeanette inferred he was giving up. They wandered slowly back through the museum's central hall, stopping briefly in a couple of side galleries. As they exited the main theater, Evan looked as depressed as he had when leaving Lyon. Jeanette wrapped her arm around his shoulders.

That evening, back at a small hotel near the train station, the three gathered around a laptop to view the images Evan had obtained of Miaskovsky's manuscript. They also listened to a digital audio file of the lost adagio movement, as reconstructed by Barry Cooper at Manchester University. Jeanette and Susan's sight-reading skills proved useful as they compared the first page. The two works were very similar – too close to be a coincidence.

Evan sat and pondered Nigel's decision to bury his own disc, 'until at a later point in history it can be uncovered and relished as an archeological treasure.' Perhaps Miaskovsky had reached a similar conclusion after hearing the unthinkable. Evan's fingers stroked the hotel desktop's glass surface as if it were the display case, thinking repeatedly – *so near, and yet so far*.

Chapter Twenty-Three

Just after dawn, they stepped onto the train bound for Krasnoyarsk, twelve hours further east. The stop at Novosibirsk had opened up the possibility of there being at least one copy of the Record, and thus some hope remained if the mission to Vanavara failed. However, even this silver lining faded as they crossed the monotonous, flat countryside and faced the enormous challenge ahead. Few words were exchanged among the three, and Evan spent most of his day preparing for the seminar he would soon present.

As they neared their final destination, it became clear why author Anton Chekhov had described Krasnoyarsk as "the most beautiful of all Siberian villages." Surrounding it were rock-outcropped mountains blanketed with mixed conifer and deciduous forests. The nearby Yenisei River allowed the city to host large passenger and cargo ships. This was also the administrative center of a large district stretching up to the northern shores of Russia, which included the Tunguska region.

From their taxi they caught glimpses of ornate churches, and fountains decorated with colorful lights. On the horizon, large factories defined this as one of Russia's prime metallurgy centers. Until the 1990s it had been a closed city, due to the military agenda at most factories. But now it welcomed foreigners, with students coming from abroad to study at several prestigious universities, and local companies adopting a more western appearance and operating style.

At the hotel, they reviewed their situation. Nigel had not yet called, and was presumably formulating a plan that would allow him to leave Moscow. In three days, they would need to board the helicopter bound for Vanavara. However, the next day's schedule was simple. Evan would go to the Siberian Federal University and remain there most of the day, while the women went sightseeing. Since Krasnoyarsk was billed as the 'City of Fountains,' Jeanette was eager to take photos. Susan suggested visiting the Regional Studies museum, founded by archeology enthusiasts in the nineteenth century, which focused on Siberian historical events and ethnic cultures. One exhibit was named 'The Tunguska Phenomenon,' and dedicated to theories surrounding the impact event.

Following a successful morning seminar, Evan had just finished lunch at the faculty club when he received a frantic call from Susan. She and Jeanette had separated while shopping, and now Jeanette was nowhere to be found; nor was she answering her phone. Evan excused himself and took a taxi the short distance back to their hotel. The scene as he entered the lobby made his stomach sink. Several local policemen and detectives were interviewing Susan in the reception area. She looked up, tears still glistening in her eyes.

"It all happened so fast," she explained. "One minute Jeanette stepped into a side street to check out some local crafts, and the next minute she was gone. I searched for almost an hour, constantly phoning her, and then walked into the nearest police station."

Evan instantly regretted not following up on Jeanette's suspicions about the man on the train. He sat down next to Susan and tried to comfort her. It was difficult to avoid panic in this foreign environment. They gave a full description of Jeanette to the police, and mailed pictures of her to detectives from their mobile phones. A search of the shopping area was already underway, and her photograph would be displayed on local television that afternoon. Evan was given numbers to call should he receive any communication related to Jeanette. All they could do now was wait.

Susan returned with Evan to his room, where he asked himself a difficult question. Should he tell Susan about the kidnapping episode in Lyon? Would that invoke her anger, since he had not shared the story earlier? Just as he was deciding to reveal everything, his phone rang – it was Jeanette's number. He paused, hoping for the best, then put the phone on speaker mode and answered. "Yes?"

The voice was male, and one Evan immediately recognized as belonging to Jacques. "I'll be brief, so I'm not traced. It's very simple. If you want to see Menard again, then bring me the black plate. I know you've come here for it. You have twenty-four hours." The only real surprise was that Jacques had not mentioned Vanavara.

Evan pondered all his options within a second or two. Should he say that the disc's location was unknown, as a stalling mechanism? Should he reveal the existence of the Novosibirsk copy? Could he set up a sham exchange, offering a regular LP instead, since Jacques had never actually held the Record?

But first things first, Evan concluded. "Let me speak to her."

After some shuffling noises, Jeanette's voice broke in, to his tremendous relief. She sounded as normal as could be expected. "Evan, I'm fine. Listen, it's Jacques and one other–" She was cut off. The male voice returned.

"That's all you need to know. You can't win this time, Blake. It's not worth a struggle. Just give me the object and we all go home."

"Sure, just like the last time, right?"

"You're in no position to argue. Call me back when you have it." The connection terminated.

Evan looked up, feeling helpless, especially since he was unwilling to give a full account of the situation to local authorities. He did, however, finally provide background for Susan, who retained her composure while listening.

Now it was time to gamble. He turned to Susan. "I'm going to contact someone in a high position – the person who I believe invited me to Russia in the first place. I only have a name, but that should be enough, if he's really so important."

Only a few miles away, Jeanette sat captive in the bedroom of a luxury apartment that Rene had rented for his business trip. Her room featured a window, but it was barred. And while the door locked only from the inside, she was clearly not free to wander about. Rene and his partner, the large man from the train, occupied the living room, with its access to the front door. She was still kicking herself for parting from Susan's company on a nearly vacant street.

Jeanette pondered whether the man she knew as Jacques had traveled on a different train, or by air. In any case, it was sickening to see his face again, after what she had suffered just two months earlier. It was equally frustrating to see her suspicions about the large Frenchman confirmed. At least this time there had been less drama – only a gun held against her back as she was led to a car. And, fortunately, these men were French. If she listened carefully through the door, she could catch bits of conversation. Finally, she knew they were all strangers in a strange land; thus, neither side had a huge advantage.

Jeanette could hear the names they were using; Jacques was now 'Rene,' and Rene used 'Marcel' to address his large partner. As the afternoon wore on, Rene repeatedly mentioned his need to leave and attend a social function organized by the hosting company, to help bolster their image as businessmen. Rene would say that Marcel had fallen sick, and was resting in the apartment.

Rene's departure brought the number of captors down to one, but a very large one, who had already displayed his dislike of Jeanette, even slapping her once. He also carried a pistol in a shoulder holster, and had threatened to shoot her, should she emerge from the bedroom. But she knew this was an empty threat; he would not risk alerting someone in the building by firing an unsuppressed weapon. He might, however, settle for stabbing.

At one point, she detected Marcel rummaging through the apartment's small kitchen – probably preparing food they had stocked the previous night. She had seen bottles of Russian vodka and loaves of bread sitting on the counter upon arrival. Collapsing on her bed, feeling hungry and defeated, she looked through her purse; it had been searched and thrown back into her room. *At least I still have my sleeping pills*, she thought with relief; these would certainly be needed if she ever got out alive.

Then a tiny spark of an idea ignited, which she almost extinguished immediately. Surely it wasn't feasible, and only worked in the movies. Still, if she could somehow get the dozen remaining pills into Marcel's food or drink, it might be enough to buy safe passage. As a scientist embarking on a new experiment, a dozen considerations popped up. Even if she ground the pills into powder, would this dissolve completely? What should the powder be mixed with? Vodka came to mind first, but what percentage of alcohol was enough to guarantee solubility? If it didn't all dissolve, the residue would be glaringly obvious at the bottom of a clear vodka bottle. Why hadn't those assholes purchased some dark red wine instead? Then she remembered, and nearly sympathized with their complaints about the local wine selection.

Next was the question of dosage. Marcel was a big person, at least two hundred pounds. Would even twelve times her normal dose be enough to make him drowsy? She was comforted by the recollection of benzodiazepines having a pronounced effect upon first exposure. Finally, she faced the problem of getting out to the kitchen and spiking the bottle. The challenges seemed insurmountable.

Yet the scheme was just too interesting to pass up. She looked around her room and found two glass ashtrays. *Thank goodness for places where smoking is still allowed!* She used them as mortar and pestle to grind up the small white tablets into a fine powder, concealing the result in a folded gum wrapper, which she slipped into her shirt pocket. Then, taking a deep breath, and shuddering at the thought of being beaten should the strategy fail, she walked up and banged on the closed bedroom door.

"Hey, I want to eat too! You need to keep me alive, you know," she yelled in French. Hearing footsteps, she stepped back, expecting the door to fly open and a gun to discharge. Instead, Marcel slowly opened the door, which was not locked, and motioned for her to come to the table, now strewn with various snacks. These included, to her excitement, a half-full bottle of vodka. Marcel was not friendly, but neither was he monstrous; perhaps he had put on the show of aggression to impress Rene. As she walked over, she glanced at the front door, a mere twenty feet away. Two dead bolts were engaged. Marcel did not watch her closely; no doubt he felt confident that he could handle any sort of outburst from her.

She sat at the table and assembled several items on a plate, then poured a small amount of vodka into a medium-sized drinking glass. Her serving brought the level in the bottle down to one third, which is what she wanted; the spiking had to result in a high drug concentration. Marcel stood up and walked into the adjoining kitchen area. He opened the refrigerator and began poking around through drawers. It was now or never. Jeanette pulled out the wrapper and dumped the powder down the bottle's throat. Within three seconds she swirled the bottle quietly several times to initiate the mixing process. All those years of preparing solutions in laboratory flasks had paid off. Her movements were as choreographed as a ballet dancer's.

Her hands returned to her plate just as Marcel turned around and strolled back. She risked a quick glance at the bottle, where a few grains of powder were still dancing in circles on the bottom. Marcel showed little interest in pouring vodka – a relief at first, but then a concern after several minutes. Had he already consumed his fill for the day? Despite a lack of appetite, she finished eating some scraps, and then announced she was going back to her room. He mumbled something without looking up, concentrating on a novel he had brought along. She shut the door behind her, and then pressed her ear to it. All she could do now was wait.

Chapter Twenty-Four

An agonizingly long hour passed. Then Jeanette heard what she was praying for: a clink as the vodka bottle contacted a drinking glass, followed by a gurgling sound as fluid rushed out. She waited breathlessly for Marcel to storm into her room in a rage after finding undissolved powder in the bottle, yet only silence followed. A cough localized him to the sofa, where he was probably reading his book – and hopefully sipping vodka. She looked at her watch: five-thirty. This could take a couple of hours, so she lay down to rest, feeling certain she would not fall asleep in such a predicament.

At eight, the sun had not set, but shadows were very long outside. Her window faced east, and the room was dim. She peeked under the door. Ambient lighting in the living room seemed insufficient for reading. Listening through the door, she thought she detected heavy breathing. Snoring would have been nicer to hear, but probably too much to hope for.

Finally, she could delay no longer. Rene would return soon, spoiling her only chance for escape. She turned the doorknob as slowly as possible, prepared to explain her exit as hunger-driven, should he be merely reading. After opening the door a crack, she peered into the living room. Marcel was stretched out on the sofa, seemingly asleep. She pushed the door another inch, just enough to see the vodka bottle on the dining table. It was empty! However, she forced herself to remain calm, and not presume the experiment had succeeded.

Emerging like a ghost, she crept quietly across the floor, which thankfully was carpeted. The front door loomed yards away – a distant horizon. She was primed to leap toward the table and feign hunger should he rouse. Her heart was pounding so hard that she thought it might be audible to anyone in the room. This simple crossing was like a dream that might suddenly evaporate into cold reality. Her mind kept repeating a stream of medical words, like a mantra for comfort, while moving ever closer to the door: Formulation – delivery – effect! Passing within a few feet of the sofa, she briefly considered taking his pistol, but then dismissed it as an unwise gamble. A nearly empty glass sat on the table next to Marcel. Apparently he had prepared a mixture of vodka and orange juice, which would have masked any drug residue or bitter flavors.

Her last hurdle was turning the two deadbolts without making a noise. Reaching up, her eyes flashed back and forth between the door and Marcel, who was still motionless. The bolts rotated easily and silently, no doubt thanks to the five star accommodations Rene had arranged. After slowly swinging the door open and stepping out, she returned it without fully closing, expecting something to go wrong – it always did at this point in a film. Instead, she found herself flying down the stairwell and bursting out onto the street, holding back a scream while frantically looking for a crowd of people or any public establishment.

She turned left and dashed down the sidewalk, almost immediately crashing into a young man who seemed to hold onto her wrists rather than back away. She uttered a brief shriek. They were in the shadows, yet his face seemed familiar.

"Hey! It's okay!" he said. "Don't you remember me? Viktor! From Lyon!"

Her expression of shock gave way to one of recognition. "Yes! But how did you – what are you doing here?"

"Listen carefully. There's no time to talk. Come with me – this way! My comrades are close by." He led her down a pedestrian alleyway that served as a shortcut between two busy streets. It was dark and narrow, with buildings towering several stories on either side. As they neared the end, a man carrying a sack of groceries turned into the alley, halted, and looked up in surprise. It was Rene returning for the evening, and he now stood about thirty feet away. Each man assessed the situation in microseconds, and each reacted aggressively. Viktor pushed Jeanette to the side, where she crouched behind a metal trashcan, and then he pulled out his pistol. Rene dropped his bag and did the same. The two men fired almost simultaneously. The sound was deafening within the confines of the concrete alley, and she covered her ears, waiting for more shots. A small inner voice kept asking, *don't these people ever use silencers?*

Both men fell, with Viktor landing beside her. He was hit in the chest, although it seemed closer to his right shoulder. He was struggling to rise, but not fast enough, and his weapon had fallen to the pavement. Through a gap between the can and the wall she saw Rene sitting up, and then trying to stand. He was making progress faster than Viktor.

"Enough is enough!" she blurted out. Rage replaced any remnants of fear – this bastard had made her life miserable. She grabbed Viktor's pistol, stood up, and took aim down the alley. All her instincts kicked in. It was like swimming; one never forgets entirely. But she refused to be rushed. Memories of her training at the shooting range flooded back, guiding her. Proper stance; a firm, two-handed grip; arms straight out and locked; sights lined up on target; take a deep breath and release halfway; pull the trigger slowly. A single round left her pistol and found its mark. Rene fell backwards.

It took a moment for Jeanette to appreciate everything that had just happened. In the few seconds she had used to set up her shot, Rene fired twice. One bullet whizzed past her head within inches, and the other passed through the outermost inch of flesh at the side of her abdomen, which began bleeding. But her shot had struck Rene squarely in the chest. She remained frozen in the firing position, uncertain whether to approach her target.

Suddenly two men from Viktor's team came running up from behind, calling out her name so she would not turn and fire on them. One took the pistol gently from Jeanette, and then ran to Rene; the other tended to Viktor. As the weapon left her hand, she noticed it was a German Sig Sauer, similar to one her uncle had taught her to use twenty years ago. Within five minutes, a police car screeched to a stop out on the street. The two men with Viktor presented identification to the officers, who appeared slightly intimidated. A local ambulance service was called.

Jeanette slumped down next to Viktor, holding her side. He sat up and looked at her. "This time you rescued me," he said with half a grin. Grimacing in pain, he leaned against the wall; his wound was serious but not life-threatening.

"We've got to stop meeting like this," she replied dryly, but Viktor's injury distracted him from hearing her joke. She held his hand until paramedics arrived.

This is one hell of a Siberian vacation, she reflected.

At the central hospital, Jeanette rested in a private room, accompanied by Evan and Susan. She had received a few stitches in her side and was expected to make a full recovery. Viktor had undergone successful surgery and was sleeping down the hall.

When the nurse left Jeanette's room, Evan gave an account of his efforts to contact Alex. After having tried for several hours without success, a man appeared at the hotel and introduced himself as Maxim, a long-time associate of Alex. Interestingly, Maxim looked like a smaller version of Alex, sharing the same chiseled facial profile and graying beard. Maxim admitted that Alex was aware of the group's travel to Krasnoyarsk, and that a small team had been assigned to watch over them. Once word of trouble got out, the team scrutinized lists of French nationals staying in town. Viktor was assigned to investigate several names, and fortunately encountered Jeanette. Soon after the shootout, police stormed the apartment and found Marcel in a deep slumber. As for Rene, he was taken to another hospital in critical condition, and 'not expected to survive,' in Maxim's ominous words.

Jeanette hopped into a wheelchair, and the three ventured down the hallway. The guard stationed outside Viktor's door signaled 'no entry,' but Maxim emerged from the room and ushered everyone inside. Viktor was just waking and still groggy, but he recognized Jeanette and Evan. Maxim scurried about the room, checking on medical equipment while arguing with nurses, as if he were Viktor's father. Evan wondered if there was indeed some relationship between the two men.

Jeanette walked up to Viktor's side. "I'm glad to see that you pulled through. I'll bet you've had enough of us, eh?"

"No, no, it was nice to see you again. Too bad I won't be able to take you out to dinner now. Maybe another time," he said with droopy eyelids.

Evan appeared beside her. "I'm going to find some kind of talent show that you can apply for. I haven't forgotten."

Viktor shook his head slightly. "Thanks, but I doubt I could leave Russia anyway. We have something here I can try. It's called 'Minute of Fame.'"

Maxim smiled at Viktor, and asked the guests to depart so he could rest. As they filed out, Viktor called after Jeanette, "Be sure to come back for our date!" She waved goodbye.

Outside, Susan pushed Jeanette back to her room, where she would be observed overnight. Evan held up his cell phone for the women, pointing to a text message from Nigel; he was planning to arrive the next day.

Later, Evan and Maxim strolled over to an empty waiting area where they could talk privately. It was still unclear whether Maxim or Alex knew of Evan's final objective. Nothing about Vanavara had appeared in any travel document. And while the Italian team's imminent arrival in Krasnoyarsk would be public knowledge, it was not necessarily linked to Evan. On the other hand, would Evan really have traveled all the way to Krasnoyarsk just to give a seminar? Surely his intentions were obvious.

Maxim looked across and asked, "What will you do now?"

"I'm not sure. Head home in a few days, I suppose." It was an honest, though incomplete, answer.

"I can schedule a small plane for your group to fly to Vanavara tomorrow, if you wish. Your colleague Mr. Thompson is welcome to join you as well," Maxim said, nonchalantly.

Evan let out a long sigh. It was no longer shocking to see all of his plans anticipated. Alex's team probably knew which brand of toothpaste he used. Evan threw in the towel. "This has been an invitation all along, hasn't it?"

"Yes, an invitation. We've gone to great lengths to insure sufficient battery power in your tracking device over the past few weeks." Maxim revealed a slight smirk. "We assumed you would find your way here, eventually."

Evan sipped water from a plastic bottle, wishing he had something stronger. One question still coursed through his head: *An invitation to do what?* For the moment, he raised a different issue. "Maxim, if you knew the details of our trip, did you also know about the Frenchmen following us?"

"We suspected that the F1602 leader would try to find you here. Rene was an obsessed man, and you were vulnerable during *any* overseas travel. But we also think he would have entered Russia on his own to search for the disc."

Evan wondered whether the whole journey had served as a tool for Alex to lure Rene onto Russian soil. Perhaps Evan's itinerary had been deliberately leaked to Rene. The thought made him shudder. *But*, he reasoned, *am I not also a threat to the disc?*

For now, Evan chose to ignore the matter. However, he made one decision on the spot regarding the Record. If he could not acquire it through peaceful means, he would give up the entire quest. He had experienced enough guns for one lifetime, and he knew Jeanette would agree.

Standing up, he shook Maxim's hand and said, "Let's go see this little town of yours." He felt that Enrico would understand if they passed up the helicopter trip to Vanavara. However, it might be awkward explaining how they had hitched a ride on a government-sponsored airplane.

Chapter Twenty-Five

The Czech-made L-410/UVP-E20 nineteen-seat turboprop commuter plane took off on Saturday morning from Krasnoyarsk's Yemelyanovo airport for the two-hour flight. Evan and Jeanette sat near the front, followed in the next row by Nigel and Susan. The latter two had bonded in the mere half-day since they had met, and were now having a friendly debate over innate musical abilities in humans. Maxim was the fifth passenger, spending his time reading nondescript documents, or wandering forward to chat with the pilots of the chartered flight.

The aircraft circled once over Vanavara, allowing them to examine the small town. It was built around a sharp bend in a river, looking like some clamp holding the waterway in place. Maxim identified the river as the Podkamennaya, or 'Tunguska under the stones' – a name derived from its occasional disappearance under a field of pebbles.

Evan pointed to the airport. "Look at the airstrip. The forest has been cleared for almost *two miles*, yet the concrete runway is much shorter. Maybe the runway was once longer, to accommodate large planes – at least, larger than the one we're in now." Maxim was sitting within earshot, but said nothing.

The landscape below consisted of low hills covered in rich green taiga, or coniferous forest. Flying even lower, they saw evidence of the wet, boggy conditions prevalent in open meadows during the mid-summer months.

After landing, the plane taxied to a large wooden structure that resembled a country lodge, but was in fact the main terminal. A van arrived to greet them, and despite their unpleasant experience with such a vehicle on their last trip abroad, Evan and Jeanette piled in without hesitation. With an unarmed soldier driving and Maxim in front, they soon passed through the community's central square. Their surroundings reminded Jeanette of villages she had visited in rural Quebec, packed with picturesque, wood-paneled cottages. The air was laden with a rich, aromatic scent from evergreen trees. Several storefronts advertised helicopter rides to the impact zone, alongside garish souvenirs and postcards portraying a wide range of explosion theories. Half a dozen tourists had already assembled on one porch, awaiting transportation to the site.

Near the town square they noticed an upright, branchless tree trunk carved into a scowling face, with highly exaggerated features. Maxim turned and explained, "That's the god Ogdy. Native Evenki believe his anger caused the 1908 catastrophe. In 1927, when Kulik first reached the edge of the devastation, his guides refused to go any further. He had no choice but return to Vanavara, and make a second trek with new guides."

Passing a spacious park along the northern edge of town, they observed an Evenki festival in progress. Local residents were adorned in traditional costumes of reindeer hide, and walked among conical tents supported by pole frameworks. It was all designed in part to appease tourist expectations.

Susan was like a child spying the circus, and she shared some history. “The Evenki are the most widespread natives of Siberia. The name means ‘he who runs swifter than a reindeer.’ About 30,000 live in the Siberian forests, with just as many in China, but a much smaller number live in Mongolia, where I studied them years ago.”

Maxim added his own statistics. “Their *official* national territory is confined to the Krasnoyarsk district, where only a few thousand live. They form about twenty percent of the entire region’s population.” His tone seemed derogatory to Evan.

Susan continued. “Their origins are at nearby Lake Baikal, with archeological records going back to the Neolithic age – at least ten thousand years. Over time, two large groups formed: the northern Evenki, who were hunters and bred reindeer, as you see here; and the southern Evenki, who were farmers, breeding cattle or horses, and living in Mongolia or northeast China. The northern culture supports a truly mobile lifestyle – lightweight tents, excellent skis, and clothing made from reindeer. Of course, factory-made clothing is more common in towns now, except at festivals like this one.”

Susan next pointed out a large drum of stretched deerskin, which sat alongside pendants decorated in animal forms. “Traditional beliefs have survived here, despite years of attempted conversion by the

Russian Orthodox Church, as well as pressure from the Communists. The Evenki created the classical form of shamanism, you know. It's the first-known spiritual practice – a belief that all elements in the environment possess a spiritual force controllable by humans, or at least by the shaman. The word shaman actually comes from the Evenki, and means 'he who knows.'"

She paused to wave at some children who were staring at the van as it passed; they did not return her gesture. "A shaman acts as a medium between people and spirits – sort of a medicine man. Each Evenki clan has a shaman who holds power over the tribe. If he, *or she,* considers a person or thing to be evil, it is! By the way, Siberian shamans have been known to use psychedelics to aid them on their spiritual journeys. One tool is a mushroom known as agaric. Well, whatever; we need to see all this in more detail."

Maxim assured them they could return later and mingle with local residents. The van drove through the small gate of a fenced compound, where a sleepy military guard greeted them. A clearing of several acres was dotted with mundane concrete buildings and communication towers. Evan made a mental note of the security configuration, in case he needed to orchestrate some daring escape later on.

They pulled up to the largest building; an aging, rectangular, weather-stained monolith, and were greeted by Alex, who had flown into Vanavara shortly after the trio had reached Krasnoyarsk. *So much for my covert journey*, Evan thought.

Everyone gathered at a small reception area just inside the door. Few staff or security personnel were visible, and the installation's purpose remained unclear. "I'm pleased to see such a distinguished group at our little research center," said Alex. "Maestro, we're honored to have you visit our country. You may not know this, but my son plays French horn in one of the very orchestras you led this week. Dr. Blake, I'm impressed with your tenacity at pursuing your dream. And Dr. Menard, I hope you're mending after that terrible incident the other day. My goodness, two kidnappings in one year!"

The four were invited on a tour of the building, but were not yet told of its function. Descending two flights of stairs, they reached an elaborate underground facility. A long, wide hallway provided access to a series of adjoining laboratories, all visible through plate-glass windows. The scene was straight from the Soviet Union of the sixties, complete with tiled walls and exposed metal piping suspended from the ceiling. Yet everything was sophisticated enough to contrast starkly with the sleepy town above.

Suddenly Evan made the connection, and walked up to Alex. "This wasn't built for the disc, was it? There must have been some other purpose, something . . . defense related?"

"You're quite observant. Much of what you see was designed as an ICBM missile site and supporting research installation. It was constructed in the early sixties, but never reached a functional state, because other sites nearby were deemed more suitable strategically. Krasnoyarsk, for example, became the main silo for this district."

"So that explains the airstrip," Evan said, "which at one time was much longer to accommodate larger planes."

"Yes, correct again. Large machinery was required back then. Later, the unused facility, given its isolated location, was deemed ideal for long-term storage and analysis of the disc, and certainly preferable to a major city, which might become a nuclear target."

They entered a room resembling an electronic workshop. Prominently displayed on a lab bench was the metal box used for the Record. The group gravitated toward the box – all but Nigel, who stayed back. Alex made no effort to detour them. "Go ahead, open it. The disc has remained in its little bed all along, and was brought to Vanavara as soon as possible after we met in May. The tracking device was never dismantled."

Evan lifted the lid and peered inside, but avoided touching anything. "Your invitation has been accepted, and we're here, so now what?" he said.

"Remember when I told you in Lyon about other considerations? Let's begin by exploring the installation a bit further. This site was chosen for the safekeeping of *another* unusual object, which you are about to see."

They were led into a square room with bare concrete walls and floor, twenty feet to a side, featuring a heavily constructed table at the center. Lining the perimeter were benches topped with even more complex electronic equipment. The four visitors surrounded the table and beheld a perfect cube, each dimension slightly over one foot. At first glance it was composed of a solid black material, but as Evan moved closer and tilted his head in various directions, he detected a thin, nearly transparent surface layer, like matte glass covering the cube's faces. The scene reminded him of a display in a modern art museum, though clearly a very special artist had been at work here.

After the group had gawked at the object, Alex spoke. "This cube was found inside the original pod, right next to the disc." He paused to let the historical connection sink in. "We believe it's made from the same material as the disc, but has a protective coating that defies characterization – some sort of transparent metal. A feat of nanotechnology, I suspect. The whole thing is surprisingly light – about five pounds."

Susan leaned very close to the cube, her nose inches away. Alex's voice broke in and startled her. "Sorry, I just wanted to warn you that the corners and edges are extremely sharp. Otherwise it can be handled safely. We've never seen adverse effects from simply touching the cube. Of course, had this object appeared in more recent years, precautions would have been taken to safeguard against exposure to unknown pathogens, as was done with the first moon rocks. But our cube and disc were handled so frequently in their first decade on Earth that all safety tests were effectively completed."

"Regarding its purpose, we know little, but there is one well-defined trademark. Every twenty-four hours, for as long as anyone can remember, the cube has emitted the same combination of acoustic and electromagnetic radiation, lasting about one minute. Of course, every possible analysis has been done in an attempt to decipher the phenomenon. The acoustic component has been described as 'white noise,' while the radiation lies in the radio and microwave bands. There may be other emissions we can't measure, but so far there's nothing destructive to human cells or tissue." Despite Alex's assurances, everyone instinctively took a step back.

"Now let me tell you another interesting observation. On several occasions, visitors to this room have included those with previous disc exposure – usually a musician or scientist."

"What kind of exposure to the disc?" Jeanette asked.

"With or without the aid of traditional audio gear," he replied. "Anyway, these subjects always had a unique response to the cube. They reported hearing jumbled or complex blends of *music*. A few even spoke of acquiring new thoughts. However, no one could articulate much further."

Evan and Nigel were listening in rapt attention. Nigel spoke for the first time since entering the installation. "When will the cube become active again?"

Alex checked his watch. "In about an hour. If you'd like, we can wait around until then."

Evan stepped forward. "Well, what a coincidence. You have two people standing here with extensive disc exposure; namely, Nigel and myself. This was all a planned experiment, wasn't it?"

Alex was unequivocal. "Of course. But I think you would agree this is necessary. You have always felt that the disc bears some kind of message, right? Well, we believe the disc *prepares* one to hear a message, which in fact emanates from this cube. I can't elaborate on the mechanism, since I know nothing beyond what I've just stated."

"You mean, after all these years you haven't found a single Russian who was sufficiently prepared?" said Evan, his voice hardening. "You didn't even subject a political prisoner to long-term exposure, and then test him with the cube? That seems unlikely."

"I can understand your cynicism. Incredible as it may seem, the politics of disc ownership have remained complex. At one time, documents existed which described such experiments, but most were destroyed during the Soviet regime, and the rest remain hidden even from my eyes. The few accounts I've been allowed to read are useless; they consist of bizarre statements, and are inconsistent between subjects."

"So you're hoping we'll be able to solve everything for you?" said Evan, his tone now hostile.

“I’m hoping,” Alex said, using deliberate pronunciation, “that your scientific curiosity will prevail,” adding ominously, “and that you wish to learn what you have become.”

The group broke up into pairs as they waited for the designated moment to arrive. Evan and Jeanette spoke in hushed tones about strategies for stealing the Record, while Susan probed Alex about the psychological profile of persons who had interacted with the disc.

A beep sounded somewhere in the distance. Alex walked over to the cube, clearing his throat loudly, as if preparing to introduce a performer before a recital. “One final comment – you may leave the room at any time, should you find the experience unpleasant. We are not going to force you to stay, like laboratory rats,” he emphasized, glaring at Evan. “This room serves as a Faraday cage, and is soundproofed, so you will not notice anything once you exit. But I hope you’ll try your best to listen. Now, please, have a seat.”

Each corner of the room was equipped with a small lab bench and high stool. After sitting, the four visitors were equally distributed around the cube.

And then it began.

Chapter Twenty-Six

It was just as Alex had described – white noise, ramping up quickly to a loud, but not deafening, sound level. The spatial origin of the noise was unclear, despite the cube being the stated source. Jeanette thought she detected a few tones buried in the mix. Evan heard a random blend of multiple tones, each with oscillating pitch, reminiscent of a test CD he used to 'burn in' new audio components.

But for Nigel, it was the tuning of an immense orchestra, with hundreds of instruments playing simultaneously. Bits of the cacophony were becoming recognizable, but in a grotesque and disturbing way. A chance melody would burst forth like a solar flare, only to dissipate rapidly. He felt extremely agitated, even as everyone else sat calmly.

After half a minute, Jeanette noticed a headache coming on, so she jumped down from her stool and walked toward the exit. Evan followed her, and Susan watched the pair retreating. In those few seconds, Nigel was forgotten. When Susan glanced back toward his corner, he was not on his chair. She raced over and found him lying on the floor, curled up, with his hands over his ears. She shouted at the door, although her voice was barely audible over the cube. Evan and Jeanette returned just as the emissions, now at a screeching crescendo, sharply terminated. Nigel's eyes were still closed, and he was shivering uncontrollably, but at least he appeared responsive. Alex had observed everything while standing near the door, without budging from his spot.

After being helped up, Nigel was guided back to an adjacent room where several sofas and armchairs had been carefully arranged, reminding Evan of a doctor's waiting room, albeit one with a potentially sinister use. Once on the couch, Nigel appeared to lose consciousness briefly, but then opened his eyes and looked around wildly. Susan brought him a glass of water, and the three monitored him for several minutes. Only then did Alex enter and occupy a chair some distance away.

As Nigel regained his composure, he spoke in a tentative manner, looking at each of them in turn. "You're wondering what happened . . . but give me a moment." He took another long sip. "This is going to sound crazy, but I *know* something now I didn't know before. It's like lying half-asleep in front of a television, and later realizing that you picked up some breaking news, even though you don't remember hearing it."

Pointing to several notepads and pens scattered on a table, he said, "I need to write down what's in my head before I forget." He frowned while writing, pausing occasionally to close his eyes and reflect. He recalled the quote from Saint-Saëns, 'There is nothing more difficult than talking about music,' which seemed particularly relevant right now. After jotting only a few sentences, Nigel looked up with satisfaction. He placed the notepad face down on his lap, as if protecting some sacred scroll, and then slumped back into the leather sofa.

Everyone took a break, and Maxim brought in coffee. The atmosphere eased considerably over the next half-hour, at which point Nigel was ready to talk again. His audience assembled, eagerly awaiting any comments. Alex's eyes were riveted on Nigel. Apparently no previous subject had been this responsive to the cube. Jeanette began recording the event with her smartphone.

Referring to his notes, Nigel struggled to express the ideas now blazing through his consciousness. "Okay, here's what I learned: Their language is like very complex music. They altered our species in the past so that, eventually, we'd be able to understand this language. The modifications were performed over four visits, spanning many years. The Record is the last step in this whole process."

He paused, regrouping. "Also, they'll visit us again in the near future. The cube is a test of our readiness to comprehend their language." He then looked around in frustration. "But I had trouble with one last point – I was dizzy near the end. It had to do with the dates of their visits – past and future. It just wasn't clear."

No one moved. Nigel noticed their stares. "I'm sorry, that's all I learned. I suppose it raises more questions than it provides answers."

Susan dove in first. "You said we were 'altered.' Could you be more specific?"

Nigel concentrated intensely before answering, digging deeper into his revelation. "I think they influenced the way human music developed, starting from the earliest stages. They guided it in a certain direction, so it would eventually synchronize with their own mode of communication – or at least come close. If I'm correct, then music today is not a random byproduct of evolution, as many claim. Instead, it resembles an alien language *by design.*"

Jeanette interrupted. "But music is so variable, and so culturally dependent. I don't see how it could be pushed in a single direction, much less manipulated genetically, if that was their method."

"Well, first of all," Nigel said, sitting up straighter, "humans have more in common musically than you might think. For centuries, most cultures have used a subset of the same twelve tonal steps, known as the chromatic scale, to build their music. There's no clear explanation for it. Typical subsets are the diatonic scale – CDEFGAB, and the pentatonic scale – CDEGA. Obviously many other scales can exist, but they all assume that one octave of pitch is divided into the same twelve intervals."

"How can that be?" Jeanette asked.

"According to one theory, music has its roots in human speech – from the tones that arise naturally in our common vocal mechanism. Think about it. Aside from animal calls, human vocal cord vibrations are the only sounds in nature we hear as tones. It would be perfectly natural for humans to base a musical system, beginning with singing, on tones heard during everyday speech."

Evan broke in. "There's actually evidence for this, from experiments done at Duke University, in Dale Purves' lab. I never really thought much about it until now. When voices from several different languages are analyzed for frequency content, the same peaks of acoustical energy – or resonances – always show up. The spacing of those peaks matches the twelve-tone chromatic scale."

All eyes were now glued on Evan, so he continued. "Even the strongest frequency *ratios* in the voice data – like major third, perfect fourth, and perfect fifth – match intervals used for common musical scales. In other words, the structure of human music *can* be linked to the physical acoustics of the human vocal tract."

Nigel tried to summarize. "Yes, it seems likely that the development of music was biased by our long exposure to the human voice, through simple speech."

Susan added her thoughts. "Well, speech *is* something that could be manipulated genetically, since it relies on throat anatomy and related brain wiring. Any modification of speech would then influence the structure of music down the road, according to your theory. Of course, such engineering would have to occur *way* back in the evolution of our species, when a speech mechanism was just emerging. And it would take many generations before a particular genetic change stabilized in the population."

"But then what's the Record doing?" Nigel asked. "If it's an attempt to genetically modify us, wouldn't that also require thousands of years?"

Susan looked confused. "The Record? Modify?"

Jeanette responded. "Susan, we never told you this, but the Record may be capable of gene transfer. Since it's the *last* step in our preparation, and they're returning soon, the disc's purpose must be some quick, fine-tuning of the brain's music circuits, to allow us to fully understand their language."

"Okay," Evan said, "let's assume the Record is meant to work over the short-term; say, one person's lifetime. Even so, there's no one around with enough exposure. Nigel was exposed for a decade, yet he can only *begin* to understand the cube."

"True; I'm probably modified more than most, but clearly not enough," said Nigel, still looking shaken.

"Nigel," Evan asked, "would you be willing to hear the cube again tomorrow? To figure out the last part of the message – about the dates?"

"No, not that soon. The experience was just too strange – maybe *because* I wasn't fully prepared to hear the message. However, after coming so close, I'm willing to spend more time with the Record. Maybe then I'll be ready for their return, if I live long enough."

Evan stood up and spoke firmly. "All this argues for the disc returning to London with Nigel."

The room fell silent, and all eyes shifted to Alex. He stepped forward, addressing everyone. "Some of these aspects were raised in the past during Russian studies, but we never got this far, simply because no one was as prepared as Nigel. So I agree, it should go with him."

Everyone stared at Alex, dumbfounded by his decision.

He smiled at their reaction. "Believe it or not, I've always felt the disc should be shared – as do others, such as my friend Maxim. But I couldn't take that step myself in Europe this summer, and endanger the rest of my team. However, given our progress today, I'm willing to release the disc into your care. All I ask is that Nigel return to hear the cube again someday."

"How long before the disc's absence would be noticed?" Evan asked.

"We can cover up its disappearance, trust me," said Maxim. "No one is checking on it regularly anymore."

The group remained in a daze, so Alex continued. "I truly believe that our extraterrestrial visitors wanted a team of top scientists to discover the disc, study it, and then release their findings to the world. I see before me now such a team: an engineer, a biochemist, an anthropologist – and a famous musician – all dedicated to sharing the truth about Tunguska."

Alex moved across the room to stand closer. "The commitment each of you has shown is impressive. Evan pointing the gun at me in Lyon, and his efforts to travel to Vanavara; Jeanette's courage in Krasnoyarsk; Nigel's willingness to take the disc again; Susan's interest in joining the team.

It's all more than I could have hoped for. I know the disc will be in good hands."

Nigel finally stood up, still trembling slightly. "Coming back to my departure – I'd like to leave as soon as possible. I don't want to be near this town when the cube starts up again, even if it's shielded. Anyway, my colleagues were hoping I'd return to Moscow by tomorrow, which means I should head back to Krasnoyarsk today."

Alex called and checked with someone at the front desk. "Nigel, there's an MI–17 military helicopter at the airport leaving for Krasnoyarsk soon; they can give you a lift."

Evan walked over to Nigel. "Are you sure you won't stay and relax a couple of days? We might take a helicopter ourselves out to the impact zone tomorrow – but as part of a tour group." Nigel just shook his head.

Everyone stepped back outside into a surprisingly warm afternoon. A van pulled up for Nigel, and a new container for the Record was offered – one fitting easily inside his check-in luggage. Alex smiled at Nigel and shook his hand. "I wish you continued success as a composer, and as a mentor for our next generation of Russian musicians. Most of all, thank you for your willingness to work with the disc again."

"I guess I'm foolish enough to continue where I left off," said Nigel, returning the smile. Alex gave Nigel a Russian bear hug, leaving Nigel gasping for air.

Nigel embraced everyone else in turn, but more gently. As he put his arms around Jeanette, he said, "I'm glad you *did* become a part of all this."

To Evan, he joked, "When you stop by London, take me to some jazz shows. Or better yet, just touch the Record, and we'll have a concert in my flat!"

He waved while strolling toward the van – the maestro leaving the stage.

Chapter Twenty-Seven

Vanavara's Evenki festival, within walking distance of the military compound, offered a welcome diversion from the day's unnerving events. Evan, Jeanette, and Susan wandered through the crowd, soaking up local cultural heritage. Many of the participants' clothing, shoes, and bags were constructed of reindeer hide, decorated with intricate leather appliqué or embroidery, and topped off with a variety of metal jewelry. A few wore fur hats, though these were shed rapidly as the day continued to warm. There were examples of traditional conical lodging, or *diu,* formed from an assembly of wooden poles covered with sewn birch bark. Tall, green spruce trees provided shade for the attendees, with the occasional beech adding color contrast. Rabbits and squirrels scurried everywhere, snatching up bits of food dropped by children.

The three stopped at a folding table where a young woman displayed a petition for signatures. She was dressed in jeans and a T-shirt, with an unbuttoned reindeer robe thrown on top in a half–hearted effort to harmonize with the crowd. Susan walked up and tried a few words of Evenki, not knowing if these were anything close to the local dialect.

The woman listened briefly, then replied in English. "You're American, right?"

"It's that obvious?" Susan asked.

"Well, we get a lot of tourists here. My name is Tatyana. I'm a student at the university in

Krasnoyarsk, but I'm here this weekend to see my parents. They run a bed and breakfast in town. Are you enjoying our little festival?"

"Yes. I know a little about the local culture, but the language I'm hearing is confusing," Susan said.

"Less than half of ethnic Evenki use their native language anymore. As for a written language, the first book wasn't even printed until 1928, after an alphabet could be devised."

"What are these pamphlets?" Jeanette asked, sifting through the mostly Russian language documents.

"I do volunteer work for RAIPON, the Russian Association of Indigenous Peoples of the North. It's dedicated to preserving local cultures and languages, and has a representative in each village. The government is now required – based on new Federal Acts – to consider our opinions. But it wasn't always that way. The Soviets tried to reorganize and 'settle' the Evenki into new villages of Russian design. Does that sound familiar – like the American Indians? Anyway, children were taken away to attend boarding schools, and men were forced to try reindeer breeding on collective farms. Families were broken up, and the gap between generations widened. Naturally, traditions took a big hit."

She pulled out scenic pictures of Siberian rivers. "Coming back to the present, our biggest concern is with plans by the state-controlled hydroelectric companies to build seven dams and power stations on different rivers in the district. For example, a dam on the Lower Tunguska alone, just north of here, would flood an area the size of Lebanon, including an old underground nuclear testing site, and several Evenki villages where people still live as our ancestors did. Another dam would affect the river running through Vanavara itself. We do what we can – send petitions to the government."

Several residents walked up to ask questions, so the trio resumed their tour, sampling native cuisine from grills set up for lunchtime. A couple of hours later, they were relaxing at a picnic table when a car pulled up on a nearby access road, and Alex emerged. Although dressed in non-military, casual western attire, the locals recognized him as someone from the base, and stepped back as he approached. His face was ashen. He sat down slowly, and several seconds passed before he could speak.

"I don't know how to say this, but something happened to the helicopter carrying Nigel. The pilot reported fog close to Krasnoyarsk. Then we lost contact. An explosion was also heard. We have military and rescue aircraft searching the area now."

Alex stayed with them for a tense half-hour, and then received a call. His near silence during the conversation was discouraging, and soon their worst fears were confirmed. "I'm afraid the helicopter did crash. And based on views from overhead, it's unlikely that anyone could have survived. We'll soon have a team on the ground to investigate."

"What kind of helicopter did you put him on?" Jeanette asked, anger filling her voice.

"A very recent model, equipped with the latest scanning and navigational equipment. The pilot described unusual readings on the displays after they took off."

Evan thought of possible interference from the Record. Then he remembered its physical construction. "Was the explosion larger than expected?"

"No, it wasn't a nuclear event. I had the same initial concern. I don't think there's enough material in the disc to reach critical mass."

It took several minutes for the shock to transform into grief. Jeanette leaned on Evan and began crying. Susan, also in tears, put her arm around Jeanette.

"I'll leave you alone now," said Alex, "but feel free to come onto the base any time; perhaps I'll have more information." He stood up and returned to the car, which drove him back inside the installation, even though it was within sight of their table.

Evan was still in denial; he wanted proof. Next he felt guilt – he should have put more effort into convincing Nigel to stay another day. Simultaneously, there was an overwhelming sense of unfairness; Nigel had welcomed the disc back into his life, yet the fruits of that commitment would never be realized. The three continued to hold onto each other for comfort. Sounds from the festival seemed distant now. They heard only the wind whistling through pine needles overhead, as each became lost in private thoughts.

After some time, Evan looked up from his meditation and noticed Tatyana standing quietly a few yards from their table, accompanied by an elderly man wearing a traditional costume. Evan motioned for them to step closer.

"Hello again," she said hesitantly. "I wanted to introduce my grandfather. His name is Liuchetkan, and he turns seventy-nine this year. Of course he doesn't dress like this every day, but as the tribe's shaman, it was important for him to attend the festival. He's very much in tune with people's emotions, and he noticed that something is wrong."

Evan described the death of their friend. Tatyana translated the news for her grandfather using an Evenki dialect. Liuchetkan then walked up to Evan. He was short but sturdy, and a gentle smile flickered within the intricate quilt of wrinkles covering his brown face. His shoulder-length black hair showed surprisingly little gray, and was wrapped in a thick headdress adorned with dangling feathers, fringes, and bells. The shaman's reindeer outfit was more elegant than most, with various metal, bone, and wood pendants hanging alongside tassels made of bird wings and tails. He also carried the shaman's ritual objects – a baton, and a drum stretched with reindeer hide. Susan whispered to Evan that many of these features had been passed on to North American Indians, not to mention other hunter-gatherer cultures.

Tatyana continued. "Liuchetkan's title of shaman was handed down from his father, after approval by clan leaders. It's a role of great responsibility. He serves as a spiritual guide, healer, and prophet, as well as a primary source of tribal history and knowledge. It's not an easy life, though. My grandfather and great grandfather suffered persecution under the Soviet system. Few examples of a Siberian shaman remain."

She helped Liuchetkan sit at the table. "Today, he sees that all of you are suffering, and would like to help. Tungus shamans are regarded as the most powerful in Siberia, and best able to guide the souls of the dead into the afterlife. They accomplish this through an ability to leave the mortal body and journey into the spirit world. My grandfather is offering to send your friend off to the next world at a ceremony tonight. You're welcome to attend."

They thanked him warmly, and agreed to stop by later. At least it would provide some sort of healing process, so far from home. Tatyana offered them rooms at her parent's inn, which they chose over staying on the military base. Later, they ate dinner at a small restaurant in town, but poor appetites made it difficult to appreciate the homemade dishes. Afterward, with the sun still well above the horizon but temperatures dropping rapidly, they headed back to the park. The crowd had thinned to a half dozen families, gathered around a few scattered campfires.

Tatyana was present and rushed over, escorting them to folding chairs located beside the largest fire. Enthusiastic conversations in Evenki and Russian floated all around as traditional dances got underway, interrupted occasionally by arguments over the correctness of specific dance steps; the ancient knowledge was slipping away from a newer generation.

When the sun finally slipped away, Liuchetkan appeared in full costume, like some phantom from the distant past. They watched him closely as he kicked off the ritual with storytelling in his native language. This was followed with chanting and the beating of a skin drum. A few other elders gathered around to accompany him. Eventually Liuchetkan started singing in a distinctive, wordless style that grabbed their attention. It consisted of a deep, richly resonant monotone superimposed on a varying set of midrange tones for melody, reminding Evan of the two-tiered sound of bagpipes.

Tatyana sat nearby and explained. "My grandfather is often asked to lead ritual songs, as he does tonight, because he is among the best Tuvan throat singers in the region. His particular style is called *Khöömei*."

Susan elaborated. "He uses resonances in his throat to produce several pitches at once. It's a very old method of singing which began in present-day Mongolia and southern Siberia."

Tatyana spoke in a proud voice. "Grandpa claims to know many songs sung this way, going back to our distant ancestors." The comment struck all three, and they sensed that something extraordinary was taking place.

The ceremony lasted for another hour until the sky turned black. The three visitors felt more at ease than at any other time that day. No matter what opinion each held of the shaman's beliefs, it was comforting to have an acclaimed religious leader perform a service in Nigel's honor. Liuchetkan's efforts seemed to transcend the specifics of time, culture, and location.

Afterward, the shaman sat next to Tatyana, exhausted. They all thanked him again for his willingness to help out. Over the campfire's flicker, Evan asked him how he came to know the ancient songs. Tatyana positioned herself between them to translate. "He says he has a sacred relic – something his father gave him. Such things are a very important part of a shaman's life."

Evan hesitated to ask the next question; it would certainly sound strange, but somehow seemed necessary. "Please ask your grandfather if his relic looks like a thin, round, black plate." After Tatyana interpreted, Liuchetkan's face froze. He stood up and started to back away, staring wide-eyed at Evan. After a few more steps he fell backward, and they all rushed over to assist. He was mumbling something while flashing expressions of terror. Evan kept pleading that he meant no harm, and was only curious, but Tatyana was not translating fast enough.

After several tense moments, Liuchetkan returned to his chair and spoke calmly again. He said he was shocked that anyone knew about his most secret possession; he had never revealed it during public rituals. While Tatyana left to get him a drink, Evan made a mental note to confront Alex later. Apparently at least three discs existed. One had been with an Evenki shaman, one was sitting in a Novosibirsk storeroom, and one was lost with Nigel. What else had Alex failed to mention?

Evan confessed to the shaman that he had once owned such a disc, but now it was lost forever. The old man's eyes seemed to pierce Evan's soul. Then, perhaps sensing that Evan's intentions were sincere, Liuchetkan volunteered a detailed account of his own relic, which Tatyana translated.

"My father Gelendzha served as a guide on Kulik's 1938 expedition to the explosion site. Being a powerful shaman, he was not afraid of the area, like some Evenki. One afternoon he noticed the Russian team pulling something unusual out of the ground; it was a large, shiny, egg-shaped object. Gelendzha was instructed not to tell anyone, under threat of death. The group set up camp that night, prior to leaving on reindeer sleds, and the object was left unguarded in a tent. As everyone slept, he crept inside to investigate. He had seen many odd things as a shaman, and felt it was his responsibility to learn more. The object's surface appeared smooth and completely sealed, yet after merely touching it, a lid opened. He peered inside but could see little, since the only source of light was the full moon filtering through the tent's canvas. Feeling around inside with his hands, he discovered a round plate – something that might have value as a pendant. He was certain it had arrived from the spirit world, and was meant for a shaman alone to possess, so he hid it among his belongings. He then abandoned the team using an extra reindeer, upon which he was an experienced rider. Gelendzha knew of places to hide in the wilderness where the Russians would never find him. He kept the plate for almost twenty years, and then passed it down to me, calling it the 'New Moon' because it was so dark and round. I've owned it for fifty years now. It has allowed me to hear the songs of my ancestors."

Evan probed further, still haunted by the numbers. "Did Gelendzha find more than one disc inside the egg?"

"Grandfather is not sure," said Tatyana, "since he was never told more details. But he says that it is certainly possible."

After some reflection, Evan chatted briefly with Jeanette and Susan. Returning to Liuchetkan, Evan spoke directly to him, wishing desperately he could ask this favor in the Evenki tongue. "There's a device inside the Russian compound that's a direct link to a great spirit's voice, but it can be understood only by those who have touched the New Moon. Earlier today we tried listening, but we weren't sufficiently prepared to understand everything. It would help us tremendously if you would go there tomorrow morning and listen, just for a few minutes. Our friend, who died today, came very close to hearing a complete message. Now he'll never have another chance to try. You're our only hope."

Evan could see Liuchetkan recoil from the very thought of interacting with the Russians, and it was not fair to push him any further. Turning away, Evan felt a weight of despair. The whole quest had worn him down, and he was ready to give up. Then he sensed Liuchetkan's hand resting on his arm; the shaman spoke in a soothing voice.

Tatyana interpreted. "Grandpa says he will go, but only because *you* have asked it of him. If your friend had unfinished business of such magnitude, then someone must complete it for him; otherwise, his spirit will never find a final resting place."

Chapter Twenty-Eight

An odd-looking group, which included an elderly Evenki man dressed in simple cotton pants and a button-down shirt, strolled up to the compound's gate in the early morning hours and was waved through without question. As they followed a winding sidewalk toward the central group of buildings, Evan imagined it as the approach to the Emerald City, where today they might learn any number of spectacular truths.

Alex, the Wizard, greeted them at the door. He had already been notified of Liuchetkan's attendance, as well as the shaman's ownership of a disc, yet he appeared unfazed, perhaps because he appreciated this unique opportunity.

Within an hour, the shaman was sitting and waiting comfortably beside the cube, having received general instructions about what would happen. Everyone else, including Tatyana, waited outside, at his request. They were able to monitor his status through a thick glass window in the door.

The cube soon began its tireless plea to anyone who would listen. Liuchetkan remained motionless during the entire sixty seconds, and then for several minutes afterwards. He rose slowly and left the room as if nothing had happened. *Perhaps the cube isn't functioning*, Evan thought. Yet microphones mounted inside recorded exactly the same event that had occurred every day for decades.

The shaman met his anxious granddaughter, and spoke in a serene manner. The small team – Evan,

Jeanette, Susan, Alex, and Maxim – waited breathlessly for him to finish. Tatyana then translated.

"Never before have I received a message so clear, even during my longest travels into the spirit world, and for me it was exhilarating. The message appeared as new ideas soaring through my mind. Here is what I learned: Great spirits want us to know their language, and it is a language of music. They even changed the way our ancestors created and heard music. How this was done, I cannot say. But these spirits will visit us again soon."

He struggled to find his next words, reminding Evan of Nigel's difficulty at the end. "One final message was foggy, as it was for your friend yesterday. I believe it said this: For the dates of our visits, look to what we have lived on the disc; most point to the past, and one points to the future." Then Liuchetkan spoke no further.

Jeanette was the first to speculate. "Does this mean we should examine the lives of musicians who have performed on the Record? Maybe there's information hidden in the date of each performance, or the musician's age?"

"Or maybe some of our most famous musicians were aliens," said Evan, before realizing the facetious tone of his statement.

Susan countered with the obvious. "I think we can give more credit to humans than that for making good music."

The session was interrupted when a staff member stuck his head into the room and summoned Alex and Maxim, who left in haste. Through a window, Evan could see them in a nearby communications room. While a discussion of Liuchetkan's comments continued, Evan excused himself and walked down the main corridor toward the voices. He heard an exasperated Maxim arguing with someone on the phone in Russian. Alex looked over, spotted Evan, and motioned him into the room.

"More information is coming in about the crash," Alex said. "Please, have a seat." Evan felt that anything he learned now would just be depressing, but he forced himself to listen.

"We're getting reports of very high levels of radiation at the crash site," Maxim explained.

"Effects of disc damage? Some fission event?" Evan speculated. "Or perhaps the helicopter already carried something radioactive."

"No, it didn't," said Alex. "In any case, it may be a long time before we can approach for closer inspection, possibly years. Evan, if you remember, what are the half-lives of those radioactive isotopes on the disc?"

Evan gazed down blankly, his inner wheels suddenly turning. Then his brain made an intuitive leap. He rose, grabbed a notepad and pen lying on the desk, and rushed out. Alex looked puzzled, but returned to his conversation with Maxim.

Evan dashed over to join the others while writing on the notepad. He approached Tatyana, holding it up in front of her. "Tatyana, please ask your grandfather if these words are close to what he *literally* heard from the cube today."

She translated. "He says yes, your statement is almost exactly what he heard, but it didn't make sense at the time, so he changed the wording a little."

Evan turned toward the others, and took a deep breath. "I know why the last part of the cube's message was confusing for Liuchetkan, and for Nigel – because it uses scientific jargon. Our shaman felt it necessary to paraphrase the message. Here is literally what he heard." Evan read his own handwriting aloud. "For the dates of our visits, look to the *half-lives* on the disc; most point to the past, and one points to the future." He looked up. "I think this refers to radioactive half-life."

Jeanette and Susan's eyes lit up. It was a concept they dealt with routinely.

Evan turned toward Tatyana and explained. "The disc, your grandfather's New Moon, contains a few radioactive elements. Radioactivity decays exponentially, and the time it takes for the original activity of a sample to drop by half is called the half-life. It's a measurement that remains the same anywhere in the universe."

Jeanette stood up. "Oh, Evan, do you think it could be that simple? But how do we group the radioactive elements from the Record into past and future?"

"Well, the most obvious way is to use class of decay. They're all alpha emitters except one, the Americium."

Alex walked in and noticed a heightened level of activity in the room. "What's happened? Did you learn something new?"

Evan was nearly out of breath, trying to log in to his laptop. "The half-lives of the four alpha-emitting isotopes in the disc, in years, may tell us how far back the extraterrestrials visited, to make alterations in us, or whatever. The half-life of the unique Americium isotope may tell us when they'll return. Of course, it's all relative to 1908, when the disc arrived, and not the current year."

Everyone scrambled over to view the screen, as Evan searched the Internet for the numbers. "Okay, here they are. The half-life of thorium-232, at fourteen billion years, is just the age of the universe, so that must be some kind of reference or base line. The half-life of thorium-229 is 7340 years, thorium-230 is 75,000 years, and uranium-234 is 245,000 years! That gives us three potential modification dates. Add in the Record and you get four modifications in total, just as Nigel related. Susan, do those numbers mean anything in terms of human history?" Everyone took a seat and waited.

Susan thought for a while, apparently feeling the pressure. "Let's take those numbers one at a time, starting with the largest. Someone visiting the earth 245,000 years ago would have found several species of 'archaic' Homo sapiens – not quite modern humans, but with a brain-size larger than anything seen before. However, none had a fully modern speech mechanism. So maybe our visitors picked their favorite starting material, altered the voice physiology a bit, and let the changes stabilize for a few thousand generations. Then – *voilà* – a creature with tongue, pharynx, and larynx deeper in the throat than any other hominoid. We know that modern Homo sapiens emerged in Africa between 200,000 and 160,000 years ago – the timing is about right."

"So those alterations would have been enough to guarantee speech?" Evan asked.

"They would have allowed better articulation of vowels, and a greater number of distinct sounds, which in turn helps to convey intent and emotion through better intonation. It's a good starting point. According to linguist Philip Lieberman, the adaptive advantages of modern speech outweighed the increased dangers of choking from that type of throat anatomy. Of course, an equally important development was the brain circuitry necessary to manage vocal mechanics and process the new sounds being heard."

Evan frowned. "I could see re-engineering the vocal tract to get a specific set of tones – that's just acoustics. But how could they manipulate neural circuits? It just seems too complex, even for an advanced civilization."

After a long pause, Susan resumed. "A large number of genes are involved in speech and comprehension – we're only beginning to learn about them. For example, take FOXP2. It's involved in our ability to acquire language, since a known mutation causes a developmental disorder in which people have trouble articulating speech. The

FOXP2 regulator protein helps to establish the wiring in the brain needed to learn sequences of movements that generate sound. But there's no single 'speech gene'; too many other factors are involved. So I agree, it would be a huge task to alter the neural control of human speech – well, huge from a human perspective."

Susan returned to the list of numbers. "As for 75,000 years ago, a couple of events come to mind. That's close to the estimated date of the Toba super-volcano, which occurred on the island of Sumatra in Indonesia. It was the largest known volcanic eruption on earth during the past two million years, and produced a ten-year volcanic winter, which surely killed many people. There's genetic evidence that all humans today descended from a small population – a few thousand breeding pairs – living in Africa at the time; those could have been the Toba survivors. Now, with such a small, localized number of humans, it would've been relatively easy for our visitors to alter everyone uniformly. Perhaps they refined their initial designs of our vocal tract and brain anatomy to encourage further developments, like a sophisticated spoken language.

"In any case, our species began a major migration out of Africa shortly afterward, and went on to populate the world. Then, beginning about 50,000 years ago, there was a huge acceleration in human achievement and artistic expression, called the Upper Paleolithic Revolution. Archeological records show much finer tool making, more intricate food preparation, cave paintings, carvings and ornaments, burial rituals, trade, and so on. It's been proposed that spoken language, and perhaps even music, played major roles in making all this happen."

"Then there's the isotope at 7340 years," Evan noted. "Counting backwards from 1908 gives 5430 BCE. That's early civilization, right?"

"Yes, it marks the beginnings of major civilizations, such as the Ubaid period of Sumer in Mesopotamia. Milestones included the first cities, and the birth of writing. Of course, the development of writing ensures that, several thousand years later, music will be preserved and passed on through scores. But it's hard to imagine what changes they would have made to us at that time. Hopefully we can ask them someday."

"Which brings us to the future," said Evan. "If all this speculation is correct, then the date of their next visit comes from Americium-242m, with a half-life of 141 years. Counting forward from 1908, you get 2049, which is only thirty-three years from today . . ." His voice trailed off as he stated the last figure. It was much sooner than anyone had expected. The room grew silent.

Jeanette broke the lull. "A return date so close argues again for the Record being a quick, final tweak to humans – something to prepare us for whatever they have to say."

It was painfully obvious that the most 'prepared' person was Liuchetkan, who would probably be gone by 2049. Evan and Jeanette would be in their seventies, but Evan's one-year disc exposure was probably not enough, based on Nigel's case. Getting hold of another disc from Alex was now crucial, since obtaining one from Liuchetkan or Novosibirsk would require two different, but equally undesirable, courses of action.

The first priority, however, was to relieve Liuchetkan's stress over being on the base. Evan, Jeanette, and Susan accompanied the shaman and his granddaughter back to the surface, and then to the compound's exit gate. After thanking Liuchetkan again for his cooperation, they promised no further disclosures of his relic. They also advised him to keep it well hidden, in case Alex should decide to gather up straggler copies.

Liuchetkan walked up, placed his hands on the arms of Evan and Jeanette, and spoke for several minutes. Tatyana let him finish before translating. "I don't understand everything that happened in there, but if a great spirit will visit someday, then you must find a way to prepare yourselves, as I was ready to hear the message today. I wish I could hand over my own disc to you, but custom requires that it stay in my family, perhaps even going to Tatyana."

Tatyana stopped, glancing down shyly, and then translated his final note of caution. "Normally when I enter the spirit world as a shaman, I negotiate with a helper spirit, and there is mutual respect and compromise. But today I sensed a power that has gone to great lengths to make you listen. Often, the one who desperately wants others to listen is not a good listener. You should ask yourself, what steps have they taken to ensure that I can *respond*, and let *my* wishes be known?"

The shaman then spoke more informally, glancing back and forth between Evan and Jeanette. "I see you two as people of the future. You each represent a mixture of ethnic backgrounds, and you are strong yet tolerant and compassionate. You are the type of couple who *should* represent us when these spirits arrive. Afterward, I hope you will guide and help others, as I have done as shaman. I am glad to have known you, even so briefly."

Evan placed his hand on Liuchetkan's shoulder. "I'm sorry you won't be here to see this special visitor."

"Oh, but I will, one way or another," was the translation.

Chapter Twenty-Nine

Evan approached Alex in the reception area and spoke defiantly. "It's time we talked about other copies of the disc. Aside from the one lost with Nigel, and the shaman's, there's one sitting in a Novosibirsk basement. How many more are there?"

Alex's answer was oblique as usual. "It was inevitable that a few copies would become scattered among the population after so many years. The two examples you cite are very interesting, though; I didn't know about them. But I agree it's time to address your question."

He led Evan, Jeanette, and Susan down a new set of stairs, leading to an even deeper and more secure section of the underground installation. After passing through doors requiring a retina scan – a post-Soviet embellishment – they arrived at a small lab. It had once served as a 'clean room,' or sterile facility, but no special procedures were in place today. At the room's center sat a large glass enclosure, and nested within was a shiny, ellipsoidal pod about four feet by two feet, just as Alex had described.

The group gathered around in amazement. Even through the glass, the pod's texture and reflective property were extraordinary. Alex opened the enclosure's side panel and touched its surface. The outline of a lid materialized almost magically. After touching a different spot, the lid lifted slowly and the interior cavity lay exposed. An empty, square-shaped indentation on one side implied a holder for the cube. The remaining space was filled with a stack of discs resting on its side, held in place by curved, foam-like molding.

Evan marveled at the sight, then turned to Alex. "This certainly explains why you weren't too worried about the loss of a few discs. How many were in this pod originally?"

"Accounting for the shaman's disc, there would have been forty-six. We knew that one was lost during the War – perhaps your Novosibirsk example. Another disappeared in the sixties in Leningrad, ending up with Nigel in 1989, and ironically destroyed alongside him."

"Hmm. Forty-six," Evan said. "Hardly exciting – not even a prime number."

Jeanette stepped forward and peered in, adding, "Most human cells have forty-six chromosomes. Just a coincidence?"

"It's hard to say," Alex replied with a shrug. "So much here is beyond our comprehension. As for the pod; it's made of a strong, non-corrosive alloy, although we can't analyze the components – there's no way to obtain a sample. In shape, the pod is a perfect ellipsoid, with an eccentricity – or deviation from spherical – of 0.847. That number matches exactly the eccentricity of the Enke comet's orbit. If you remember, a fragment of this comet may have caused the Tunguska event in 1908. Just a coincidence?" He threw the phrase back at Jeanette with a friendly grin.

Evan was suddenly upbeat. "With so many discs available, perhaps it's not asking too much if we take one?"

"I think something along those lines can be arranged," he said.

Maxim then appeared and began chatting with Alex privately. The two seemed to be reaching some kind of agreement. Evan joined the women as they looked over sheets of data gathered from the pod.

Alex returned and offered to continue the tour. "We are currently very close to the original silo built decades ago. Of course, there's no missile inside, but I think you may still find it interesting." He led them down a long corridor, pointing out various rooms filled with complex control panels, as if he were a museum guide.

A final, thick metal door swung open, and they entered a dim cylindrical chamber, at a point halfway up its total height of 150 feet. A metal platform clung to the inner wall, allowing them to step out into space. The opposite wall loomed fifty feet away. Alex punched buttons on a utility box, in an attempt to activate a series of interior work lights that were apparently seldom used. As they stood motionless and waited, their eyes adjusted to the darkness, and they could sense that the entire silo was filled with some sort of scaffold or latticework, perhaps a support for the aging concrete walls, which were beginning to show hairline cracks.

Suddenly a vast array of hundreds of small light bulbs was activated, illuminating the entire scaffold and blinding them momentarily. Once they had a clear view, it still took time to grasp what they were seeing. The lattice served as an enormous storage rack for countless objects of uniform size and shape, like an overblown, three-dimensional wine cellar. Once everything in their visual field gained perspective, they realized that each of these stored objects was a single pod. They turned to Alex, speechless.

"My friends, may I present the last and greatest secret of the Soviet Union – and of Russia, for that matter. Let me explain. What Kulik found at the epicenter in 1938 was not a single buried pod, but a tunnel leading straight down to a large, artificial chamber where many pods had been deposited. These 'eggs,' as we call them, were moved here, discreetly and gradually, during the sixties. This defunct missile silo provided the perfect cover, not to mention a safe, long-term storage site in a remote location."

Alex sauntered over to the opposite side of the platform, even though it offered a symmetrically equivalent view. "There has always been a desire to mine the valuable isotopes trapped within these brilliantly designed discs. That motivation overrode anyone's interest in the disc as a communication device, or as a guidepost into nanotechnology."

Evan found his voice, though it was now somewhat squeaky. "How many pods are in here?" Incredibly, only moments before, he had been asking how many discs were contained in a single pod.

“This silo holds a little over twenty thousand pods, and thus almost a million discs.”

“What about the cube? Does each pod also contain a cube?”

“Yes,” Alex said, to their astonishment. “Obviously these discs, along with the cubic testing devices, were meant for widespread distribution. But again, our visitors didn’t foresee issues associated with a human political system.”

“That chamber at the epicenter – what do you know about it?” Jeanette asked.

“How and when it was created remain controversial topics. Some say our visitors used the Tunguska event to cover the commotion required for excavation. In fact, eyewitnesses reported multiple explosions lasting more than half an hour after initial impact, but that may have been a simple release of methane from the permafrost layer. Some even believe the primary impact was *deliberately caused* as a diversion for chamber excavation. But most think it was dug in the days following the impact, using sophisticated methods that generated little seismic disturbance; only a few local natives would have noticed anything odd. We’ll probably never know for sure.”

Alex guided them back off the dizzying platform and into a nearby refreshment room complete with tables, chairs, kitchenette, and vending machines, but no other occupants. Although most of the facility was empty, he still closed the door for privacy. Evan, Jeanette, and Susan were numb with the escalating amount of information, and welcomed the break. As they sat and tried to fathom everything, Alex prepared a pot of coffee.

Evan began shaking his head. “Why are you showing us all this, Alex?”

“Eventually, word will get out about these discs; maybe not in my lifetime, but someday. There will be a worldwide outcry for Russia to share its treasure. Investigative teams will no doubt arrive soon afterward, and then the final truth will unfold.”

“*Final* truth?” Jeanette asked. “You mean, there’s *more* to all this?”

“You might as well learn everything today.” He walked over and sat down slowly at the table, apparently as exhausted from telling the story as they were from hearing it. “The underground chamber at the epicenter was never cleared of all its contents, because it’s a vast collection. Only a small fraction of the deposited pods was actually transported to this silo. We don’t really know how many pods remain, perhaps millions. Our speculation has always been that the total number of discs delivered to earth in 1908 is roughly equal to the human population at the dawn of the twentieth century – a little over one billion. In other words, the plan was for everyone on earth to receive a disc and become prepared to hear a message. Of course, individual disc ownership isn’t really necessary, since the sharing of a single disc within a family is conceivable.” This last statement, though practical, was uttered so nonchalantly that Evan found it comical.

The coffee machine finished its task, and Styrofoam cups were passed around. Oddly, the beverage was tolerable to all, perhaps because at this point even tea would have tasted the same. They drank in silence for several minutes.

Evan then explored a new direction. "It's tempting to assume that our job is to distribute these discs around the world like Santa Claus. But something still bothers me, and our shaman friend alluded to it. So far, we've been set up to *hear* their message, without any obvious plan for us to *respond*. Of course, maybe they're assuming we'll decipher the cube's language and electronically reproduce it. But what if their *only* plan is for us to obey their commands after they arrive to rule the planet? Perhaps a byproduct of our 'preparation to hear' is an inability to resist."

Jeanette spoke next. "I agree with Evan. If the Record really does alter humans using gene delivery, for *any* purpose, then it's debatable whether the pods should be distributed." She remembered the sight of laboratory mice lapping up gelatin packaged with nanoparticles of DNA. "Maybe something like this has happened before, during those ancient visits. Maybe they introduced a gadget that every human wanted to own, as a trick to induce changes in us. Do we really want to repeat the same mistake our ancestors made?"

"It would be interesting," Susan said, "to re-examine human history and look for the sudden appearance of a novel object that eventually gained widespread usage."

"I'll offer another, even more troubling thought," Evan said, now on a roll. "Perhaps that drop in the number of our species 75,000 years ago was not due to some super-volcano, but from trial-and-error genetic experiments, with the designers experiencing extensive 'failures.' The only humans that survived, or were allowed to survive, were those born with a vocal tract and brain circuitry guaranteeing a particular path for speech and music."

"It's important to remain skeptical," Susan said, "but let's not go too far. It would be a shame if extraterrestrials arrived in 2049 and *no one* could understand them. It's in our best interest for at least *a few* humans to hear the message – good or bad news – and act as interpreters." Susan was staring at Evan and Jeanette as she spoke, and the implications for the couple made them squirm.

"These are all important considerations, many of which I have weighed myself," Alex said, trying to quell the rising anxiety. "It could certainly be argued that nothing should ever leave this place. But, like I said, the primary library of discs will eventually come to light, and it's better if an in-depth analysis of a few has occurred by then, before politicians decide to spread them around the globe."

Alex stood in front of them. "I propose that you distribute the forty-three discs from the first pod among top academic institutions around the world for open study, especially with regard to biological effects, and create a public database for the results. Once conclusions are reached about the designer's intentions, you can reveal the existence of the other pods at your discretion."

"Is this ultimately why I was invited here?" Evan asked. "So I would 'steal' a few discs and pass them around for analysis, while you deliberately looked the other way?"

"Yes, that's what I've always wanted, but I couldn't really proceed myself. Right now, I'm tired of everything. I've had enough," Alex said with a sigh. "I assume you have a plan to abduct a pod?"

"I know of a way, in a couple of weeks," said Evan. "Can you box up the pod to look like something innocent, and have it delivered to the airport?" Evan felt no need to mention the Italian team's departure; Alex no doubt knew of every flight scheduled in and out of Vanavara for weeks. He had probably counted on Evan to show up during the Italian group's summer expedition.

Still, Evan thought, once word got out that Alex had facilitated a pod's release, thereby initiating a global research effort, the man would be placed on every blacklist his government could devise. Evan spoke to Alex quietly in the corner while Jeanette and Susan chatted. "You're an engineer by training, right? Why don't you come with us, and study a disc with me back in Boston?"

"Thank you, that's a tempting offer. I appreciate your concern, but there's no rush for me to decide – the absence of one pod will not be noticeable in a place like this. And after the news leaks, I have some options that may surprise you. Besides, I have a family here in Russia. I can't leave right now."

“One other thing,” Evan said. “I run a big risk too, if I encounter one of your colleagues who’s less eager to part with such a treasure.”

“Leave that to me. Your flight back will be uneventful.” Alex then addressed the group. “I look forward to reading many interesting scientific articles in the near future, and I hope you three will be chosen to oversee the whole project. I’m confident you’ll make a large impact on the world – something that will last for many generations.”

Evan stared into space, astonished at how he had voiced this very ambition to David Rollins in London nearly one year ago.

“Now,” Alex said, “let’s head back up into the warm Siberian sunshine.”

As they emerged, Evan almost expected to see a hot-air balloon prepared for their return to Kansas.

On the following evening, Enrico Facchini arrived in Vanavara. Once notified of Nigel’s death, he had asked a helicopter pilot to fly him from the site into town, so he could offer his condolences. He found Evan, Jeanette, and Susan at the inn, sitting in the cozy den next to a stone fireplace. Distraught, Enrico sat down and leaned forward, looking at the floor, his hands clasped tightly together. “This is terrible news. The loss to the music world is incalculable. It just seems unreal. What was Nigel *doing* in Vanavara anyway?”

The trio looked at one other; they had already decided on a course of action. Evan spoke. “Enrico, we’ve discovered something we’d like you to take back to Italy. It will receive much more attention than any fragment of a Tunguska asteroid or comet. It's a collection of ancient artifacts, and we think your university should have the first shot at an investigation."

Evan proceeded to give the briefest possible overview of an incredible pod, cube, and set of discs that the Italians could transport out of Russia. Enrico appeared confused, and then frightened, as if he had entered an insane asylum. Twice he rose to leave, but after an hour they had convinced him that the fairy tale just might be true.

Finally, Evan pulled out a single Record. "Enrico, if you don't mind, there's something I'd like to try. I remember how much you love Italian arias. There's a turntable over in the corner, which our host found in her attic. I'd like for us to hold this record at the *same time*, and set it on the player together. I know it sounds strange, but please indulge me."

Enrico agreed, befuddled. After several minutes, music emerged from the small speakers. It was an Italian aria, and both men recognized the voice as Rosina, from her performance at the 2008 Bologna Music Festival. But this time, it was a soothing sound for Evan, and his pain did not surface. He glanced over and smiled at Jeanette, sitting beside him on the sofa. She surmised what had happened, and snuggled closer.

Something then caught their eyes, and all looked up. Through a large window in front of them, the night sky was in full view, and the show had just begun. The northern lights were condensing into ghostly apparitions of green and blue against a black-velvet canvas. Unfolding like a thin, silk sheet blowing in a calm breeze, the vision moved in perfect harmony with Rosina's voice.

Chapter Thirty

The air inside Bologna's lavish Teatro Europauditorium was charged with anticipation as hundreds of scientists gathered to hear the keynote address. When the speaker finally approached the podium, thunderous applause erupted, and many rose in a standing ovation.

"Thank you very much," Evan said, once the clapping had subsided. He paused, waiting for a hushed silence; that moment when one could hear a pin drop. "Today I'm pleased to open the 2017 Conference on Materials of Extraterrestrial Design. It's incredible to note that only one year ago, before public disclosure of the artifacts, such a title would have been preposterous. Yet, as you know, an international committee plans to hold this event annually, rotating through each of the forty-three sites chosen for analysis of an alien disc.

"Over the coming week we've scheduled almost sixty research presentations. At the next conference, this number will undoubtedly increase. The importance of sharing all this information, especially through publication in new journals and open-access online databases, cannot be over-emphasized."

An image of one disc blazed across the huge screen behind him. After several seconds, it was replaced with a photo of the pod's interior, showing the cube and stack of discs restored to their original positions. Although most had already seen such pictures, murmurs of awe filled the room. Evan gestured dramatically toward the screen with his arms, as if the view were not captivating enough. "During these proceedings, you'll hear updates on efforts to understand the disc's structure, function, and impact on biological systems. Our knowledge of the biological impact is building slowest, since experiments involving humans are highly regulated, and thus far no animal model exists to simulate the human response. I'm told the situation is reminiscent of early attempts to understand infection from the Human Immunodeficiency Virus.

"Nevertheless, much has been learned." A magnified image of the disc's surface immersed the audience in a forest of unearthly projections resembling stretched mushrooms. "For example, several properties of the detachable nanospheres have been revealed using human cell cultures. As Dr. Menard suspected early on, the particles are capable of entering cells and releasing DNA. It's been possible to sequence individual strands of this DNA using the latest nanopore technology."

A slide appeared summarizing the molecular biology studies. "The alien DNA is transcribed by our bodies into RNA, and part of that RNA contains genes encoding proteins. Some of these proteins bind and regulate cellular receptors in the brain, affecting synaptic transmission and even nerve growth; other proteins remain a complete mystery. This alien RNA has other functions as well. It can modulate cellular gene expression by mechanisms ranging from RNA-interference to long-noncoding RNA; the latter derives from 'junk DNA' previously thought to play no role in our cells. Finally, some of the alien-derived RNA possesses a catalytic function, like ribozymes, which allows enzymatic modification of our cellular nucleic acid. It's interesting that the disc would contain RNA enzymes, since these have been proposed as the first genetic material on earth, based on their dual role in catalysis and information storage.

"We will also hear how the nanospheres can promote the growth and connectivity of neurons. DNA fibers originating inside the particles can coalesce and provide structural scaffolds for nerve growth. In one study, a nanostructured gel formed spontaneously and filled the space between existing nerve cells in culture, encouraging new ones to grow. Combined with the proteins encoded by the same DNA, there are implications for modification of brain circuitry.

"But the ultimate influence of all this foreign material on the human body remains unclear, since extrapolation from cellular experiments is always challenging. Still, the cell-based studies are generating new ideas for drug delivery and gene therapy.

"In terms of simply locating nanospheres in the body, some hope lies in the fact that the particles behave as tiny, semiconducting nanocrystals, like the 'quantum dots' already in use for biological imaging and diagnosis. When such dots are illuminated with ultraviolet light, they emit a wide spectrum of colors, which helps to locate and identify cell types and biological activities.

“Because of the low concentration of nanospheres in the human body, external imaging methods like MRI have not been helpful for localization. However, functional MRI studies, which follow oxygenated blood flow, are showing how brain activity in humans during disc exposure is unlike anything ever seen before, especially when the subject is asleep.

“Labs with more of an engineering bent, like my own, have started looking at the amazingly complex scaffolds within the nanospheres, constructed largely out of DNA. We’re only beginning to scratch the surface, figuratively and literally. Decades may pass before we can assess the disc’s *inner* construction. However, there have been some interesting advances regarding the distribution of radioactivity within a disc, as will be reported later this week by a team from the Russian Institute for Physics of Microstructures.”

A rumble of discussion coursed throughout the hall, spawning pockets of heated debate, as the crowd reacted to the ongoing controversy over past Russian secrecy about the pod. Many felt that Russia had forfeited any opportunity to participate in the current global initiative, and should be ‘punished’ by permanent exclusion. Others wanted to set politics aside, arguing for the value of past research only now seeing the light of day. Ultimately an international oversight committee chose inclusion, consistent with the spirit of a worldwide research effort. Evan, while on the committee, was one of the few scientists who understood the absurdity of sending a disc to Russia last year for 'study,' when that country still concealed an enormous stockpile. Russia's request had clearly been a ploy to cover the fact.

Raising his voice, Evan tried to bring the proceedings back to order by changing the subject. "As you know, a number of volunteers have stepped forward to help evaluate the long-term effects of disc exposure. Obviously, they are motivated by the hope of someday communicating with extraterrestrial beings. It was decided that a select group of volunteers should have access to a disc at each research center, but only if they agreed to be monitored closely over the years. These dedicated individuals may well be our future ambassadors when, and if, the extraterrestrials return. Let me emphasize that the set of visitation dates – past and future – remains a hypothesis; efforts are underway to confirm the proposed time points.

"Later this week, we'll hear from scientists exploring how humans might have been altered in the past. This is difficult to infer from the genetic record – but not impossible, since we know that viruses have integrated their DNA into our chromosomes over millions of years.

"Researchers are also scanning history for evidence of prior alien artifacts. Dr. Susan Henderson at Harvard has been focusing on the proposed 5430 BCE visitation date, which lies within the scope of current archeological methods. She has developed interesting theories about possible tools used for genetic manipulation of humans. These include some of the simplest objects of that period: domesticated grains like wheat and barley, which were widely coveted and consumed."

A final slide appeared as a backdrop. It was an illustration of human anatomy taken from the groundbreaking sixteenth century work *De humani corporis fabrica* by Vesalius. "These are exciting times – as significant as the Renaissance. Yet these are also early days, and we must proceed with caution. An incredible phenomenon is being viewed through the filters of human perception and logic. Blinding biases and mistaken assumptions can accompany any great scientific leap, and we must learn from the errors of the past.

"On a final note; tonight at seven there will be a performance in this auditorium by the local Philharmonic Orchestra, featuring several works of the late Nigel Thompson. Ironically, he was the guest conductor here only a few years ago. It is but a modest attempt to honor this marvelous composer, who gave his life in pursuit of a deeper understanding of the disc. Now, let's move on to the day's first presentation."

The three scientists had finished dinner and were working on a second bottle of wine when he entered the restaurant. They studied the figure negotiating a path through the crowd, his profile illuminated sporadically by islands of table candlelight. Upon reaching their table, he paused, as if waiting for an invitation to sit, and then occupied the fourth empty chair without speaking. They poured him a glass of red wine while he removed his coat.

"Hello Alex," said Evan. "I was worried you wouldn't be allowed to attend."

"There was a family-related delay, but no government interference. I'm sorry I missed the first day of talks. At least I can stay for the rest of the week." He took a long sip of wine, closing his eyes while savoring the rich flavors.

"Your family is doing well?" Jeanette asked.

"Yes. Naturally, they're disappointed about not seeing Bologna, but hardly surprised. For many years in Russia, one member of a family was allowed to travel while the rest stayed behind as hostages. Some things never change. You'll have to tell me how you arranged for my exit."

"Quite simple, really," Evan said. "About a week after the very first announcement, two Russian 'diplomats' requested a meeting with me in Boston. I arranged lunch at a public spot. They asked whether my intention was to reveal everything about Vanavara. This was during the initial outrage over your country concealing a *single* pod and set of discs. I promised to remain silent as long as you, Maxim, and your families were not harmed. They agreed, but said your government privileges would be revoked, which I expected. However, I insisted that you and Maxim be allowed to attend one annual conference, so I could verify your well-being."

"Thank you very much for your efforts," said Alex. "Still, I can't help but worry about your own safety. It would be very convenient if the three of you – the only foreigners to know the *full* truth – suddenly disappeared."

"Well, I told these 'diplomats' that Jeanette, Susan, and I had each placed a special clause in our wills. If something suspicious happens to any of us, a detailed written account of Vanavara will be released to the media."

"Good idea. However, if Maxim and I ever find a way to get our families out, even leaving ourselves behind, don't hesitate to reveal the facts, if you feel the world is ready for it."

Alex ordered a small entrée, and the group relaxed as a violinist began playing in a small courtyard outside the restaurant. The warm September evening was enhanced by fragrant scents of olive and lemon trees wafting in through the open patio doors.

Over coffee, Alex scanned a book of abstracts summarizing global research efforts. "It's intriguing, these people who volunteered for long-term disc exposure. I noticed this doesn't include any of you," he said without looking up.

"We . . ." Evan trailed off.

Jeanette took over. "We decided that our contributions were best made through research. Also, Evan and I didn't know how such exposure might affect our future child. We're worried enough as it is, although at five months now, everything seems normal." She rubbed her stomach in a slow circle.

"Ah. I see," said Alex, smiling at Jeanette. "Congratulations. I'm actually relieved that you didn't volunteer, pregnant or not."

They all looked over at Susan, who finally spoke. "Me? Volunteer? After watching Nigel and these two deal with the disc, I decided I could pass up hearing a concert with Paganini playing his Stradivarius." They all laughed.

Alex reflected for a moment. "If those volunteers really are the only ones who can interpret an alien language, I wonder if they'll become the next prophets of our planet, like the high priests of some ancient civilization, communicating exclusively with the gods."

Susan continued the thought. "Perhaps they'll even be the seeds of the next major world religion, generating yet another set of unverifiable claims and rigid doctrines, against which science will once again do battle."

"If so," replied Alex, "then I expect all of you to lead the rebellion, since I may not be here in thirty-two years."

Evan leaned forward, his face highlighted eerily by the candlelight. "But remember, those volunteers will hear something that has always been present in our own music, just below the surface." He leaned back and searched his thoughts. "Nigel always enjoyed sharing quotes of past composers, and one of his favorites was from Delius: 'Only that which cannot be expressed otherwise is worth expressing in music.'"

"Then here's to Nigel," said Jeanette. Four glasses clinked together. Out in the courtyard, the violinist broke into a display of virtuosity. His playing glowed with a sense of optimism and possibility. No one at the table recognized the tune, but it felt right for the moment.

www.ingramcontent.com/pod-product-compliance
Ingram Content Group UK Ltd.
Pitfield, Milton Keynes, MK11 3LW, UK
UKHW040022200726
13854UKWH00001B/311